MW01222368

Also available from Headline Liaison

A Private Affair by Carol Anderson
Invitations by Carol Anderson
The Journal by James Allen
Love Letters by James Allen
Aphrodisia by Rebecca Ambrose
Out of Control by Rebecca Ambrose
Voluptuous Voyage by Lacey Carlyle
Magnolia Moon by Lacey Carlyle
Dark Deception by Lacey Carlyle
Autumn Dancing by Adam Chandler
Vermilion Gates by Lucinda Chester
The Paradise Garden by Aurelia Clifford
The Golden Cage by Aurelia Clifford
Green Silk by Cathryn Cooper
Sleepless Nights by Tom Crewe and Amber Wells
Hearts on Fire by Tom Crewe and Amber Wells
Seven Days by J J Duke
Dangerous Desires by J J Duke
A Scent of Danger by Sarah Hope-Walker
Private Lessons by Cheryl Mildenhall
Intimate Strangers by Cheryl Mildenhall
Dance of Desire by Cheryl Mildenhall

Island
in the Sun

Susan Sebastian

Copyright © 1997 Susan Sebastian

The right of Susan Sebastian to be identified as the Author of
the Work has been asserted by her in accordance with the
Copyright, Designs and Patents Act 1988.

First published in 1997
by HEADLINE BOOK PUBLISHING

A HEADLINE LIAISON paperback

10 9 8 7 6 5 4 3 2 1

All rights reserved. No part of this publication may be
reproduced, stored in a retrieval system, or transmitted,
in any form or by any means without the prior written
permission of the publisher, nor be otherwise circulated
in any form of binding or cover other than that in which
it is published and without a similar condition being
imposed on the subsequent purchaser.

All characters in this publication are fictitious
and any resemblance to real persons, living or dead,
is purely coincidental.

ISBN 0 7472 5689 6

Typeset by
Letterpart Limited, Reigate, Surrey

Printed and bound in Great Britain by
Cox & Wyman Ltd, Reading, Berks

HEADLINE BOOK PUBLISHING
A division of Hodder Headline PLC
338 Euston Road
London NW1 3BH

Island
in the Sun

One

Saffie and Rachel relaxed on the waterfront on Mykonos, languid and content after their day on the beach. They watched in amusement as a group of children fed the resident pelican with scraps from the local fishermen's haul. At tables all around them, holiday-makers were enjoying the warmth of the evening. Many were eating salads or hot dishes from the many tavernas and bars. Some were attending to their boats, or chatting to the Greek owners of the fabulous yachts moored alongside. Bazouki music came evocatively from the bar in the square beyond.

'Talk about Greek gods!' said Rachel, nudging her friend and indicating to her right.

Saffie turned to watch as a man on a fine chestnut mare came slowly down the hill-path. He rode with leisurely ease, holding the reins in his left hand as he guided the horse down the incline. He wore only loose black trousers and his naked torso was bronzed in the hot sun. A dark red bandana with long trailing ends restrained his jet-black curls. Saffie was transfixed by this unexpected vision. She smiled with admiration at the young man's powerful physique. She was exquisitely moved by his graceful posture as he rode easily along. She wondered whether man and horse had been galloping wildly over the parched earth beyond. Her warm body responded naturally to this image. Ever responsive to male sexuality, she smiled inwardly as she experienced the familiar glow of arousal. Her small breasts, loose under the soft tee-shirt, ripened. Awareness spread through her slim brown thighs to between her parted legs. The magical holiday atmosphere, and her euphoric state rendered her more receptive. This proximity to such a desirable male made the moment perfect.

Instinctively, she thought of the friezes from the Parthenon, at present still in the British Museum. She recalled the reliefs of the handsome ephebes – or knights – on these friezes. Many, the pride of their generation, were naked on horseback; others wore only cloaks. She imagined this beautiful man, devoid of his remaining clothing. Her pleasure increased as she pictured his generous penis, extended, perhaps, like those of the satyrs. They had seen many of these legendary beings recently on Greek plates and vases. When she was most aroused, Saffie fantasised about wildly sexual men, blessed with such over-large phalluses. She had heard that ancient Greek men went about naked. A resumption of such a habit would certainly add to the pleasure of their holiday. Perhaps it would be fun to visit the nudist beach on the next day.

Saffie's unreasonable hope that the stranger would tether his horse here and quench his thirst at one of the tables was dashed as he took a water-bottle from the saddle bag and drank thirstily from it. His need somewhat appeased, he poured some of the remaining water over his body and arms. Saffie watched as the liquid ran down his pectoral muscles and biceps. She was filled with sensuality as she imagined licking the warm liquid from his hot flesh. She would begin with his strong, brown forearms, and then move on to his chest. Her tongue would lap hungrily as she moved down towards his belly, and further, to where the thick black hair increased. She would breathe in the musk of his hot prick as she trailed the juice from her mouth lovingly over his quickening member . . . She smiled wickedly at the vivid nature of her imaginings. She levelled her cool gaze at the lovely young man.

As he neared them, the stranger cast an arrogant glance over the crowd on the front. Saffie wondered whether he resented the tourists. His dark eyes met hers before she could look away. They were filled first with enquiry, and then with sardonic amusement. Saffie realised that the man was very aware of his attractiveness. She flushed as she realised how revealing was her avid gaze. She was filled with a kind of anger at herself and at him. This emotion was, however, tempered by her reflex response to the man's undoubted beauty. He did indeed look the archetypal Greek god. His features were of a classical, delicate mould. His cheek-bones were high and angular, his chin clean-cut and his mouth was full and passionate. The sable curls fell beguilingly over his brow despite the head-band. Perhaps he was a descendant of one of the youths who had modelled for the perfect statues they had admired in the museum at Athens?

He rode past them, but she continued to savour him as he went slowly towards the windmills at the edge of the beach. She kept every aspect of him clearly in her mind as he disappeared round the headland. What a wonderful painting he and his horse would make! Her fingers itched to make some rapid sketches. Her body yearned to have him. Perhaps she could follow him and entice him back into one of the deserted windmills. She would take him on the hot earthen floor. She closed her eyes as she almost felt him within her, so potent was her imagination. Her vagina squeezed in response. The warm liquid of arousal wet her silken pants. She opened her eyes and turned to Rachel, meeting the young woman's laughing eyes. She widened her own in acknowledgement of the man's obvious appeal and then grinned.

'I know what I would like to do with him,' said Rachel.

Saffie nodded her agreement.

'I think I need another drink,' Rachel decided, standing, 'and the loo!' she added, smiling knowingly at her friend.

Saffie inclined her head, seeing the sun glow in her companion's long golden curls. She wondered whether her friend found it necessary to appease her longing immediately by herself. She smiled affectionately; she couldn't blame her! Saffie watched Rachel for a moment as she stopped and spoke briefly to the Greek waiter, indicating their table. The waiter nodded and went to fetch them another couple of ouzos with water and ice. Like Saffie, he could not help but regard Rachel as she made her way to the taverna. Her tall slim figure weaved its way elegantly between the loitering tourists. Rachel was pretty, but it was her smile and warmth of personality which drew people to her. And, Saffie admitted ruefully to herself, she was very sexy, especially in her brief white shorts and tangerine top.

Reaching for her sketch-pad, Saffie was surprised at how aroused this lingering view of the sun-bronzed horseman had left her. Despite her weariness and the heat, her hand was deft as she executed rapid lines in an attempt to re-capture him on paper. She smiled in thanks as the waiter brought their drinks. He looked with interest at her drawing, and nodded in appreciation. As he left he shook his head at the English girl, with her short black hair and green eyes.

'Purely artistic interest, hey?' Rachel teased as she returned.

Saffie shook her head as she reciprocated her friend's smile and put away her pad.

'So – shall we go to "Apollo's" again tonight?' asked Rachel, reminding her, 'There's the disco.'

Saffie nodded her agreement and took a sip of her ouzo. They had had a good time at the club on the previous night, despite their tiredness. The music was excellent, and the atmosphere lively and cosmopolitan. Also, they had danced and chatted with quite a number of good-looking young men. And sometimes, Saffie had simply enjoyed watching the youths dancing.

'And I expect you'll want to go to Delos tomorrow?' Rachel added in a tone of mock resignation.

Saffie smiled, experiencing a rush of excitement at the prospect of visiting the ancient sacred island. They would reach it in one of the kayaks moored on the jetty close to the windmills. She planned to make several sketches of the ruined temples.

'So – shall we eat here?' she asked Rachel, meeting her friend's clear blue eyes.

'Oh . . .' Rachel sighed contentedly, 'Not yet. I'm happy just to laze around for a bit longer, then go back, have a shower and get changed. We can eat later. What do you think?'

'Fine.'

Rachel leaned back and closed her eyes, putting her slim brown legs up on the opposite chair. She folded her hands over her firm belly and let her mind drift off. Saffie regarded her thoughtfully for a few minutes before resuming her sketching. She still felt very turned on and sensitively attuned to people around her. Without really planning to, she began to sketch Rachel. She luxuriated in drawing the long loose curls which shone in the golden sun-light. Her pitch of arousal seemed to increase as she concentrated on her friend's shapely body. She drew her long legs, the alluring curve of her firm thighs and the mound of her pubis, visible under the thin white shorts.

Saffie took a deep breath and a long draft of her cold drink before continuing with the lines of her companion's soft round breasts. She looked at Rachel's face. Her tan was deep and her lashes long on her high cheekbones. Her generous mouth pouted slightly in her sleep. Saffie smiled affectionately at her and put her sketch pad on the table.

She was unbearably aroused and could not concentrate on her work. She poured more water from the jug into her glass and drank from it. She looked around at the other people on the quay in order to distract herself. On the adjacent table a young couple were sharing a large dish of strawberries. The young woman indicated to her partner that they should eat half each. She drew her elegant hand over the centre to signify this. Saffie smiled. The girl was exceptionally pretty, with long dark ringlets framing an elfin face, and huge black eyes. Her male companion was even more beautiful, dark and definitely Hellenic.

Saffie decided that she was too restless to remain seated. She glanced at Rachel, who seemed to be still asleep. Turning over the page of her pad, she scrawled 'Gone for a walk, back soon' on the blank page. Taking up her tumbler, she drained the contents, then stood and stretched. She picked up her camera from the table and hung it around her neck. She would go and photograph the windmills. The air was hot all around her as she began to walk towards the gift-stands of leather goods and jewellery. She touched the worry-beads as she passed, and looked casually at the postcard reproductions of Athens and the islands.

Unhurriedly, she went on past the café-fronts, and through the groups of strolling holiday-makers, and made her way to the end of the concrete promenade and on to the beach. It was pleasant to walk along the sand. Saffie glanced up at the small domed church as she passed, admiring the pots of geraniums growing in profusion, on the adjacent steps. As she continued along the beach, she gasped as she saw the horse and its rider. The young man was engrossed in conversation with another, equally handsome youth, who stood, stroking the horse's head. They made a very picturesque group. The second man had long chestnut curls and was tall and strong.

Saffie remained for a moment in fascination, then withdrew to the side of a building and directed her camera. But, as she took the photograph, they turned to her. The rider seemed annoyed, though his friend smiled at the attractive young visitor. Saffie's legs felt weak as she backed away into the narrow alley of white-washed houses. Without really knowing where she was directed, she climbed the steep steps at the end of the short street. A group of children ran past her, and a black cat eyed her warily from its lair of kittens high up in a niche in the white wall.

She wanted to see him again. She turned at the small square. She was now above the church and windmills. Still lingering, she went back towards the beach. She could hear the sound of horse's hooves advancing. She stopped as she heard mens' voices. They were coming nearer. She could not see them; they were on the other side of the tiny old houses. Saffie held her breath. Her heart beat faster. She strained to hear. Her Greek was excellent, as her multi-lingual father had taught her when she was young.

'Niko . . .' said the man's rich voice, 'don't let him get you down. We'll sort something out . . . It will all go to plan. You shouldn't allow him such power over you. You really don't need him. You should go away – forget it all. Start a new life.'

'You know I cannot, Yianni— My family . . .' replied Nikos.

Saffie was intrigued, but could not hear the other's response. Neither could she follow as the narrow street was opening out into another little square. She almost flattened herself against the wall as she saw the men emerge into this square, cross it and begin to ascend a steep path. The rider's friend was holding the reins, and she had a feeling that he was the one she had heard speaking first. She wondered what he had meant. All kinds of colourful explanations inveigled their way into her mind. She had as a child been told that she was nosy. Indeed, she had sometimes found herself almost missing her bus-stop, so involved had she been in over-hearing people's (in truth, probably mundane) conversations. In this case, however, her imagination had already been engaged.

So – it was 'Nikos' . . . Saffie was happy to discover that their 'Greek god' really *was* Greek.

She wandered back to the front, deeply engaged in thoughts of why the handsome young man was so despondent and who the powerful 'he' was. Rachel was wide awake and looking out for her. Refreshed from her nap, she was eager to change and eat and go out for the night. Saffie noticed that the engaging young couple from the next table had gone.

6

Eleni lay naked on the huge bed. The window was wide open and the fragrance of honeysuckle wafted in on a gentle breeze. She listened vaguely to the birdsong, and the sound of splashing water. Feeling the warmth flow gently over her languid body, she looked dreamily over to the profusion of flowers on the window-sill. She drifted her fingertips teasingly over her firm breasts, tweaking at her hardened nipples. Her hand continued on, over her hollow belly to her pubis. Even before she touched herself, she experienced an increase in her sexual receptivity. The glow was pitched to sharpness as she pinched the ripe bud of her clitoris between finger and thumb. Her pleasure increased as she pushed her forefinger further, parting the tender labia to feel the liquid, gathering. She did not penetrate, but idly, spread this liquid over her clitoris. It was a sleepy, relaxing movement.

Then she lifted her hand peremptorily and turned onto her front to watch Nikos showering. She smiled to see the water splash over his black hair, causing it to straighten and cling to his forehead and neck. He had washed and rinsed it, and was now engrossed in lathering soap over his lithe, firm body. Eleni writhed gently on the bed, pressing her crotch repeatedly into the hot mattress as she watched him. His large penis, always seeming semi-erect, moved against his left thigh as he soaped his upper body. He lifted his arms gracefully as he washed, and then began to attend to his lower body. The lather and water streamed over his shoulders and chest, down his back, over his tight, glistening buttocks and frothed at his crotch.

As he took his long penis into his right hand to wash it, Eleni experienced a lance-like stab of lust. She wanted to go to him, to take him, hot and wet, into her arms. To feel the water cascade over her, and to thrust his stiffening rod into her ready vagina. Her breasts swelled, eager for a man's strong touch. Perversely, she remained on the bed, watching him through cat-like eyes. She pinched her burning clitoris between her bent fingers. It beat gently, and she controlled her arousal, stroking herself softly.

Though he did not turn to her, she knew that Nikos was aware of her desire. Teasingly, he grasped his erect penis in his left hand and began to masturbate rapidly. Eleni's aching body pulsated as, in response, she jerked her pubis against the bed. She was riveted by Nikos as he brought his foreskin over the purple end of his prick, and then drew it back to its root. He held on to the shower rail, and continued his regular rapid movements. As if he was alone, and was engaging in this private activity in a business-like way, merely to appease his fretful lust, so that he could think more clearly.

Clear water continued to gush over his straining body as he kept his attention on his swollen prick. All the time, he looked down at it. Eleni squirmed in delight, massaging her sensitised breasts, feeling at her tightening abdomen as she thrust faster downwards. If she carried on like this, she would soon reach orgasm.

Suddenly, Nikos stopped and released his cock, now holding on to the overhead bar with both hands and looking at her through liquid, beguiling eyes. Eleni slowed her rate of self-stimulation and gazed at his swollen lips. The thought of his powerful kiss sent spasms of joy shooting through her body. Nikos' dark eyes glanced to the side, and then he turned his head to the side. Slowly, he put out his long tongue and began to lick at his wet shoulder. Eleni looked at his huge prick rearing and yearning towards her. She narrowed her eyes as she concentrated on its purple head. She imagined licking off the gathering liquid from its hole.

'Niko . . .' she murmured longingly.

Smiling a little, Nikos shook his head slightly and put down his left palm to his other shoulder. Now, he began a sensual, narcissistic journey. He fondled his shoulder and then traced his palm down his strong arm, then up again to his neck, which he caressed lovingly. Eleni groaned in anguish, though she prayed for him to continue. Languidly, Nikos put his left index-finger to his lips and with lowered eyes inserted his finger and began to suck on it.

'Oh, God, Niko . . .' Eleni moaned as she felt her senses quicken in her stomach. All delicate tendrils of exquisite sensitivity responded in her groins. Her sex began to throb deliciously.

Nikos removed his wet finger from his mouth and began to trace it round his pouting lips. His cheeks became flushed, his breathing quickened. He moved his hand slowly down his chest, caressing as it descended. His eyes were hooded as he looked at her. He moved his tongue over his lips. At any moment, she could

8

have him. She could make him do exactly as she wished. Eleni watched as Nikos began to run his hands rapidly and strongly over his body, closing his eyes in pleasure.

She saw that he bit savagely at his lower lip and he squeezed his own buttocks, his fingers between. Dreamily, he traced the crack. He opened his eyes wide to her as his index-finger brushed against his anus. His cock reared impatiently. Eleni felt the heat of her cheeks increase, her throat constrict, as she realised that he couldn't wait any longer. This self-arousal was driving him crazy. His lust was even stronger than her own. Deep inside, she recognised the primitive tingle of fear and pleasure as he left the shower, his dark eyes burning.

Instinctively, she rolled over and dropped her knees to open herself to him. She watched him as he came towards her, aware of his animal power. She saw him eye her red and glistening vulva with desire. Eleni moaned in longing. She was impatient for him to be inside her, part of her. She cried out in joy as she felt his hands under her bottom and his huge prick thrust straight into her. Its hard length went along her clitoris as he filled her vagina. Her pleasure ripened. She gripped him tightly within her muscular passage. She looked up at Nikos as he supported himself and watched her as he began to fuck her.

For seconds only, he was slow, easing his cock almost out of her body, and then ramming it back home, making her body shudder with his force. Each time he re-entered, he slid along her clitoris. Soon they were lost, all control gone. Eleni did not know where his body ended and hers began as she cleaved to him. Nikos was agile and fit and strong. Now he kneaded her breasts painfully as he pushed repeatedly into her. Expertly, he continued to stimulate her thrusting bud, banging firmly against it with his sharp bone at each jerk into her. Her movements echoed his perfectly. As one they strove for that ultimate release, each concentrated on the supreme seat of pleasure.

Eleni thought that all her consciousness was in the place where their bodies met, and his penis was as sensitive to her as her own body. She clenched the powerful muscle of her vagina ever more tightly round him as he thrust along it. He pressed his pubis rhythmically against her hard tense ridge as his body pounded hers. Her breasts strained within his palms as he squeezed tightly, now holding her suffuse nipples between his finger and thumb. She felt a pull to her vagina, as though invisible threads connected these places of sensation. She loved the way he pressed her nipples so tightly. Sometimes she thought that this manipulation alone could bring her to climax. But Nikos would not be able to deny his greedy cock its ultimate need.

Nikos moved his hands back to her rear and lifted her so that he could insert even more deeply. Eleni gave a gasp of pleasure as her body was jerked powerfully. She felt his swollen phallus hit against the neck of her womb. He fingered her anus tantalisingly. Eleni was sure that she could contain no more pleasure. Attuned to her, Nikos recognised that her orgasm was imminent and remained still, holding close against her clitoris as the growing waves of pleasure peaked and crashed wildly. As she came, Eleni's mouth sought his, kissing him hungrily.

'Niko. Oh, God, Niko . . .!' Eleni cried.

She rocked against him, eager for more, and Nikos continued more quickly now, concentrating on chasing his own orgasm. Eleni delighted in this rare masculine selfishness as he strained and moved his prick inside her exactly as he wished to. He raised himself and looked down at where he entered her, and then he continued, hot and frenzied for a long, long time. Eleni continued to have orgasm after orgasm, until, at last, Nikos ejaculated powerfully, taking her once more to ecstasy. As he relaxed, pulsating within her, Eleni held him gratefully, experiencing another orgasm against his strong throbbing.

Then Nikos kissed her tenderly, taking her onto her side as he rolled over, his prick still inside her. He pulled her naked body against his, caressing her breasts and shoulders, kissing her neck and tousling her dark curls.

'You're beautiful . . .' Eleni whispered as he lapsed into sleep.

His smile was like that of an angel's. Eleni's satiated body glowed as she held her lover close.

'Niko . . .'

Eleni awoke with a start. It was dark. She shivered a little and automatically reached for the sheet to draw over them. It wasn't really cold, it was the difference in their temperature now and their intense heat of a little time ago. She took Nikos' prick in her

10

hand. Already it was full. She smiled. Again came the tapping on the door and the call.

'Niko?'

Then the door opened and Yiannis entered. Eleni smiled at him, and he smiled back beautifully. He was smartly dressed and ready to go out. Eleni got out of bed and headed for the shower. Yiannis caught her round the waist and drew her naked body to his. She put her arms around his neck and kissed him deeply as he caressed her. He ran his palms all over her body, immediately arousing her. She felt his penis harden against her labia, under the soft cloth of his trousers. His hands moved over her small bottom. He squeezed her tight buttocks and inserted his forefinger gently into her tight hole. She began to throb against him.

'Yianni . . .' Nikos said sleepily, in greeting.

Eleni released him with laughter and stepped inside the shower. Soon, she was luxuriating in the warm stream of water.

Yiannis looked at Nikos. The moonlight painted his body, so that he seemed to be made of marble. His beautiful eyes were limpid and sensual. Nikos smiled. His wet prick yearned against his thigh. Yiannis turned away.

'Come. We will go to "Apollo's".'

Nikos shook his head slowly. Yiannis tried to control the surge of disappointment.

'Eleni will go with you. I must work.' Nikos got out of bed, regardless of the effect his nakedness had on Yiannis.

Yiannis eyed his semi-erect penis. Nikos pulled on his black trousers and tee-shirt. He shook his long curls free. Yiannis wanted to kiss those perfect lips; knowing that he could not made him want to hit Nikos. Instead he remained for a moment watching Nikos drink water from the glass on the bedside table. Then he went towards the shower.

'You will come to "Apollo's", Eleni?'

'Yes, of course. That will be good.'

Eleni dressed in a tiny black dress. Yiannis watched in admiration. Eleni was very slim. Her black curls reached almost to her slender waist.

'See you later, Niko . . .' she called as she slipped on her sandals. Eleni was always quick and decisive. Yiannis envied her single-mindedness. He met his friend's dark eyes as they left. He thought of him as they walked down to the club. Now, he would sit in the lamplight and write. Later, he would walk in the darkness when everyone else was asleep. Or still dancing.

The music was wonderful, vibrating through the warmth of the velvet night. The atmosphere was electric, shot through with youthful energy and the desire to enjoy. People from all countries were gathered for a short space to dance to the same music, to drink and to have fun. Everyone was friendly and welcoming. In between dances, Saffie watched from the relative coolness of the doorway. She leant against a pillar and drank wine. Rachel was dancing with the young Greek man Saffie had seen at the table next to them earlier. They looked very good together, a contrast: Rachel with her golden curls bright in the flashing coloured lights, and the young man, dusky and debonair.

Saffie often enjoyed watching from the perimeter, savouring life to record later in her art. Rachel danced well, full of joyful exuberance. Saffie smiled at her friend's obvious enjoyment. As the music slowed, she was held close by her partner. They entwined as if they had been lovers for weeks, and Saffie wondered whether she would be going home alone tonight. Her body responded in empathy as she watched them. Her attention was taken by some newcomers. It was the lovely young woman she had seen with Rachel's dance-partner, and – Yiannis. How very interesting. She glanced at Rachel, to ascertain whether her partner had seen his friend enter. She hoped the friend would be just as happy with her current partner, Yiannis.

They were greeted warmly at the bar by the bar-man, as well as some of the young people. They were obviously popular here. Saffie took the opportunity to replenish her own glass, and thus have the chance to take a closer look at Yiannis. On her way to the bar, she refused a request to dance from a young Norwegian whom she had previously partnered. The young woman was ordering their drinks, whilst Yiannis was talking to a group of young men, whom Saffie had decided earlier were gay. She could not blame them for being interested in him. He was very attractive, with his dark chestnut curls and warm brown eyes. His smile was friendly and generous, extended incidentally to her as he became aware of her interest.

12

'Have you ordered one for me?' asked Rachel, as she and her young man joined Saffie.

'Georgiou . . .' called Yiannis' friend across the bar.

'Eleni . . . Yianni . . .' Georgiou shouted back in greeting and waved.

Yiannis and Eleni pushed their way through the crowds to join them.

'This is Rachel – and—?'

'Saffron – Saffie,' said Rachel.

'Hello, Saffie,' Georgiou took her hand graciously, 'These are my friends, Eleni and Yiannis.'

Friendly greetings were exchanged all round, and then the group retired to sit at a recently vacated table by the door.

'Niko.'

Nikos started and looked up from his writing.

'Constantine.' His tone was resigned.

'You are all alone?'

'They've gone to "Apollo's".'

'Good,' said the older man, 'Have you had chance to consider my – ultimatum?'

Nikos sighed, put down his pen and looked out into the blackness of the night.

'Yes.'

'So – we will go ahead with the project?'

'I don't see how we can get hold of such – gifted and obliging women so quickly.' Nikos' tone was sarcastic.

'Time is money, Niko. I am a busy man. However, I am keen to undertake this – I believe it will make money. You are an artist, Niko – you understand.'

'This wasn't what I wanted though . . .'

'It will be fun. You are young. An experience. Think what you will get out of it.'

'Yes,' Nikos sighed again. 'That which was already mine, before—'

'Discretion, Niko. You should have been more discreet.'

Nikos moved away as the man reached out to touch his hair. Constantine laughed, adding,

'Tomorrow, Niko . . .' and then he was gone.

★ ★ ★

It was good to talk and drink with their new friends. Saffie and
Rachel got on very well, but it was invigorating to meet other
young people. Eleni was very friendly and amusing. She seemed
to know many people at 'Apollo's' and called them over to meet
the young women. Sometimes, it was necessary for her to stand
on a chair and call loudly to them over the music. Saffie laughed
at her. In time, Eleni went off to join some people at the bar.
Saffie saw how much her company was enjoyed by those around
her. She had a gift for making people feel light and happy. She
was a pleasure to watch, and when she suddenly did a little dance
for them, everyone clapped and cheered. Saffie smiled, already
she liked Eleni. Rachel and Georgiou, engrossed in each other,
had returned to their dancing.

'You want to dance?' asked Yiannis, indicating with outstretched hand the crowded dance-floor.

'I'd like to go for a walk,' said Saffie, smiling back into his
warm eyes.

'Okay.'

The relative coolness of the night air was welcome. They
walked down towards the waterfront. It was natural for Saffie to
take Yiannis' hand as he held it out to her. She smiled at him, and
he returned this charmingly.

'Do you live here?'

'No, my home is in Athens. We are just staying here for a time.'

'What do you do?'

'Oh. I lecture, and I am an actor.'

'How wonderful.'

'Sometimes . . .'

Saffie noted the slight preoccupation in his response. They had
reached the quay and leaned against the low wall at one end.
There were still many people strolling about or sitting at the café
tables.

'And you?'

'I illustrate books.'

'That is – wonderful . . .'

They laughed. Saffie realised how relaxed and easy she felt with
this man. It was as if he was an old friend. She imagined that he
would have that effect on anyone. She recalled his care for his friend.

14

'I saw you earlier,' she had to confess.

'Yes. I know. You took our picture. That is very ironical ..'

The last was said more to himself. Saffie frowned.

'Your friend . . .?'

'Ah – Nikos . . .' He turned to her, smiling. 'He is very beautiful . . .?'

Saffie wondered whether he was mocking her, but then she became aware of the underlying sadness of his expression.

'You are beautiful too, Yianni . . .'

His smile lifted.

'And you too, Saffie.'

Once more, they laughed together. Without discussing it, they walked onto the beach. The windmills were eerie in the moonlight. Saffie shivered.

'Are you cold?'

'No. I saw Nikos, coming down the hill on his horse.'

'Like a Greek god?'

'How do you know?'

'I think that Nikos is well aware of his appeal, Saffie.'

'And, is he as—'

'Sexy as he appears? Oh, no doubt of that.' Then he added mysteriously, 'Though sometimes I think that he does not always like the effect he has on people.'

Saffie was intrigued. Only ever simmering beneath, now Saffie's previous arousal returned forcibly. As did her annoyance with the man who could merely pass her by arrogantly, on horseback, and leave her desperate. This feeling was however tempered a little by the knowledge that he himself was vulnerable. Yiannis was also beguiled by him. Of this she was sure.

'Is he – your lover?'

Yiannis laughed and shook his head.

'Oh, you have the artist's perception, Saffie . . . How strange – that you should take our picture, that you should . . . And that you should arrive. I have the feeling that you are a liberated as well as an intelligent young woman. You know, you may be able to help Nikos.'

'Help him?'

'What about Rachel? Is she as liberated and free-thinking as you?'

Unbidden, and a little disturbing, came an image of Rachel making love. Saffie had come in on them by accident, and had been captivated by her friend.

'Perhaps . . .'

'I really do think you can help. But it may take some time. When do you return to England?'

'It doesn't really matter. I always bring work with me. We are travelling around. Rachel is between jobs. She's in computing; a contract-worker. Taking the opportunity to discover Greece.'

'And does she like it?'

'Yes. I'm sure she'll love it as much as I do by the time we go home.'

'Good. And you will come back – to Hellas?'

'Oh, most certainly.'

'That makes me happy.'

They were passing the windmills. There were signs that one had been used as a home once, and another had an open door. Saffie recalled her fantasy of earlier. She shivered in a sudden cool gust of wind. Yiannis put his arm around her. Her body responded instinctively to his masculine warmth and strength. Sensing this, Yiannis pulled her closer. Soon, they were in a close embrace, and Saffie was left in no doubt that, whatever his interest in Nikos, Yiannis was as aroused as she. It did not really matter that the mysterious Nikos was a catalyst in their attraction for each other.

She pulled him very close as she received his first, tender kiss. It was this reality, rather than fantasy, which she acted on. Yiannis was gentle. His almost too tentative touch fired her, making her nerves flame. Her mind followed his hands as he caressed her back and buttocks. She longed for him to touch her breasts, to slip his hand between her thighs. People passed, interested in them. Saffie took Yiannis' hand.

'We could go inside the windmill,' she suggested.

He nodded. She noticed the languor of his eyes, his parted lips. She wanted to feel for his prick. As they went towards the windmill, she could scarcely walk for thinking of him – his swollen crotch pressed against her clitoris. They closed the door as best as they could. A little moonlight came in through chinks in the thatched roof.

'Wait, Yianni . . .' She pushed him against the wall and took off her short dress and pants. She could feel him, breathing rapidly. She smiled at her own power. She went to him and pressed her naked body against his clothed one. As he reached for her breasts, she forced his arms back against the wall. Yiannis allowed himself to be held there, though Saffie was aware of him, writhing and impatient. She was excited by his restrained strength, by the certainty that he could take her any time that he wished, and that he chose compliance with her. Her breasts tingled in anticipation of being touched at any instant by this new man. Her hungry vagina secreted greedy juices, ready for him.

She shoved him, harder, against the wall and kissed him deeply, inserting her tongue into him. His mouth was very hot. She bit at his tongue and lips. All the time, she pressed her breasts and pubis against the softness of his light clothes. She knew that his prick was urging to be free. She felt its movement against her. Yiannis thrust his thigh between her legs, but she closed them, denying herself even this.

Still restraining his arms, Saffie kissed his warm neck, breathing in his heady masculine scent. Yiannis was beginning to moan now. She moved her hands to his, and he clenched his fingers through hers. Holding her palms against his, Saffie began to force her crotch repeatedly against the warm sheath of his clothing. She imagined his cock, straining to be released, and her breasts thrust in a reflex action against him, becoming agonisingly suffuse.

Further aroused by her own denial, Saffie increased her rate of pressure against Yiannis' bulge. Then, suddenly, she released his hands, and tore her nails down his back to his buttocks. Squeezing them tightly, she knelt and kissed the bulk beneath his soft trousers. Yiannis cried out as she unzipped his flies to release his aching prick. She licked at it, enjoying its clean, spunky odour. She ran the edge of her tongue along the serrations under his hood. Yiannis shuddered. She slipped one hand between his clammy legs and fondled his balls, which were large and hot. Then she took his prick into her sucking mouth.

Yiannis was beginning to remove his shirt. Saffie prevented him, and then stood to divest him of his clothes herself. She gloried in the strength and energy of his body as she caressed him roughly. Then she urged him to the ground and straddled him.

Grasping his prick, she raised herself and thrust it up into her vagina, grunting with fulfilment as she lowered herself, tensing her muscle all the while. She felt her throat and face flush as she took him deeply into her. This sensation spread throughout her body at the joy of having this virile stranger. Yiannis held her waist to support her as she moved slowly up and down the length of his prick. He remained still as she leaned forward to rub her clitoris along him. Saffie realised that Yiannis possessed insight and sensitivity. He responded to her intuitively. Again the feeling that she had known him intimately for a long time overwhelmed her. She smiled blissfully. Yiannis acknowledged this with a slow sensual smile of his own.

As he seized her dangling breasts and massaged them, the exquisite feeling in the pit of her belly and thighs expanded and joined with the acute burning in her womb. Yiannis began to jerk hard but slowly, upwards into her, nurturing the wonderful growing awareness in her nerves. Her vagina began to throb, squeezing his penis. The patient Yiannis now lost control and began to ram more strongly into her, rocking her body with his powerful need.

Saffie leaned forward to kiss him, biting his mouth hard as she continued to fuck him. Yiannis held onto her breasts, yanking them as he neared his orgasm. He closed his eyes and shook his head. He squeezed her nipples tightly. Saffie welcomed the pain. She moved along him faster and faster, as the tight bud of feeling in her clitoris began to explode into myriad spasms of pure pleasure. At the same time, Yiannis cried out in Greek as his hot liquid began to shoot along his penis and out of him. Saffie was aware of his throbbing in unison with her own heady orgasm. Her body was filled with joy.

She clung to him as their hot sweating bodies moved together in enjoyment of each other. Yiannis continued to hold her close as they lapsed into a satiated sleep.

She awoke from erotic slumber to find herself on her back on the floor, with her legs parted and Yiannis trailing the head of his erect penis repeatedly over her clitoris. Saffie smiled, enjoying the pressure of his prick, now parting her labia and rubbing tantalisingly along its opening without entering. She looked up at him in admiration, melting in the tenderness of his eyes, reaching out to

18

feel the bright hair. She took a lock of it between finger and thumb. It felt like silk. She rubbed it lazily through her hand.

'Hello,' said Yiannis as he bent to kiss her, handling her breast as he did so.

'Hi,' Saffie grinned, taking his tongue into her mouth, and seizing it between her teeth.

Yiannis entered her, groaning in sweet anguish as he did so. Saffie entwined her legs around his. Yiannis pressed against her ripe red bud. She kissed him repeatedly, holding on to his muscular buttocks as he made love to her slowly, raising her once more to a consuming orgasm.

When they woke again, it was light and someone was entering the windmill.

'Here you are!' said Eleni, coming in and sitting beside Saffie. She completely disregarded their intimate state.

Yiannis grinned at her, not troubling to move from between Saffie's legs. In fact, he kissed Saffie and caressed her breast gently. Saffie felt his prick stiffening against her clit. She chuckled inwardly, pleased that he was so potent.

'I've been looking for you,' Eleni's dark eyes slid towards the reclining Saffie. 'Constantine called on Nikos last night.'

'How is he?'

'Naturally Nikos didn't get much sleep.'

Saffie's imagination ran amok. Who was Constantine, and how had he deprived Nikos of sleep? Eleni reached out idly and touched Saffie's nipple. Saffie was amazed at her own response as a surge of desire swept through her. Yiannis smiled at her in realisation as her body moved against his. Saffie blushed. Eleni seemed unaware of the commotion she had caused as she stood.

'So – you'll be back soon?' she enquired of Yiannis.

'Yes . . .' he replied, his fingers fiddling casually with Saffie's labia and clitoris.

'Have you seen Rachel?' asked Saffie.

'Sure – she's gone back with Georgiou, to the house.'

'Tell Nikos I'm on my way,' Yiannis assured Eleni as she left. He turned back to Saffie and kissed her, stroking her breasts gently as he did so.

'Where's the house?' she asked.

'I'll take you. It belongs to Constantine, though he has more

19

than one property and is staying elsewhere.'

'Who is staying there?'

'Nikos, Eleni, Georgiou and myself. There were some others but – well, they had to leave . . . Shall we get dressed? There is a possibility of early walkers looking in.'

'Okay,' Saffie laughed, beginning to retrieve her clothes.

The day was already warm as they made their way up to the house. They stopped at a café on the quay for coffee. They sat and watched a couple of the boats being launched. Saffie recalled that they had planned to visit the small island of Delos today. She glanced at the handsome Greek man beside her. Yiannis smiled as if in remembrance of their passionate night together. He ran his finger along her inner arm. Saffie felt her body tingle, recalling the pleasure he had given her. She allowed a moment to pass silently by before enquiring:

'So – who's Constantine?'

'Oh – he's a sort of "friend" of Nikos' family,' Yiannis explained, adding quietly: 'Though I doubt Nikos thinks of him as such right now.'

Intrigued, Saffie awaited further enlightenment, though she decided against questioning Yiannis when he lapsed into silent thought.

The house was at the top of the hills, with a view over the small-holdings and the terracotta rooftops of the white houses and occasional windmills, down to the harbour. It was a large villa, standing in a generous garden and surrounded by open land. Bushes and flowers filled the well-tended garden. There were also neo-classical statues and a pond and fountain. Yiannis shouted out for Nikos as he entered. Nikos was in the kitchen, looking surly and tired. He glared at Yiannis from his position at the sink, then almost sneered at Saffie. Saffie didn't think he'd actually been doing much; perhaps he was just annoyed that there wasn't a clean cup. Yiannis ignored him and went to turn on the kettle.

'Coffee?' he asked Saffie.

'That would be lovely.' She sat on a wooden chair by the door. 'Nikos?'

Nikos shrugged, and went to sit at the pine table by the window. He picked up his pen and scowled as he looked down at his blank paper. Sometimes, he glanced surreptitiously at Saffie. Saffie smiled as she watched him. Though he was partly hidden by the vase of flowers on the table, she occasionally had a good view of his clean-cut profile. Yiannis handed her a glass of fresh orange from the fridge. She drank it thirstily. He took one over to Nikos, who tried to communicate with him without Saffie seeing. Yiannis went to the sink and began to wash the dishes Nikos had abandoned. Saffie was aware of the tension between them. She wondered where Rachel was. Yiannis finished the pots, made coffee and brought her some.

'What would you like for breakfast?' he asked.

Saffie shrugged. She *was* hungry.

'Ham, cheese, salad and bread?' Yiannis suggested.

'Yes, that would be lovely. Thank you.' She smiled at him.

Yiannis returned this. As this exchange lingered, Saffie was aware of Nikos' annoyance. She was puzzled by his unfriendliness; saddened too as – under clandestine scrutiny – he proved to be even more attractive close up. His black curls hung over his perfect face as he leant over the table. His eyes were dark and expressive as he glanced occasionally at them. The jet lashes were very long. Saffie smiled secretly in pleasure as she looked at him.

'I think I'll take this out in the garden,' she said to Yiannis. 'Is that all right?'

'Sure. Please do.'

Nikos began to shout at Yiannis almost as soon as she had left the room.

'Why are you wasting your time? We have to find some new people. You can't just pick up English tourists to fit the bill. Constantine will be back later. You can't just go out like that and pick up anyone – expect them to take part in this, this farce!'

'Sshhh . . . Niko – I didn't . . .'

'And Georgiou, he came back with her friend.'

'I know. It just happened. But – don't worry . . . Despite it not being planned, I think it will work . . . They are free to stay – for long enough.'

'You've told her?' Nikos asked in astonishment.

'Of course not. Niko, calm down . . .'

' "Calm down"! I don't know how to get out of this whole mess. It's a ridiculous situation.'

21

'Then leave. Don't comply.'

'I have to,' Nikos scoffed.

'Well, then, we will. Get an agreement that this is all. After that – you can get the photographs back.'

Saffie wandered around the garden with her coffee, looking at the fountain and pool and at the lovely view beyond. She saw Eleni come from the house. She felt a little confused at seeing her; her body recalled her piquant touch. Nevertheless, she smiled.

'Do you know what they are discussing?' Eleni asked her.

'Mmmmm . . .' Saffie could not lie.

Eleni smiled.

'Ah – you understand Hellenic?'

'Some. I've been visiting Greece for many years. My parents loved Hellas, my father taught ancient Greek.'

'So – that may be fun for you. Don't worry. Nikos is – worried. He's not usually quite so hostile to guests.'

'Where's Rachel?'

'She and Georgiou have gone for a walk. They'll be back soon.'

'It's a lovely house.'

'Yes. But it's nothing like Nikos', on Naxos. That is really something.'

'They were talking about us.'

'Yes. I think Nikos got the – wrong end of the stick? You are merely welcome here as friends. Nothing is expected of you.'

'But – what kind of trouble is Nikos in?'

Eleni looked surprised.

'Yiannis told you?'

'No. He hinted . . .'

Eleni hesitated visibly before responding.

'Constantine, who owns this house, is making a film. Two of the actresses left unexpectedly.'

'Ah – and Nikos is an actor?'

'He can act well, but he wants to devote himself to his writing.'

'And Yiannis?'

'He acts sometimes.'

'Oh, yes – he said. So – what is the problem? Were they in this film of Constantine's?'

'Yes – they had to be.'

22

'But, they weren't keen?'

'Not really . . . You see – it is a particular type of film.'

'Ah – a pornographic film?'

'I suppose some people would say that, but – it will be artistic. Constantine is talented. He has had much success.'

Saffie smiled. She could not help but be aroused by the thought of Nikos and Yiannis in a sex-film. Eleni was interested in her response.

'You are not – disgusted – by that?'

'No. I can only think how wonderful it would be – with Nikos and Yiannis— They are both very attractive men, aren't they?'

'Of course. But, you see, Nikos is reluctant to do the film, which is really why the actresses left. I mean – it is hard to get sexy when the leading man is shouting and sulking.' Eleni smiled ruefully at Saffie.

'Yes. I can see that. But, why on earth is he making it?'

'Well, Constantine has – a hold over him.'

'What?'

'Nikos' family is proud, and also extremely wealthy and successful. Nikos will inherit his grandfather's fortune. Also, his responsibilities and standing. His grandfather, Stavros Mandreas, is in his nineties now, though he still has all his faculties. He has great pride in Nikos. Nikos' father is dead. Constantine was his father's friend. He found out something about Nikos that he threatens to tell his grandfather – unless Nikos makes this film for him. As you say – Nikos is handsome – he would look well in such a film.'

'It was photographs . . .' Saffie realised, thinking of the conversation she had just overheard, and recalling how Yiannis had said it was ironical that she should take their photographs.

Eleni smiled.

'Actually – they were very good pictures.'

'Of you and him?'

'No.'

Eleni laughed and whispered to Saffie, 'They are of Nikos and Yiannis.'

Saffie turned to her, her smile broadening. Eleni's black eyes met her own. She nodded and put her finger to her lips.

'And so – you see – despite all those stories of ancient Greek

23

love, many older modern Greeks strongly disapprove of homo-sexuality – especially Nikos' grandfather.'

'So – they are gay?'

'No more than you are. But the photographs would shock old Stavros. Oh, they were taken many years ago, by one of their friends. Nikos was tremendously annoyed when Constantine got hold of them.'

'Wouldn't the film shock Stavros?' asked Saffie reasonably.

'He won't see it. It's not to Constantine's advantage for the old man to know. Constantine wants to make money . . . though, to give him his due – it will probably be a good, artistic film.'

'I'm sure it will be . . .' agreed Saffie with interest. 'What are the photographs like?'

Eleni smiled at Saffie's curiosity.

'Oh . . . you would like them, Saffie. Ah – here's your friend now. I'll go and see Nikos.'

Rachel and Georgiou waved to them as they approached the garden from the lane. Saffie watched Eleni return to the house, then went to meet Rachel, who was smiling radiantly from Georgiou's embrace.

'I think that Saffie, at least, would be willing to take part in the film,' Eleni announced to the men as she entered the kitchen.

Yiannis was preparing breakfast. Nikos looked up at her, astounded.

'What are you two up to? Yianni, you told me . . .'

'I didn't arrange it . . .'

'Don't blame Yiannis. We just got talking. She can understand Hellenic – so she knew how you were talking about them . . .'

'You can't do this, Eleni . . .' protested Nikos, coming over to them from his table.

'She's sexy enough, Niko – and receptive,' pointed out Eleni.

'That's not the point. It's unethical just to entice women and then get them to take part in Constantine's seedy film.'

'We didn't really do that, but you've not done anything to hire new actresses . . . and, Niko, it was down to you that they left. Constantine is getting impatient. He could go to your grandfather out of spite . . .'

'Look, Niko,' added Yiannis, 'you know we haven't got anything

24

to lose. They are intelligent women. Saffron is an artist herself. And she can speak Hellenic. We can put it to them, discuss it . . .'

'Tttt . . . I don't know – maybe . . .'

'Think about it.'

'It just doesn't seem ethical. They are here on holiday . . .'

Eleni and Yiannis exchanged a smile at their friend's meticulous scruples. Eleni could only think how much the lovely Saffie would enjoy Nikos. He himself had no doubt of his attractiveness and sexual prowess. Why did he complicate matters so with so much thinking? It must be to do with him being a writer. He seemed sometimes to agonise for hours over things that would not have given her a second's concern. As for herself, she was more like Yiannis, happy to live life to the full, grasping at every opportunity to do so.

She began to help Yiannis with the meal, taking things to the table outside. Georgiou and Rachel went upstairs, ostensibly to have a shower. Saffie was sitting on the bench at the far end of the garden, her drawing-pad on her knee, sketching the view to the harbour below.

Nikos could not concentrate on his writing. He watched the English woman through the window. Saffron. Saffie.

She was completely engrossed in her work. He envied her this. He was keen to go and look at what she was doing, but he was held back by the awkwardness of the situation he believed himself to be in. By now, the ebullient Eleni would have disclosed all to her. Things were always so simple to her. And indeed, seen from that viewpoint, he had to agree. It was like a godsend. They desperately needed two young women for Constantine's film, and here were two very sexy women. He was torn between his natural integrity and his apprehension of Constantine carrying out his threats.

It was ridiculous really, that such a juvenile indiscretion could carry such potential cataclysmic disaster. For Nikos had no doubt that his grandfather, Stavros, would disinherit him if he saw the photographs. They were very incriminating. Or could be seen as being so. Stavros had extremely old-fashioned ideals, and Nikos could not afford 1990s worldliness about this. He himself may be sexually liberal, but Stavros would not – could not – understand this. He would consider that his grandson was insufficiently masculine – or something equally ludicrous. If Nikos had not been so concerned, he would have laughed uproariously at this misconception, but he had an extended family to care for. Stavros had never really liked his daughter-in-law. Now that his son had died, he would probably be pleased to pass on his estate to his own daughter. He was close to Nikos, but would reject him if he believed that Nikos was unreliable. He would consider him to be vulnerable – at a disadvantage in an increasingly difficult and competitive business world. He would think that Nikos' cousin, his daughter's son, would be more trustworthy. Nikos sighed.

He continued to watch Saffie. He was aware of her interest in him, and he had to admit that his own response to her was as dynamic. She would perhaps be sympathetic, but his pride prevented him from revealing his plight to her.

He saw the sun gleaming in her thick black hair. Her limbs were brown and smooth. She wore a dark blue cotton dress. Everything in him urged him to go out into the warm garden and look at her drawing. How easily he could sit beside her, and begin a friendship. He had no doubt she would be friendly. He lit a cigarette and pushed his writing away from him.

'The meal is almost ready, Niko,' said Eleni, coming to put her arms around his shoulders and kiss his head. 'She is very nice – no?' she teased as she looked out at Saffie.

'Go and tell Georgiou and Rachel it's all ready, 'Leni,' called Yiannis.

'I'll go,' offered Nikos, relieved to have the opportunity to be alone for a few minutes.

'That's very good . . .' said Eleni admiringly, seeing the familiar landscape accurately recorded on the white page. 'You are very talented.'

Saffie smiled and closed her book, going with Eleni over to the table in the shade of the old olive tree. It looked very appetising, laden with croissants, sesame rolls, baguettes, meats, cheeses, fruit and salad. There was also a bottle of wine.

'It's almost lunch,' joked Yiannis.

'Yes, Yianni – ten a.m.' agreed Eleni, sitting down and pouring orange from the iced jug.

★　★　★

Still deep in thought, Nikos pushed open the door of Georgiou's room. He smiled affectionately, filled with wonder as he was confronted with the sight of the two young people engrossed in making love. Rachel's soft golden-brown body was entwined with his friend's darker brown muscular one. Her long golden hair was strewn over him, mixing with Georgiou's black curls. She was leaning over to kiss Georgiou passionately. Nikos smiled at his friend's obvious ecstasy as her slender hand moved to grasp his full penis firmly. Nikos felt his own greedy member strain jealously as she pulled on Georgiou. He watched as, expertly, she jerked his cock rhythmically, taking his foreskin over the bulbous head, and pulling it sharply back towards its base.

Her other hand was under his muscular buttocks, her fingers seeming to Nikos to go between, perhaps even to rub against, his anus. Georgiou reached for her ripe breast. Slowly, he traced the outline of its fullness. Rachel moaned in pleasure, her leg went over his as she pressed her erect clitoris against his thigh. Georgiou began to knead her swollen teats in abandon, tweaking at her hardened nipples. Nikos' body beat in accord with Georgiou's as his friend grasped Rachel's bottom and pulled her on top of him.

Rachel released his prick. Georgiou groaned in despair at this sudden abandonment. Nikos smiled as Rachel slipped between Georgiou's legs, and began to bounce against his cock. His eyes narrowed lasciviously as he watched her smooth round behind rise and fall with increasing rapidity. Each time she fell against Georgiou's prick, she lingered for longer, squirming against him. Nikos knew that she found it increasingly difficult to move away from that delightful place as the spasms of sexual joy shot between them.

It was obvious that Georgiou was longing to thrust his aching prick deep into her warm moist muscular place. He tossed his head from side to side in sweet suffering. Nikos smiled at his voluptuousness. As, at last, Rachel positioned herself to allow his suffuse cock to slide easily into her, Georgiou opened his eyes and saw Nikos. He smiled sensuously. Nikos wanted to be in his place. He smiled slightly and mouthed: 'Food'.

Georgiou blinked his eyes in understanding and turned to kiss Rachel. She was now moving very rapidly along his stiffened

27

member. Soon, Nikos knew, the impatient Georgiou would come. But he would be ready for love again very shortly. Rachel was beginning to strain and gasp. Nikos watched as they tensed and writhed, tearing at each other as they sought release, and then he turned away unwillingly from this beguiling sight.

He leaned against the door at the top of the stairs. His body, always sensual, burned with sexual longing. He prayed that Eleni would come to see why he had been so long. He would lift up her short dress and push his hungry cock into her crimson hole. He would ram her hard against the wall, and she would respond and smile in pleasure. But she was too interested in Saffie at present, he told himself, filled with sudden jealousy.

With immense self control, he prevented himself from going to his room and wanking quickly to appease his wild longing. Instead, though distracted, he went downstairs to face the nerve-wracking ordeal of getting to know Saffie.

'Niko . . .' Eleni greeted him with a knowing look. She recognised his lustful expression and exploited his condition mercilessly. She laughed and kissed him teasingly. She knew that he needed to fuck her. She lingered near him, touching him secretly. He pushed her off impatiently, embarrassed in front of Saffie, who was regarding them with keen interest. After the initial, natural meeting of their eyes, Nikos decided to remain aloof. Saffie was fascinated by his state. His intense sexuality came towards her in waves.

'Did you tell Georgiou and Rachel?' Yiannis asked Nikos.

'Yes.'

Nikos avoided Saffie's smiling eyes.

'So – Constantine is inviting us to dinner tonight?' Eleni asked Nikos.

Nikos poured coffee. Saffie saw the dark eyes glowering. He was becoming angry with Eleni.

'I am sure he would be only too happy for us to take our new friends along,' Yiannis added.

Nikos glanced at him darkly, wondering what they had been concocting together.

'You would be very welcome,' he said graciously to Saffie, who smiled once more and nodded.

'We had planned to go to Delos today,' she recalled, turning to

Yiannis. 'Do you know what time the boats leave?'

Yiannis laughed.

'I think you should speak to Nikos.'

Saffie looked at him in question.

'I have a boat,' Nikos explained simply.

'We will all go!' exclaimed Eleni. 'You can make a picnic, Yianni.'

'Cheers.'

'Niko?' entreated Eleni, kneeling and putting her head on his lap. She was too near his swollen penis and smiled at his discomfort. She squeezed him playfully as she rose. Saffie saw the desire smouldering in his eyes as his gaze followed the pretty Greek girl. Her skirt barely covered her pert bottom, her shapely, olive-brown legs parted invitingly at the top. Saffie felt her own sex pulse in sympathy. Simultaneously, she was vicariously excited by the prospect of Eleni's sexuality, and dynamically moved by Nikos. As well as her own feelings, it was as though she was poised between them and their sexual relationship. To be within this milieu of sexual promise and freedom was certainly stimulating.

'Nikos would never refuse to visit his beloved island,' Yiannis explained to Saffie. He raised his voice to shout, 'Georgiou – come and eat – we are going to Nikos' island!'

Saffie regarded the handsome Greek man with a new, intellectual interest. If he knew the sacred island well, then he could help her. She had visited it before, but the scheduled boat-trip only allowed for a brief visit. She was excited at the prospect of spending many hours amongst the pure white marble ruins. Ancient strictures forbade people to sleep on the island overnight, but perhaps they could hide and defy this? How magical – to explore the ancient island by moonlight. Then, her spirits fell slightly. It would not be possible tonight. They were dining with Constantine.

'We'll go then?' she asked Nikos. This was important to her.

Nikos inclined his head, recognising her interest. She felt that he respected this.

'You will draw?' he asked.

Saffie nodded.

'I'll go and tell the others,' Eleni said, with an exaggerated sigh.

'We ought to go back and get some things,' Saffie said.

'Oh – you don't need much. I can let you borrow some shorts if you like. Eat first and enjoy your meal.'

'Can I have a shower?'

'Sure – later, while Yiannis gets the picnic.'

'You can help, 'Leni . . .' insisted Yiannis.

'Sure . . .' she laughed.

Eleni went to Yiannis and hugged him from behind. Yiannis turned and kissed her passionately. Saffie watched Nikos regarding them through narrowed eyes. She wondered how he dealt privately with the liberal sexuality between them all.

'Come, then – Saffie.'

Released from Yiannis' embrace, Eleni held out her hand to Saffie, who took it as she stood. Once more, she was surprised at the flash of sensuality between them, and wondered whether the men noticed her flush. As they went into the house, they encountered Rachel and Georgiou, still entwined and tousled. Rachel smiled at Saffie, like the cat who had got the proverbial cream. Saffie smiled at the sexual interpretation of this.

The room Saffie was shown into was large and airy, containing only a bed, under the opened window, a large wardrobe on the opposite wall, and a table and chair in one corner. There was a shower-unit in the opposite corner. Eleni lay on the bed, watching Saffie as she went to Nikos' desk. She trailed her fingers over the pile of books, and tried not to look at Nikos' strewn papers.

She turned to smile at Eleni, but was made serious by the look in the young woman's beautiful dark eyes. As an artist, she had always been aware of the integral attractiveness of people she encountered. She admitted to herself that she was interested in women, but she had never taken it beyond this. She recalled Eleni's effect on her that morning, when she had reached out so naturally and touched her breast. Her vagina glowed now in memory of this. She told herself that her receptivity then had been due to arousal with Yiannis. But then, she had been interested in Eleni and Georgiou at the quay, when she had regarded them merely as strangers. It would never have crossed her mind that same beautiful girl would touch her so intimately within hours. And her initial awakening had been merely from watching Nikos ride arrogantly by. This would have been missed if it had not first been appreciated and pointed out by Rachel. Already, they all seemed intrinsically bound.

It occurred to Saffie that she was in the midst – no – part of a group of highly sexed and attractive young people. The four Greek friends certainly seemed liberal in their own sexual liaisons. The prospect of being part of this appealed to her. The thought of sexual indulgence at will was liberating. It entered her mind that making Constantine's film would really only be one step from their normal life together. She scarcely flinched as Eleni came to her and stood close.

'Nikos . . .' she murmured, 'He is very, very sexy . . .'

Swiftly and delicately, her hand cupped Saffie's cusp. She caressed her breast delicately and then moved to kiss her, just putting her pointed tongue fleetingly between her lips. Saffie was ragingly turned on, and felt bereft as Eleni moved away.

'Please – help yourself to anything in here . . .' She indicated the wardrobe. 'I should help Yiannis with the food. You just turn the shower dial round to the right.'

'Thank you, Eleni . . .'

'You are most welcome.' Eleni smiled warmly.

Two

Constantine Stephanopolous sipped from his glass of champagne as he listened to the caller on the other end of the receiver. He looked out of the window across the expanse of shore towards the azure sea. The firm set of his jaw belied his relaxed attitude as he reclined on his chair, feet up on his desk. He was a man in his early fifties whose appeal had been increased, rather than diminished, by time. He was all the more distinguished for the silver in his once raven hair.

His strong, well-sculptured face was endowed with character in its finely etched lines of experience. His lithe body was still agile and powerful if a little stockier than in his youth. He kept himself fit by swimming and working-out. His dark brown eyes were intelligent and perceptive, conveying, to those he surveyed keenly, his astute understanding. The hands which cradled the phone and lifted the crystal glass were well-shaped and sensitive. They had brought many women supreme pleasure.

He was a passionate man, used to achieving his desires and gaining full enjoyment in his hedonistic life. He was also a man quick to anger and frightening in his occasional rages. He surrounded himself with people eager to fulfil his needs.

'I can assure you that the film will be completed on time as promised. Your loan is not misplaced,' he said crisply. Though his tone was arrogant, his deep voice was musical and persuasive, conveying a confidence he did not quite feel at present.

He replaced the receiver with control and squeezed the empty cigarette packet beside it. Perhaps it would have been easier to demand finances from Nikos. But, although the young man would one day be extremely wealthy, he could not, at present, command such sums as would be worth Constantine's while. In any case,

Constantine's creative mind was obsessed by the concept of the film he had planned. He had not thought that Nikos would be so unwilling, nor have so many scruples.

Indeed, it had been the seductive and professional photographs of the young man which had inspired him to formulate his plan. Nikos! He felt suddenly violent and out of patience with him. He grabbed up the receiver and keyed in his number. The phone rang on and on. Constantine had a sudden fear that the man would defy him and go off with his eminently suitable and attractive friends. He was afraid that he had lost not only the two willing, though replaceable, actresses from Paris, but also the enticing and imaginative Eleni. He was certain that she, as well as Yiannis and Georgiou, would do as he wished for Nikos' sake. Indeed, they had seemed quite keen on participating. Eleni was one of the sexiest young women he had ever met. He smiled to think of her, some of his impatience evaporating. His lecherous body recalled her eager love-making.

Surely they would arrive this evening for dinner as arranged? Nikos dared not risk him revealing his youthful indiscretions to his stern patriarch. Constantine took another fresh packet of cigarettes and patiently placed them in the silver box on his desk. Then he lit one and smoked slowly, looking out over the sea.

Saffie and Rachel relaxed in the stern of the yacht. Rachel lolled sleepily against her friend, languid and content. Yiannis and Georgiou took turns at the wheel. Eleni stretched out along the bench one side of the boat. Nikos, sitting opposite, seemed engrossed in making notes. Saffie looked over the side, smiling to see dolphins. As they neared Delos, she moved to Nikos' side, to drink in the wonderful first sight of the island. On top of the glistening white ruins, she imaginatively transposed the ancient image of temples, houses and statues. Once a huge bronze statue of Apollo, whose island this was, shone in the Mediterranean sun.

The port was then bustling with sailors and merchants from around the world. There had been hundreds and hundreds of statues; a theatre, and temples to gods and goddesses. This had been a strategic military, political and trading centre. Its importance was reflected in its wealth and luxury. There had been festivals and games to honour the deities. Now the earth was parched by the hot sun, and the ancient ruins gleamed like white bones. All the marble statues were long gone.

They passed the ancient sacred harbour and found space beyond the kayaks. Yiannis moored the boat and they disembarked. Rachel had not visited Delos before, and wanted to climb the steps up the hill of Mount Kynthos, in order to gain a good vantage point from which to see the island. She and Georgiou therefore set off through the later, Roman ruins. They could hear Georgiou telling her that, according to myth, Leto had given birth, first to Artemis, and then to her twin brother, Apollo, on this island. Eleni and Yiannis, who knew the island well, strolled off to the deserted area, beyond the ruins, and the stadium.

'And when he was born,' said Nikos to Saffie as they set off for the avenue of lions, 'flowers appeared everywhere, and music played.'

'God of music and of the arts,' Saffie added.

She smiled. It seemed that they had been left together by common consent, or, more probably, the others had paired off naturally and desired privacy more than a view of the remains.

Nikos accompanied Saffie to the area which was once the sacred lake, where she photographed and sketched the marble lions which still guarded the filled-in lake. Nikos was a quiet companion, though he answered various questions she put to him, displaying an extensive knowledge of his history. Saffie thought he was thoughtful rather than sullen. She found it difficult to concentrate on her work with such a desirable male close to her. He too was an artist and appreciated her need for quiet.

'I often come here,' he told her.

'You have the boat – but you don't live on Mykonos, do you? Eleni said you have a house on Naxos.'

'That's true. But I spend much time on Mykonos, at Constantine's house. Mainly to come here.'

'How lovely, and – you write. Novels?'

'Yes. And short stories, plays – and some poetry.'

'You have been published?'

'Yes.'

They continued in silence for a time. Saffie was increasingly aware of the dynamic effect the man had on her.

'You know,' she said at length, 'I'd love to come here at night. When there is absolutely no one around and there is silence.'

'Except for the old gods and the frogs in the cisterns, lizards . . .'

'And the full moon.'

'It will be full tonight. We could return.'

Nikos' dark eyes met hers. He was serious. Her heart leapt. Without even thinking, she nodded. Nikos smiled. She wanted to kiss him. Increasingly, she was disturbingly aware of his powerful sexuality. She turned away from his intense gaze. They walked slowly through the ruins, past the place where the statue of Apollo had stood, and towards the region of the ancient gymnasium.

'What about your dinner with Constantine?'

'Ttttt . . .' he was annoyed at the thought of this. 'Afterwards, we will come.'

'Well, Yianni – do you really have hopes of our new friends agreeing to do Constantine's film?' asked Eleni.

'We have to persuade Nikos, first!' Yiannis sighed. 'I think that may be more difficult.'

Their eyes met in their mutual exasperation with their recalcitrant friend. They were sitting against an old wall, looking down on the small synagogue near the sea. Yiannis ran his finger slowly down Eleni's back. He took a handful of her silken black hair and put it to his mouth to kiss. It was fragrant and warm. He reached out and slipped his arm around her slim waist, pulling her gently back on to the verge. She smiled up at him as he leant over to kiss her. Yiannis grasped her breast and began, with circular motion, to press down on it. The burning of his unruly member increased.

Eleni's kiss was sweet and strong. He felt her body writhing beneath his. He unfastened the buttons of her tiny dress and released her breasts. Hungrily, he took one of her pert nipples into his mouth and began to suckle greedily. Eleni tossed in pleasure, nudging at his crotch with her pubis. Yiannis sucked strongly, bringing her to the edge where pain and pleasure met. One hand caressed and squeezed her other breast, whilst the other trailed slowly down her belly. He slipped it under the loose silk of her soft pants. And inside, where, immediately, he found her ripe bud of pleasure and pressed it hard between finger and thumb.

He moved as she slipped her hand down to his cock. She squeezed it hard. He knew that she was impatient for him to enter her. As she released his naked prick and teased him, he inserted his finger deeply into her tight passage. Keeping his thumb on her clitoris, he began to jerk his fingers rapidly into her. He moaned as she responded by masturbating his yearning penis.

Yiannis released her and lay between her legs, pressing on her sex with his for a few minutes. Then he moved his hot, sucking mouth to her other breast. Her little dress was around her waist. Otherwise, she was naked. Yiannis sat astride her, smiling sexily and looking at his red raw prick lying against her brown belly. Her mouth was open, the tip of her pink tongue coming hungrily between her lips. Her hair was tangled in the dried grass. He leant to lick at the soft skin. He trailed his burning tongue down to her clitoris and tongued her.

He felt her squirm in enjoyment as he spread her labia and licked powerfully at the opening of her vagina. He forced his tongue within. At the same time, he touched her secret, tighter hole with the delicate edge of his forefinger. He thought she would come as she began to toss wildly, groaning and swearing and moving her head from side to side as his mouth was at her sex.

'Yianni!' she commanded.

Yiannis raised her abdomen and looked lustfully at her moist scarlet lips, and sodden hole. He narrowed his eyes in anticipation and then pushed his cock deeply into her. He groaned as he felt the powerful muscle grasp him tightly. Then he abandoned himself to the familiar pleasure of fucking her long and hard. Each thrust brought him nearer his release, but, with long practice, he had learned to control this.

They became hotter and hotter in the burning sun as their naked flesh slapped rhythmically. They were as aware of each other's approaching orgasm as their own, and controlled their rate until they reached their peak at the same time, clinging to each other, kissing and fondling. Until they drifted into vermilion dreams.

'You must consider yourself a guest,' Nikos said in a very serious tone.

Saffie realised that this was what he had been building up to during his preoccupied silence.

'If people try to persuade you to — participate, you must feel under no obligation, none at all . . . You understand . . .'

'I understand.'

Saffie smiled affectionately. Certainly, Nikos seemed to be a supremely honourable man, as well as an exceptionally attractive one. His scruples endeared him to her. She wondered fleetingly whether he was so deviously clever as to depend on this for her co-operation.

'Have you been to this area before?' he asked, indicating the expanse of the ancient track.

'No.'

They walked across the stadium until they came across the satiated lovers, deeply asleep in each other's arms.

'You must not – be jealous.' Nikos looked at her in concern lest she should show such an emotion.

'I'm not,' Saffie assured him. 'They look very beautiful.'

'Yes . . .' Nikos agreed.

Her sex pulsed at the sight of them, and the thought of them making love. She moved a little away from Nikos, probably as a counter-reaction to actually wanting him so much. He glanced at her. She wondered whether he misinterpreted her gesture as shyness, or, she thought incredulously, unwillingness!

'Yianni,' Nikos called softly.

Yiannis was lost in sleep, his face buried in Eleni's breasts, his leg over hers, his hand between her thighs.

'Yianni . . .' Nikos repeated. There was tenderness in his tone.

Eleni stirred, opening her eyes slowly to see Nikos. Saffie registered her smile of glorious happiness. She reached out her hand to him. Nikos knelt beside them and kissed her softly.

'We should return to the boat, to drink and eat,' he said.

Eleni nodded and then shook her head and kissed her lover until Yiannis awoke. He too met Nikos' eyes. Saffie was surprised

to see Nikos tousling Yiannis' thick hair before standing. She was
moved by the affection and freedom between these young people.
Their care for each other was obvious.

'We'll see you soon. We'll go and prepare the food – yes?' He
turned to Saffie with this last word.

She nodded, catching Eleni's amused glance, and recalling
Nikos' reluctance in the kitchen earlier. However, it was the
possibility of sex with Nikos, and not preparing food with him,
that she thought of as they made their way back across the
island. She wondered how he would react if she approached
him as she had imagined on the previous day. He seemed so
hell bent on not taking advantage of her with Constantine's film
that he was blind to her obvious interest in him. So an approach
on her part may be the only way. Would he push her away as
he had done Eleni earlier? She did not have an opportunity to
implement her plan as Nikos really did get on with laying out
the food Yiannis had brought. There were pies, rolls, meat and
cheese, olives, honey, fruit, salad and wine. Soon, Rachel and
Georgiou returned to the boat. Saffie had an opportunity to talk
to her friend as Georgiou helped Nikos. The men were engaged
in quiet conversation.

'So . . .' Saffie began, '—you're okay with your Greek god?'

'Yeah . . .' Rachel smiled smugly at her. 'He's fantastic.'

Saffie's green eyes flickered across to where Rachel's lover
was opening wine, his back to them. Instinctively, she glanced
appreciatively at Georgiou's small, neat behind. She met Rachel's
eyes in approval. It was easy to imagine that he was as adept a
lover as Yiannis. And somehow, Saffie expected Nikos to be even
more accomplished.

'Has he said anything about Nikos' dilemma?' she asked
quietly.

'This film, and Constantine?' Rachel's clear eyes met hers.

'What do you think?'

'I'd be happy to take part. It would be fun, don't you think?'

Saffie shrugged.

'Perhaps. I'm certainly keen to meet this Constantine. Tonight,
dinner at his?'

'Right.'

'Hi!' called Eleni as she and Yiannis climbed aboard.

Georgiou brought round a tray of chilled wine, which they all accepted gratefully.

After an enjoyable and protracted late lunch they returned to Mykonos in time to shower and change before driving across the island in Nikos' black Mercedes. Eleni sat next to him in the front. Saffie was aware of their intimacy as she herself reclined against Yiannis, who put his arm around her, as if to reassure her.

Constantine eyed the young English women with blatant approbation. Saffie witnessed Nikos bristling at his host's obvious assumption. He took Constantine to one side as they drank their cocktails, no doubt to disillusion him. Saffie was interested in the dynamics between the two men. Though Constantine was supposed to wield such power over the younger man, Nikos' bearing and attitude was proud, almost haughty. Everyone was quite at home in this older man's house. At table, the conversation and laughter flowed as freely as the wine. Saffie sat next to Constantine. Throughout the meal, she was aware of Nikos' frequent sidelong glances towards them.

She thought that Constantine was certainly a charming host, and a very charismatic man. He was the kind one met rarely – an older man with immense personal presence and self-confidence, in some ways more attractive than most younger men. He was still extremely handsome and, no doubt, thought Saffie, a very experienced lover. She was aware of her receptive body's response to this.

He talked fluently on many subjects and apparently, he was very interested in art history. Saffie wondered whether he was shaping his film in his mind, picturing them together. Would he himself take part?

After dinner they split into various groups, several – including Saffie and Nikos – went into the warm garden. The night was filled with the perfume of flowers, the scent of lemon groves and the myriad sounds of cicadas.

'Ah, Niko, I'm sure you will not mind at all if I should steal your lovely friend away, just for a short conversation.'

As the older man placed his hand firmly on Saffie's shoulder and steered her away, she was aware of Nikos watching him darkly.

'Do sit down, Saffron. A delightful name. You're not cold at all?'

'No. I'm fine,' Saffie assured him, sitting on the marble bench under the cypress tree, aware that its position conveniently shielded her from Nikos. Doubtless this was Constantine's intention.

'Now. I am well aware that you are an intelligent young woman, Saffron, and so I will waste neither your time nor my own. I gather that you know about the film I intend to make, and the problems we have encountered?'

Cloistered away with him, Saffie was strongly aware of the man's persuasive charm, and – disturbingly – of the powerful magnetism of his body. As he continued to talk to her, this power was translated in her mind into believing that he was requesting that she become his mistress, not merely take a part in his film.

'I would be honoured if you should agree to participate. Take some time, tell me tomorrow. What will be asked of you will not be difficult for you. Indeed, I cannot for one minute believe that you will find the experience other than liberating and enlightening.' He touched her arm fleetingly, sending waves of lust through her body. 'These beautiful young people are all fascinating, each in their own way, are they not? Already, you will be aware of the freedom between them: the attraction, and lack of possessiveness. That is partly what inspired me. It is quite unique. And now, here you are on holiday, out of your ordinary life, and you have somehow become part of this special group. Tell me, Saffie, how did that happen?' Constantine leaned even closer to her, riveted, awaiting her revelation.

'It was Nikos. When I saw him . . .' She shrugged.

Constantine nodded, understanding completely.

'And, by chance, we met the others at "Apollo's" . . .'

'You have much in common with them, you and Rachel,' Constantine commented in an assured tone, as if he had been closely examining the reason for their inclusion. 'You do realise that you will be asked only to do that which is enjoyable. In fact, perhaps merely to record on film what you will doubtless experience in any case, with Nikos and Eleni, Yiannis and Georgiou. As an artist, you will understand that. As you know, sexual relations between these four are very free. You and your friend have already been charmed by this. Already been included. You cannot leave now, can you?'

Saffie's mind did not go willingly towards the possibility of leaving Nikos.

'You will undoubtedly become further involved. They have that power. It is this I wish to capture. I could get many willing actors to take part in my film, but they have, well, something very special. They are liberal and unashamed. They are free with each other, and chosen newcomers, and they are not envious. That is because they are secure. The bonds between them are unbreakable. Think, Saffie – by agreeing to do the film, you will be freed to do that which is in your most secret fantasy, if you wish ... There is no shame, no false modesty with them.'

Saffie flushed, believing that this man had the power of omniscience, that he realised how much she needed to fuck Nikos.

His mellifluous voice continued: 'All I ask for now, Saffie, is your assurance that you will give serious consideration to the possibility of being in the film.'

They sat in silence for a time. The heady atmosphere of the friends, together with this fantastic request, mingled in her head. Constantine's melodic voice bewitched her senses. She really believed that he was offering her a once in a lifetime opportunity to indulge her sexual desires. Her mind spun. She re-lived her first sight of Nikos – was it really only yesterday? She recalled her sensual sketch of Rachel. She thought of her night with Yiannis, and Eleni's knowing touch. Her body was flooded with the memory of Nikos' proximity. It was as if all these events conspired to bring her here, to this man's garden. To be offered indulgence and sex and the freedom, by way of his film: to enjoy all this more fully than in life.

They *were* all attractive and desirable young people. This older man, now watching her carefully and patiently awaiting her response, was himself extremely desirable.

Saffie realised that she was very aroused. Her day had been beguiling to all senses. She wanted to be loved tonight. She could be touched by anyone – Yiannis, or Eleni, Georgiou or even Rachel. Most of all, she wanted Nikos. She nodded slowly at

42

Constantine, whose eyes smiled. His face flooded with relief. Saffie felt that she should wonder what she would be asked to do, and why Nikos was so very reluctant for them to participate. If she had been prescient, she would have had some inkling as he arrived to take her away from the predatory Constantine.

'Don't forget Delos,' he whispered to her.

Saffie wondered whether she was drunk as he led her away. She was glad to be near his warm, potent body. But she would have been as happy for Constantine to have kissed her. It was as if his hypnotic voice, with its promise of sexual freedom, had already liberated her. Or was it the overwhelming need to have Nikos, which had possessed her since she first saw him, which convinced her? She did not care. She smiled at Nikos, and he took her in his arms and kissed her passionately. Her body soared in intense relief. As she embraced him, she sighed happily. It was comforting to hold the corporeal Nikos close.

Just before they were about to leave, Saffie went to the bathroom. On her way back, she encountered Eleni, who had obviously been waiting for her.

'Nikos is an exquisite lover,' she whispered.

Saffie was not sure whether her body thrilled at this affirmation of her imagining, or the closeness of Eleni's body as she pressed it gently against hers.

'And . . . he's very big,' Eleni added, touching Saffie's crotch fleetingly but acutely through her thin dress. Saffie's sex pulsated in response. Eleni smiled and leant to kiss her lips. Her kiss was softer than any man's, and tantalising in its swiftness. She left Saffie hot and ready outside the bathroom. Yiannis was ascending the stairs. He grinned at Saffie, recognising her state and came to kiss her. Her breasts swelled and burned against his shirt as she embraced him.

'Ah, Saffron, good,' said Constantine's cultured voice.

Yiannis released her with difficulty and went into the bathroom.

'Come. I would like to show you something which will convince you, I'm sure. You will not regret remaining a little longer for this, I can assure you.'

Naturally, Saffie thought of the photographs of Nikos and Yiannis. She very much wanted to see those. Her body glowed in expectation of this as she followed Constantine along the corridor and into a room filled with chairs and a screen.

'Do sit down,' he invited as he went to the projector.

Saffie did so.

'This will perhaps illustrate something of what I told you – concerning the sexual dynamics between Nikos and his friends.'

Constantine darkened the room and set the reels going. Nikos, dressed in an ancient Greek chiton, or long tunic, of pure white, with a gold embroidered border in the Greek 'key', and a long scarlet cloak, or himation, sat alone in a room on a kind of throne. He wore a garland of intertwined bay leaves on his sable curls. On his lap, he held a switch of long twigs fastened together. His pose was perfectly still. Saffie saw that his ebony eyes were smouldering with repressed anger. His body seemed filled with tense, violent energy. Her heart beat increased. His full lips expressed petulance. His demeanour was impatient, despite his reposed expression.

The room was almost bare, except for a tall vase. The floor was of marble. It wasn't difficult to be imaginatively transported back two and a half thousand years to believe that this waiting figure was not Nikos, but an Emperor from that classical age. A servant – it was Yiannis – clad in a short white tunic, and with a similar fillet of leaves, entered. Saffie's heart raced. Perhaps Constantine had forced them to re-enact some of the scenes from the coveted photographs. That would explain Nikos' anger. She looked forward to seeing that.

Yiannis spoke to Nikos, but the sound was off. Nikos inclined his head in a regal gesture and Yiannis turned and stretched out his hand to the entrance. A woman – Eleni – clad in a long white robe – was led in by Georgiou, who was naked. Saffie smiled at his firm body and eyed his semi-erection. His prick glistened with moisture as if he had just been making love. Eleni was secured with rope, which bound her wrists. Nikos said something to Georgiou and both he and Yiannis left the chamber, leaving Eleni and Nikos alone.

For long minutes, Nikos remained on his dais, looking at Eleni. The robe fell in delicate folds around her slim, shapely form. It was as lovely as those on statues or sculptures. Indeed, both actors looked the part. Eleni's long hair fell down her back and over her shoulders and breasts. As the camera went closer, Saffie was aware that she was quivering slightly in trepidation. She admired the woman's acting ability, for she surely must feel at ease with Nikos. Eleni's sloe-black eyes were round with fear. The outline of kohl made them appear even larger, and more stunning.

She seemed to whimper slightly as Nikos rose slowly from his chair and descended the two steps before it to confront her. He certainly appeared imposing and terrifying as he looked into her eyes. Eleni began to shiver as he walked around her.

Saffie's body tensed in anticipation of what he would do to the slave girl. He held the fierce-looking switch, with its dry sharp twigs, in his left hand. Disdainfully, he completed his slow circular tour of her. Saffie felt the hairs on the nape of her own neck rising as Eleni shuddered in fear. Nikos unfastened the rope. It fell to the floor. With a gesture of his head and arm, he indicated that Eleni should strip. Eleni backed away, shaking her head and imploring him with outstretched arms. Nikos widened his dark-circled eyes in command, and with trembling hands, Eleni began to obey. So caught up was she in the film, that Saffie began to feel great pity for the woman, although her strongest sensation was that of sexual expectation.

Eleni unfastened the gold clasp at her shoulder and the robe slid over her naked body to the floor. She stepped away from it. The camera lens now caressed her lithe body, sliding over her slowly. She was very lovely, her loveliness increased by her coy pose as she stood with her thighs pressed tightly together and her arms crossed over her firm breasts. The eye of the camera was Nikos' slow, sensual gaze as it travelled with pleasure over the body of this slave-girl. This captured Persian princess. A virgin, it seemed.

Saffie smiled and shook her head in wonder. She was aware of the powerful double effect of the dynamics between Nikos and Eleni: emperor and captive slave girl; friends and familiar lovers.

Nikos brushed Eleni's hands forcefully aside with the switch. His eyes were hooded in sensuality as he looked at her young, untouched breasts. The camera lingered lovingly on her swelling orbs. Eleni shook her head slowly, her passionate mouth drooping in misery. Nikos brushed the twigs against her legs, compelling her to part them. The camera went gradually in to show the moist pink tip of her clitoris.

Suddenly (the gesture startling for its contrast to the preceding lack of speed), Nikos inserted his finger into her sex and then withdrew it, arching his eyebrows to Eleni in recognition of its wetness. Eleni shook her head and continued to beg him not to do whatever he planned.

Saffie, however, strongly wanted him to. Nikos put his soaking finger to his mouth and extended his long tongue to lick it slowly, his eyes narrowing in enjoyment. Then he reached out the switch and began to trail it over Eleni's quivering body, beginning at her breasts, which he encircled several times. He ran it roughly down her body to her crotch. Eleni winced in pain as he teased her delicate bud with the sharp ends. But her breasts were thrusting and her mouth parted.

She began to writhe against the switch. She held out her arms to Nikos. He sneered and snatched away the twigs. But he moved quickly to her back and began to hit her buttocks with hard strokes. Saffie was delighted to see his prick extended under his fine linen robe. She squirmed deliciously in her seat.

Nikos continued to whip Eleni mercilessly, concentrating mainly on her breasts and buttocks, though sometimes he teased at her genitals. As Eleni collapsed, he forced the switch between her parted legs. Eleni was calling out to him – probably, Saffie was sure, begging him to fuck her. She reached out for his stiffened penis, which nudged greedily at the restraining material. Nikos shook his head once peremptorily and stopped whipping her. His smile was cold and cruel as he regarded her writhing in sexual longing on the marble floor.

Her hands groped at her breasts and vulva. He shook his head once more, refusing her even this. He reinforced his lack of consent and his dominion over her with a forceful lash of the switch on her stomach. Eleni lay, trying not to writhe. Nikos raised the whip to show that she must stand. Eleni did so. With a widening of his kohl-rimmed eyes, he indicated for her to advance towards where he stood, before his throne. Eleni came, with her head bowed and her hands over her eyes. Her long raven hair partly hid her pert breasts.

Saffie squeezed her thighs together tightly and repeatedly, not really caring that Constantine observed her, so intent was she on watching Nikos as, very slowly, he parted his robe. His lovely eyes were flooded with sensuality, the tip of his tongue clenched tightly between his teeth. Saffie was absolutely certain that it took all his willpower not to throw Eleni to the floor and penetrate her. She thought of him, kissing her in the garden and her vagina contracted, secreting hot liquid, which stained her pants and dress.

She gasped audibly as Nikos revealed his long, thick phallus to Eleni. Constantine smiled. Eleni feigned shock. Saffie smiled. Eleni's eyes opened wide, though she could not take them from this (supposedly new) display of rampant masculinity. She looked up at Nikos. She knew what she was expected to do. She seemed to sob in fear as she crawled towards him. The camera gave a glimpse of her dangling breasts, and between her parted buttocks to her spread sex.

She closed her eyes and, opening her mouth, she took Nikos' swollen penis in. She gagged (effectively) and then let him deeply into her throat. Expertly, she moved the tightened muscle of her mouth along it. She held onto Nikos' buttocks as she sucked.

The camera moved to Nikos' face. Saffie took a sharp breath at the sight of its lascivious beauty. Nikos breathed quickly as his body moved in accord with the strong jerkings of Eleni's mouth. He pushed right into her. He reached out and held tightly on to the thick black hair as she sucked. Empathising with Eleni, Saffie wanted him to force his burning wet cock into her dripping hole. She wanted this herself as her vagina pulsed in longing. Without thinking, she began to touch her clitoris evocatively through her (really Eleni's) thin dress.

Nikos bit his lip and threw back his head. His movements were becoming more rapid. Saffie imagined his hot spunk shooting in to Eleni's labouring mouth. But unexpectedly, he released her, swept his cloak over his angry cock and flung himself on his throne. He called out. Yiannis and Georgiou returned. Georgiou was still naked. Perhaps they had been watching. His penis stuck out hugely. Nikos nodded to Yiannis, who went to Eleni. Eleni cried out and ran away from the throne, shaking her head and attempting to hide her nakedness with her hands and hair.

Yiannis strode swiftly after her and cornered her. He forced her against the cold wall and fingered her sex strongly. Eleni began to slide down the wall. Yiannis grasped her wrist and yanked her away. He dragged her back to the space before Nikos and flung her to the floor. Saffie was filled with a mixture of rage and lust as Yiannis forced Eleni's legs apart. Eleni struggled wildly, pretending to fight him off. Yiannis grasped at her breast, squeezing her nipples cruelly. Eleni arched her back and tossed her head.

The camera looked between her legs as Yiannis pulled them wide apart. Her labia were deep crimson and swollen, and her hole was wet and ready. Dripping. Yiannis nodded to Georgiou, who advanced immediately, holding his thin, long cock. He wanted to kiss Eleni, but Nikos forbade this with a movement of his arm. Georgiou rubbed the head of his prick over her genitalia before pushing himself urgently into her. Eleni continued to struggle. Georgiou drew up her knees to prevent this. Her legs went around his waist. He supported himself on his hands as he rammed deeply into her, shaking her body with each thrust. His buttocks began to clench and pump rapidly.

Yiannis sat with her head between his legs and continued to knead and tear at her breasts. Saffie knew that Eleni's pitch of excitement was rising. She was now moving in accord with Georgiou's body. No longer a Persian virgin, but a highly-sexed modern Greek. The camera moved to Nikos, who watched with dignity. That he was intensely moved showed in the high colour of his cheeks, and the liquid sensuality of his eyes. Saffie admired his self-control. Once, his eyes met those of Yiannis, and Saffie experienced a piercing longing shooting up her.

Yiannis stood, allowing Georgiou to force his tongue between Eleni's lips, to grasp her hair and suckle her dark nipple as he continued to fuck her hard.

Eleni was now extremely aroused, tossing and writhing. Saffie remembered her potent kiss. Eleni contracted her body as Georgiou bit and sucked her swollen breasts. Their coupling became wildly abandoned and feverish as they neared their mutual climax. The camera lingered on their abdomens. Saffie had no doubt that all this was real. They clung desperately together, kissing and biting, clawing at each other's flesh until, at last, they arched and peaked, their bodies throbbing in unison.

The camera went to Yiannis, who was just pulling his tunic over his head, revealing his muscular body and standing phallus. He shook his hair free and dropped the garment. Georgiou rose from Eleni, who once more attempted to rise. He restrained her as Yiannis advanced. Eleni appeared to call out in anguish. Nikos observed them with seeming detachment. Yiannis entered her quickly, moving rapidly along her tender muscle. It was not long before he had re-awakened her. Eleni was obviously receiving intense pleasure.

Nikos gestured to Georgiou, who shook Yiannis. Yiannis withdrew from Eleni, his prick still long. Purple and stiff. Saffie watched breathlessly as Georgiou urged Eleni over onto her front. She was whimpering and reluctant. Saffie was sure that anal intercourse was not new to Eleni, though she herself had never had it. The camera honed in on Eleni's parted buttocks, on her tight secret hole and her ruby lips dripping below. Yiannis caressed her breasts and bottom tenderly as she continued to undulate her body frantically.

Georgiou took a bowl of ointment from Nikos and inserted his fingers. Then he lavished the dripping cream between Eleni's buttocks, and forced his finger into her anus. Yiannis manipulated her breasts. Nikos nodded and Yiannis knelt between her thighs. He put his arms around her waist and pulled her onto all fours. Georgiou supported and stimulated her. Yiannis grasped his cock and wiped the tip over her opening, covering it with ointment. Then, positioning himself with care, he pushed his tumescent prick against her sphincter muscle. His face expressed his rapture as he allowed the head of his penis to enter her tight passage. Gradually, by degrees, he stuffed his phallus into her. Filling her. He pulled her buttocks sharp against him. The camera showed a view between his legs, of his tightening balls and ramming backside.

Slowly and carefully, he slid almost out, and then fully into Eleni who now wriggled in delight. He reached to her clitoris and fiddled with it. He pressed his fist against her ridge. Georgiou played with her hanging breasts and then slipped under her to lap at them. The camera panned to Nikos. With a shock Saffie saw that his naked desire mirrored her own. He was beautiful.

Constantine stopped the film. He had the decency not to illuminate the room. Saffie considered that he was all too aware of the state she was in. Her body was raging with longing. She would welcome any of these potent men into her maddened body. Constantine left her. He himself could have appeased her, but that was not his plan. She would not have been surprised if he had locked her in in order to enhance her suffering. To encourage her to participate. Saffie had needed little persuasion, and now she was only too eager.

She swallowed hard. Her mouth was dry. She hoped for Yiannis, or Georgiou, or Nikos – especially Nikos – to come to her. (Even Eleni or Rachel would suffice.) But she was left alone in the dark. She licked her parched lips and then sucked on her finger. She pressed her closed palms between her thighs. She pushed them further up. Her sex thrilled at this touch. She returned one finger to her mouth and sucked lasciviously on it. With the other, she pulled the fine elastic of her pants to one side and touched her clitoris. With a sensual moan, she fingered her sensitised bud and then moved her finger to her vagina, which was well-lubricated by her arousal. Inserting her fingers deeply, she pressed on her clitoris with her thumb. She was already very near to a gentle, releasing orgasm. She bit her finger savagely and then rubbed it hard around her lips as she masturbated. Then she moved her hand down to her breasts and began to squeeze them as they swelled urgently against her palm. She pressed and massaged. Her orgasm beat gently around her fingers, echoing against her thumb. It gave her a little release, but also had the effect of intensifying her need.

She felt someone's arm around her and a face come towards her to kiss her. Saffie did not know nor care who it was. The touch of another was piquant and sweet, and when slim fingers stole over her naked flesh down to her crotch, she urged her pubis up to meet them. As she came to a sense of her surroundings, she realised that it was Eleni. She pulled the woman close and melted gratefully into her warm embrace. Eleni manipulated her sex with an expert knowledge that few men could match. Soon, she brought Saffie to a stronger orgasm, fingering her breast as she moaned in relief. Then, she held her close.

'I see that Constantine has persuaded you?' she whispered, kissing her hair.

'How do you, you know, lose yourself in front of the cameras?' Saffie asked.

'It isn't difficult. By then, you'll be as familiar with Nikos and Yiannis and Georgiou as I am – well, nearly. That is necessary, don't you think? To be used to their bodies?'

Eleni smiled to feel the reflex throbbing of Saffie's sex at the prospect of this.

'You want Nikos, don't you?' Eleni's voice expressed her certainty.

'Do you mind?'

'No . . .' Eleni laughed easily. 'We do not seek to own each other. We have known each other for very many years.'

'He *is* sexy.'

'Yes. He is. Which is why Constantine can even think of making this film. But Nikos has been enraged by his very talent because of the situation he has been placed in by Constantine. He feels like a whore – as though his integrity has been compromised. You can hardly blame him. We take part to make it easier for Nikos. Constantine did well there. He only asked Nikos – and – perhaps Yiannis. But, naturally, Nikos is not pleased at this. He feels that Constantine is using – devaluing – the bonds between us.'

'Do you think perhaps that is true?' asked Saffie.

Eleni shrugged and smiled.

'These things do not worry me. Nothing will change my feelings, my respect, for my friends. No. In fact, I find it exciting to – make-believe with them. It adds a new aspect . . .'

'And – the others?'

'Georgiou will do most things, where sex is involved.' She laughed. 'He is insatiable. Nikos calls him a whore. He is equally attracted to men and women. But he is lazy. Yiannis . . .' Eleni hesitated, smiling gently to herself. 'He will do anything for Nikos.'

'And Nikos will go ahead now, and complete the film?'

'I hope so.' Eleni sighed. 'Yiannis advised him to obtain an agreement in writing. That is the best he can do. I do not doubt that Constantine will get greedy, and want another film – and another. But he has to return the photos. And, you know, Stavros Mandreas cannot live for ever. He is a very old man . . . Will you help, Saffie?'

'You already know that I will do the film.'

'But, you can do more. You can persuade Nikos. Get him to see it through this time. It's wearing, abandoning films because he gets in a temper with Constantine. Also, it will be better for him to finish this. You can probably help him to release the potential that Constantine demands. With those actresses, Nikos felt compromised – his pride was hurt. He did not want to do it. He admires you, Saffie. If you can persuade him that you will enjoy it, that you will not be damaged . . .'

'Alright. I'll certainly try my best. I really do want to participate . . .'

'Good . . .' The young women smiled at each other, 'And, Saffie, beware – he is very jealous.'

'But, I thought I had to—'

'Not of us. Of Constantine. He does not want him to get you first. Under the circumstances . . .'

'Quite.'

Saffie smiled, glorying in her power; recalling her own attraction for the distinguished older man.

It was with different eyes that Saffie surveyed the young men as she returned to them in the safety of Eleni's company. She felt that she had been introduced to them intimately. She anticipated her prospective sexual adventure with pleasure. Nikos met her eyes fleetingly and with a trace of his former arrogance. Was he aware that she had been watching a clip of their old film, or did he suspect that she had been with Constantine? Yiannis and Georgiou were too engrossed in Rachel to notice her. Saffie raised an eyebrow at her friend as she lounged on the chair by the edge of the garden, her legs raised on to the table as she flirted and laughed with the young Greeks. Perhaps she really had no qualms about the sexual licence the film would permit?

Nikos was silent as they drove back to the house. Saffie now sat beside him, wondering whether he still wanted to go to Delos. Then she recalled Yiannis' earlier comment that Nikos would never refuse to visit his beloved island.

★ ★ ★

The moonlit sea-journey to Delos was like a dream. She was alone with this beautiful Greek man in his boat. She would have been happy for the journey to have lasted hours. The anticipation of making love with him warmed her blood. She lay back in the boat and watched him. It was exhilarating just to do so, he moved with such natural grace. When they arrived, the island was deserted and lonely and eerie in the moonlight which flooded the white buildings.

Saffie was aware of Nikos' sexual potency deliberately restrained. The dynamic tension was like a coil unfurling within him. Perhaps he was keeping a distance because of his feelings about the film. She knew that he was still angry with Constantine. Nikos' controlled power excited Saffie. Her absolute need for him increased with the knowledge of his energy. When he allowed it release . . . The prospect thrilled her. She recalled Eleni's lascivious description: she had no doubt that Nikos was her lover.

She thought of him in the film extract she had seen. He had done so little, but his power was all-pervading. Would she be able to convince him, as Eleni had requested? She herself wanted to. But she would have to tread carefully with this proud and sensitive man, who already felt threatened and vulnerable. Saffie could see that his friends would be able to see the venture as fun. As for Nikos – he felt that he was selling himself to an unscrupulous man. He was much too serious about it. But that was because of his breeding and background, and, indeed, part of the very thing he was protecting. For the qualities which differentiated people were intangible. Could he come out of this with his honour intact?

Still in silence, they moored the boat and went on to the moon-drenched island. The swollen orb was radiant and white, painting the white ruins of the temples. It was enchanting. Magical. Saffie knew that Nikos shared her sense of wonder. They walked around in silence in the peaceful night. After a time Saffie ventured to take his hand. He did not refuse. Saffie felt the sensual promise of his masculinity transmitted through this casual touch.

'I will do the film, Niko.'

'I knew you would,' Nikos replied cynically, adding. 'Constantine is very persuasive.'

'Actually, it wasn't Constantine . . .'

'Eleni then – she can wrap people round her little finger.'

'Niko. It's because of you . . .'

'You pity the poor rich boy?' he scoffed.

'No. Actually, I believe it will be fun. A liberating experience. As simple as that.'

Saffie decided that it would only elicit a sardonic response if she confessed that he was the most desirable man she had ever met; that his dark beauty was as beguiling as any god's. She would not have him treat her with disdain because he would not accept admiration, or because he was so scathing of people who were impressed by his natural gifts. She smiled, realising that they were still holding hands.

'I warned you not to feel pressured . . .'

'Yes, you did, Niko, and I don't. I honestly think that I will gain much from this experience.' As she spoke, Saffie knew that this was true. Its validity was demonstrated by Nikos' tangible presence. Her stomach tightened in excitement.

They continued to stroll around the island in the warm night. Saffie decided that she had to resign herself to this man's gentlemanly reticence. But, though her mind might respect his scruples, her body was not so rational. Her need for him was all-consuming. She was sure Nikos must be aware of the almost fevered pitch of her sexual arousal. She could scarcely attend to his conversation. All she wanted was sex with him!

'Let's climb Kynthos,' Nikos suggested.

They negotiated the wide steps of the small mountain in quietness; Saffie looked at the ruins spread around them as they ascended. At the summit, they sat to drink the wine Nikos had brought. They toasted each other and the moon, and then Nikos poured some of his wine onto the dark earth.

'A libation to the god,' he explained.

'Apollo?' Saffie asked.

Nikos smiled.

'Perhaps, under the circumstances, it should be to his wilder brother, Dionysus, god of drama – and of ecstasy?' he asked, lifting his glass and keeping her eyes. Saffie felt herself colour under his piercing gaze. God of ecstasy! She knew of the Dionysian – or Bacchanalian – rites, where revellers, liberated by wine, and frenzied with desire, indulged in wild orgies. The atmosphere between them changed subtly with this reference, or because of the heady wine. Perhaps Nikos accepted Saffie's choice. In any case, he seemed more relaxed as he leaned back and drank. Saffie was relieved.

'So . . .' he drawled, 'do you think this is a good opportunity for us to lose our inhibitions . . . get to know each other . . . prepare ourselves?'

Saffie's heart leapt wildly. Her vagina began to burn in anticipation. With immense effort, she controlled her crazy body. It was hard to keep still.

'Yes. I do,' she replied candidly.

'Okay,' he agreed.

This seemed to Saffie a cold-blooded beginning. Nikos continued to drink wine.

'You are prepared then, for what he'll require of you?'

'Such as?' she challenged.

'Such as being fucked by one man after another; such as buggery and beatings and sex with Eleni or Rachel. Such as sex with more than one person – of either gender – at any one time. Sex in groups. Sado-masochism . . . Phalluses inserted, anything that takes his fancy,' Nikos ended bitterly.

Saffie felt her sex throb in anticipation of these delights.

'Yes,' she replied confidently. Perhaps a little more so than she felt.

'You are an unusual woman.'

She shrugged.

'So where would you like to begin?' he challenged, a twinkle in his dark eyes.

'I think you should take your clothes off.' She was only half-joking.

'Alright.'

Saffie sat and watched, bewitched, as Nikos stood. Slowly, he stretched his arms out to the side. The loose white sleeves of his shirt hung down. He looked like a poet, or a Renaissance prince. Nikos raised his arms above his head. He turned his head to one side and then brought his arms slowly down and crossed them over his chest, and lifted the bottom of his shirt out of his waistband. Then he looked down at her, sucking in his cheeks as he did so. Slowly, he began to unbutton his shirt, beginning at his throat. All the time, he retained Saffie's gaze. The man was certainly confident of his effect on her. Perhaps he was always aware of her attentions and played some elaborate game with her. When he had unfastened his shirt, he teased her by opening and closing it like some sleazy strip artist. All the time, she thought, he moved as though in tune to a slow, lascivious rhythm. And like one of the frenzied audience, her body responded. She could scarcely restrain her hands from going to her breast and vulva. She stroked at her swollen breasts. Nikos smiled seductively over his shoulder as he turned, wiggled his tight behind and revealed one shoulder. He licked at this and then let the shirt fall over his bottom. Taking an end in each hand he pulled the garment across his behind and then cast it to the ground. Crossing his arms across his chest, and still with his back to Saffie, he rippled his fingers over his body lovingly. He began to grind and thrust his abdomen. Then he moved one hand down to his crotch.

Saffie could not see what he was doing, but from his sense of enjoyment, thought that he was caressing himself. He turned to let her see as he fondled his bulging prick. He did this with loving attention to himself, tracing the swollen shape of his cock beneath his trousers. He looked down at it in interest, his lashes against his cheekbones. Saffie could no longer prevent herself from squirming in delight. Waves of hot pleasure swept over her sensitised body. Nikos smiled and released his penis, still grinding his abdomen in circular motion. His ebony eyes incited her. Saffie found it very difficult to remain where she was. Her body yearned to go to him. If she did, she imagined that he would prevent her with an imperative shake of his head, as on the film. When he touched his rigid member once more, Saffie pressed her sex clandestinely. Secretly, she rubbed at her erect clitoris, nurturing its gathering potency.

Nikos let go of his prick, removed his other arm from across his bare chest and began to massage his buttocks. He thrust his pubis forward rhythmically as he did so. Then he moved his left hand to his stomach, flattened it on it and inserted his outstretched fingertips under his waistband. Saffie's sex pulsed as she imagined them feeling his extending cock; pinching exquisitely at its end. With the other hand, Nikos began to unfasten the tiny buttons of his black trousers. When this was done, he allowed them to slither to the ground and stepped away from them. He was wearing only black satin shorts which, miraculously, contained him. He lowered his eyes at her.

Saffie stood and went to him, putting her hands on his buttocks and pulling him hard against her. It was very good to feel his erection against her belly. Nikos bit hungrily at her ear, deliberately increasing his rate of breathing to excite her. Saffie ran her palms repeatedly over his firm buttocks. She thrilled at the feel of the strong muscles beneath the soft satin. He held her still and brought his mouth down on hers. He kissed her hard. Saffie felt that she had somersaulted in space when he released her. This first private kiss convinced her that she had been right about his sexuality and the chemistry between them. Naturally, her hand went to his crotch. She pressed on his swollen member. Then she began to insert her fingers into the top of his brief garment. She had just begun to feel the hardness of his bone when he pushed her hand decisively away.

'Now you,' he whispered.

Saffie took off her sandals and ran her hands over her hips and midriff, and down to her abdomen. She feathered her fingers tantalisingly over her vulva. Deliberately, she enticed him with an alluring expression. She pouted her lips, and narrowed her eyes provocatively. Then she caressed her bottom, and pulled her dress up to tease him, giving him a glimpse as she massaged her burning flesh. Her hands darted hungrily between her buttocks. She fiddled briefly with her sex. She was so turned on that it was difficult to lift her hands from her fanny. She wanted to make herself come. She grasped at her breasts and rolled them, further excited by his dark eyes on her.

Swiftly, she pinched her nipples, smiling at Nikos' eyes narrowed in desire for her. She put her hands between her legs and pressed on them. Her vulva beat erratically. She pulled the leg of her sodden pants to one side and encircled the opening of her vagina with her forefinger. She knew that Nikos watched her with longing. She inserted her finger briefly. She wanted her pleasure from the man so close to her, but did this for his sake. She took off her wet pants and pulled down her dress. Then, smiling coquettishly at Nikos, she slowly dragged up her hem to display her generous, now engorged, sex. At last, becoming impatient, she drew her dress over her head to reveal her naked body to the Delian moon and to Nikos.

Nikos came to her. He stood close behind her and thrust his arms under hers to seize her breasts. He kneaded and massaged them roughly, sending darting stabs of lust through her vagina. He nudged against her crack with his hidden cock. She felt the silken material whisper against her soft skin. She reached backwards to grasp at his straining muscles. He released her breasts and caressed her belly and shoulders. He bit savagely at her neck. He inserted his finger into the tight puckering of her anus. Saffie gasped, assaulted by so much sudden pleasure. Nikos pulled her gently against him, cradling her and tracing the outline of her breasts slowly and with infinite tenderness. Her abdomen tingled in awareness of his penis rocking against it. She wanted him to ram it sharply into her forbidden hole.

She raised her face to kiss him. He returned this gently. He continued to stroke her breasts. She was stunned at his tender care. She had considered him too self-centred to be capable of such generosity. Nikos turned her round and embraced her tightly. His mouth found hers and his tongue urged open her lips. Saffie sucked on it hungrily. His hands now caressed every inch they could reach, stirring her nerve-ends to eager life. Then he traced over her naked body with the tip of his extended tongue. He knelt before her to complete this. Like an acolyte. Saffie luxuriated in his attention. She saw, in wonder, how the moonlight sculptured his perfect body.

This ritual under the full moon on this empty sacred island was like a baptism. In time, Nikos urged her to the ground. Here, he continued his sensory exploration of her body. Preventing her from touching him yet, he watched her eyes as he ran his fingertips from her sensitive inner ankles up to her silken thighs. He caressed her hips, and inner thighs, and then her buttocks, pulling them gently apart as he did so. He kissed her belly and her groin. He licked her breasts, lingering at her nipples, and then all the way down to her open sex. He lapped lovingly at this, sucking at her swollen labia. Saffie grasped his extended cock, feeling him shudder as she squeezed it. Holding her bottom, he raised her hips and inserted his tongue fully into her vagina. Saffie submitted to this delightful indulgence. She felt his tensile tongue within her, stroking at her taut muscle. It was as if she was being taken slowly to heaven. All she had to do was lie and be pampered by this beautiful man. Nikos moved his mouth to her clitoris and teased gently at it. For a moment, he squeezed it between his lips, and then made a point of his tongue to lick it. Saffie writhed in delighted abandon, glad to be at his mercy, trusting him to pleasure her.

'Are you ready?' he whispered unexpectedly, moving his head from between her legs.

'Yes . . .' she groaned.

Nikos kissed her as he pulled down his shorts to release his rampant prick. He held it, and made it take the place of his exploring tongue, rubbing it against her bulging clitoris. It was warm and comforting. Almost familiar. Saffie raised her lower body and he slid his cock hard against her clitoris as he entered her. She cried out as his swollen member filled her entirely. She felt a wonderful relief at this consummation. Once within her, Nikos remained still for a moment. Already, Saffie could feel her muscle throbbing around his wet cock. His dark eyes met hers in acknowledgement of this. He took each yearning nipple between thumb and forefinger and squeezed very tightly. Saffie felt her body tense in pre-orgasmic pleasure. Then, he merely nudged her clitoris with his pubic bone and held her as her body released its long-nurtured joy. Her body jerked in spasms around him. This orgasmic warmth spread throughout her body.

She smiled as he gently caressed the smooth skin of her ripe breasts. Then Nikos narrowed his lovely eyes and began to move his long rod up and down her vagina. At first his movements were slow, as he savoured her. Gradually, he increased his pace. He was a practised lover. Soon, they had ascended into a rapid and hard thrusting as he raised his fit body high and rammed into her with force. Her body shuddered at each impact as Nikos built up his relentless rhythm. Deep within, Saffie knew that this was the kind of sex she had always wanted. Forceful and powerful, yet at the same time, tender. The initial reflex fear at his supremely masculine power was immediately submerged in the sheer joy of his strong body as it banged against hers.

For a very long time, Nikos slammed into her. Saffie's spread sex raised to meet him as she moved in time to his urgent pumping. She had never believed that sex could last so long at this pitch. She smiled blissfully. Her body felt gloriously alive. Nikos bent to kiss her, his hot mouth bringing her even more pleasure as he bit at her tongue and lips. Saffie cried out as he touched her breast, unable to prevent her supreme release as her entire body began to spasm dramatically.

'Come, Niko! Now . . .' she demanded, longing to feel his prick throb with her vagina.

Niko held her tightly as the burning fluid shot from his balls and along his cock. He gave a long agonised groan, as though unwilling to let it go. Saffie knew that he had wanted to hold back for longer. She felt his sex pulsate strongly in unison with hers as their bodies beat in time. They cleaved and clung together, their flesh inseparable, and kissed deeply as their orgasms and heart-beats mingled.

Saffie gazed up at the white moon. She lay content in the warmth of Nikos' arms. She listened to the small animal noises all around them. If she raised herself, she could see down to the scattered white ruins below. She did not think that Nikos slept. Already, his penis was re-erect. Saffie smiled. Did he feel cheated? What a potent, greedy, generous man. She raised herself onto her elbow and looked down at him. His fathomless eyes met hers. Saffie was moved by their stillness, and by the almost petulant droop of his lovely mouth.

She smiled at him and took his member firmly into her grasp. She thrilled to see his expression change subtly to one of extreme lasciviousness. Saffie eased herself on top of his warm, pliant body. She met his mouth with hers, and pressed her vulva hard against his penis. Nikos held her gently, kissing her hungrily. His prick moved under her. Saffie continued to masturbate on him, enjoying this: she could come, like this, using his trapped cock to undulate against. She could tease him. She squashed her clitoris hard against his prick. Nikos played with her hanging breasts. In a moment, Saffie knew, he would simply turn her over and take her.

She raised her abdomen and eased his rod into her. Nikos

sighed with relief. He moaned in pleasure as she tightened her grip and began to move frantically up and down his length.

'Niko?'

'Yes?' he murmured vaguely, concentrating on his own pleasure.

'I've never had it from behind.'

Nikos stopped moving.

'You mean—?'

'Both.'

'And – you want me to initiate you?'

'Yes.'

Nikos slipped his penis from her and Saffie turned on to her belly. She shivered as Nikos applied cream from his trouser pocket lavishly between her buttocks, concentrating, in little sensual circles, on her orifice. She cried out in exaltation, as, with one hand, he fondled her breast, and, with the other, he entered her anal opening. Saffie experienced decadent pleasure at this very personal act. She liked the feeling of unaccustomed pressure and fullness. Nikos withdrew his finger, and prepared her for his sweet invasion.

Saffie spread her legs and raised her bottom as Nikos positioned her. He stroked between her crack with the tip of his prick, causing arrows of expectation to shoot up her. Then, on his way to locate her vaginal opening, he trailed his stiff rod along her perineum, that delightful, sensitive place between apertures. Saffie grinned to herself, feeling drunk on Nikos. Carefully, he entered her vagina from behind. The unusual position and tightness gave Saffie increased stimulation which was further enhanced as his fingers manipulated her labia and clitoris. She was a mass of expectation, on the brink of fulfilment. She nurtured her impending orgasm skilfully. She was aware of the weight against her anus. Moving against Nikos, and feeling his strength along her back as he thrust, she thought she would come, regardless of her attempts. Then Nikos withdrew his penis and immediately pushed its end against her back passage. Saffie was flooded with dark joy and excitement.

'*Yes,*' she told him urgently.

Nikos continued to masturbate her as he eased the end of his prick gently into her. She felt her muscle expand, to accommodate his size. He inserted his fingers into her vagina, keeping his thumb on

61

her clitoris, as his lubricated member slid inch by inch into her tighter hole. When he was fully in, he released her and grasped her breasts as he raised himself and began to fuck her, anally. Saffie positioned her fist under her sex, and raised her bottom to meet each thrust, feeling them echo throughout her body.

'Do you like it?' Nikos whispered hoarsely.

'Oh, yes . . . Niko . . .'

In response to the certainty in her tone, Nikos let go, giving in to his own dark desire as he sodomised her. Saffie was aware of his intense joy as his body took on its own wild control and rhythm. He gasped and moaned, wriggled within her, grasped her buttocks as she held tight and still, shuddering dramatically as he emptied his seed into her forbidden hole. Saffie felt her own glorious orgasm reverberate through every part of her. In time, Nikos held her close as they kissed and lapsed into a contented languor. For the rest of the night, Saffie was filled with erotic dreams of future sex with this wonderful man . . .

They awoke as the morning sun lapped over their naked bodies. Nikos smiled at Saffie and kissed her. Then he stood and stretched luxuriously. Saffie rose to be entwined in his strong embrace, smiling at his renewed desire. The tip of his phallus kissed at her clitoris. Down below, the island's treasures glistened in the bright day, cradled by the azure sea.

'We'd better go and see what Constantine has planned for us,' Nikos said at last, reluctantly releasing her.

'Yes.'

'And at night,' he asked, 'will you come to me alone?'

'Oh, yes, Niko.'

He smiled beautifully at her.

'Let me dress you . . .'

She stood, like a child, as he did so. They held hands tightly as they descended the hill and walked across the island, back to the yacht.

Three

'Do you want a shower?' Nikos asked as they boarded the boat.

Saffie met his limpid eyes, beamed and nodded. Nikos echoed her response and gestured to her to follow him below. They traversed the luxurious yacht, through the main cabin to the bathroom. Nikos turned on the shower, beginning to undress, taking off his shirt, and then going to stand before the waiting Saffie. Tenderly, he lifted her dress, standing very close to her. His proximity was like electricity activating her. She lifted her arms as he drew the small garment over her head, and acquiesced as he removed her pants. His eyes swept over her nakedness, rendering her acutely receptive. Saffie unfastened his trousers and grasped his stiffened penis. Nikos moaned and pulled her to him, kissing her with longing. Saffie felt the shape of his yearning member lovingly: already it had given her so much pleasure. She traced the thick vein along to the bulbous end. Nikos tightened his hold on her. Then he reached for her breasts. Saffie yielded. His tongue was hot and agile within her mouth. His hands caressed her body, teasing her tingling nerves.

They made love under the cascading water, already like passionate lovers. They were as eager as if it had been days or weeks since they had last coupled, rather than an hour or so.

Saffie knew that few men could touch her like this, giving her joy and satisfaction at the same time as awakening her ever more deeply. Her reciprocal arousal of Nikos' lithe body seemed to give him as much enjoyment, and she hugged her wonderful happiness secretly within herself. Still, they embraced and kissed as they made coffee, whilst wrapped in soft towels. Later, as Nikos steered the yacht through the foaming blue sea, Saffie stood behind him, holding him and kissing his hair and neck, breathing

63

in the subtle musk of his fragrance. She was sure that he shared her feeling of euphoria.

A little before they reached Mykonos, she went to sit at the side of the boat. In a daze, she watched the sparkling sea and paler blue sky, thinking that this man acted like a drug on her. No sooner had she had him, she knew that she had to have him again. Her soft body glowed in the warmth of the day, lapped by the soft sea-breeze. She looked at Nikos through lustful eyes, enjoying the perfection of his body. All of her tingled with the memory of his touch. She looked idly at the other boats they passed. Some of the passengers waved or called to Nikos. He greeted them in return. As he directed the yacht into the harbour, Nikos turned and grinned at her. Her heart raced. She went to kiss him.

They purchased melon and grapes which they ate, laughingly, as they climbed up to Constantine's house. The sweet juices trailed from their mouths. It was hotter as they rose. Saffie felt the sun strike her legs and her bare back. They held hands as they went along the narrow track to the garden. Yiannis smiled knowingly at them from the gate. Saffie felt Nikos tense as, at the same time as they entered the garden, Constantine emerged from the house. Saffie witnessed the dark look Constantine shot at her young companion, and glanced quickly up to see the look of supreme arrogance which Nikos gave in return. Instinctively, she put her arm around her lover's waist. But Nikos merely kissed her head briefly and disengaged himself. Then, to her intense chagrin, he was gone.

Saffie had a sudden irrational dread of facing the older man alone. However, she was rescued by Eleni, who came across the garden to her, kissed her and took her arm. Saffie was grateful for this friendly greeting. She was aware of Constantine's speculative gaze. His intelligent eyes seemed to burn through her thin dress, as if he imagined Nikos' caresses arousing her. Saffie told herself that she was tired, and prey to imaginings. Nevertheless, her wayward body responded sensually to his look. Eleni led her towards the house, and therefore Constantine, and said, as they neared him:

'Constantine is eager to begin to discuss the film.'

'Yes . . .' he agreed, taking her cue, as if reminded how impolite he must seem to this newcomer. 'Naturally, I wish to waste no time. As you may know, I am already behind schedule. I very much hope,' he seemed to Saffie to refer to her obvious consummation with Nikos, 'that your decision is in the affirmative, Saffie?'

Despite his warm tone, Saffie retained an impression of his initial hostile attitude towards Nikos. There was something between the men that she could not quite grasp. She was sure that it was not merely the hold Constantine had over Nikos because of the photographs. Constantine was talking about the film. Now released from the dynamism of Nikos' presence, Saffie was tired. She wanted to sleep, and to dream of her night with him. Eleni sensed this intuitively.

'You go and lie down, Saffie. I'll bring you some orange juice,' she suggested, pushing Saffie gently towards the house, away from Constantine, who sat reluctantly on the garden chair and lit a cigar.

Saffie could smell the pungent aroma drifting up to her open window as she undressed. She went to draw the light muslin drape. As she did so, she caught Constantine's eye as he looked up. He smiled lazily in appreciation of her nakedness. Saffie interpreted her immediate desire as being derived from her vulnerable sexual state. She smiled as she lay on the bed gratefully. She closed her eyes, her mind immediately flooded with the warm voluptuousness of her body. She caressed her breast languidly, amused by her own greed as she began to imagine a potent prick nudging her glowing clit. She licked her lips slowly. She was drifting off dreamily as the door opened.

Nikos rode Calypso hard over the dry ground. He was eager to get far away from Constantine as quickly as possible. The countryside seemed to fly past him as he galloped along. Naturally, Constantine knew of his night with Saffie: there was not much that the man missed, especially when it concerned sex. Most particularly any liaison concerning him. Nikos resented his knowing, almost mocking expression. He felt that he would never be free of him. If they did this film – what then? Would he demand another, and another? Or would he devise something else?

He swung the horse towards the beach and galloped along the shore-line. This was invigorating and released some of Nikos' pent-up energy. He allowed the mare to splash through the water, enjoying the drama of this. In time, breathless, he slowed, and trotted for a while, to allow Calypso to cool. Then he dismounted, crouched and dipped his hand into the sea. He splashed his face and neck with water. Then he walked along the edge, speaking softly to the sweating horse.

Saffie hoped it was Nikos, or Yiannis entering her dimmed bedroom. She did not open her eyes. There was a gentle, tantalising kiss on her parted mouth and a fleeting touch of her exposed bud. Saffie opened her eyes to see Eleni looking down at her, her black eyes expressing affection.

'He *is* wonderful, Nikos, is he not?' she asked as her fingers trailed gently over Saffie's sex.

Saffie's body purred into life at this too gentle touch. Her naked breasts swelled, and her vagina secreted sudden moisture. She lifted her crotch closer to the woman's hand. At the same time, she reached up, put her arm around Eleni's neck and pulled her down to kiss her. Eleni's abundant hair fell around them. Her kiss was urgent and seeking as her tongue went into Saffie's parted mouth. She moved so that she lay along the length of Saffie's body. Saffie felt the sharp bone of her pubis against her own. She was light and soft and warm. Her tender kiss was as cogent as any man's.

Saffie let her hands run down Eleni's back to her bottom. Eleni squirmed in pleasure as Saffie caressed her. Saffie lifted her short dress and traced her fingertips over the other woman's peachy buttocks, warm under the soft silk of her pants. She felt Eleni's gentle fingers on her breast. Her light touch aroused Saffie poignantly. Eleni raised her head and looked into Saffie's eyes. The women smiled. Saffie felt that this was safe and comforting and familiar. In the back of her mind, she wondered why she had never experienced this before. It was so easy. So friendly. She was sure it would be so with Rachel.

She helped Eleni lift her light dress over her head. She grasped handfuls of the lovely hair and kissed it, smoothed it over Eleni's olive-brown shoulders. Eleni lay back on the bed, and Saffie, raised on one elbow, surveyed her slim body in admiration. Eleni smiled.

'Touch me . . .' she urged, her eyes becoming softer.

Saffie looked at the well-shaped mouth. Eleni put the tip of her tongue tantalisingly between, moving her hands down to her own breast and crotch. Shyly, Saffie reached out to Eleni's flattened breasts. Eleni smiled invitingly. Saffie encircled the dark brown area around Eleni's nipple. Eleni's body writhed gently in response. Saffie knew that the woman was hot. She thought of the film of her, pretending to be a virgin slave-girl, under the thrall of the Grecian potentate, Nikos. She removed her hand and trailed it slowly down, over Eleni's concave stomach to the elastic of her pants. Eleni's dark eyes challenged her. Saffie slipped her fingers tentatively inside, feeling the soft hair. Eleni smiled reassuringly, then rose and grasped Saffie and pushed her back onto the bed. Then, kneeling beside her, she began a long and exciting exploration of her body. She leant and kissed her neck and then cupped her breasts firmly, feeling each erect nipple with a slender thumb. She smiled to see the pleasure reflected in Saffie's face.

She moved so that she straddled Saffie's thigh, her knee against Saffie's moist vulva. She pressed her knee against Saffie's pubis as she held each nipple tightly, rolling and pulling on them. Saffie tossed her head from side to side as sexual joy welled up from deep within. Her face flushed, her eyes became hooded and sensual and she panted between her parted lips. Eleni stroked and caressed her flesh lovingly, sometimes kneading and pressing. Slowly, but surely, she worked her way down to Saffie's sex, leading in evocative strokes over her belly and groin until Saffie prayed silently for her to touch her eager clitoris, to insert her long fingers deeply into her yearning vagina.

Instead, Eleni released her, leant to kiss her and then began to lick her throat and neck with her hot tongue. Saffie tossed her raging body in abandon as Eleni sucked at her nipples. She gasped in delight as, at last, Eleni touched her erect bud. She raised her body in response and Eleni increased her pressure, so that she pressed rhythmically and repetitively on Saffie's clit. Saffie felt her pitch of arousal increase to a pre-orgasmic state. As if she knew, Eleni pushed her fingers into Saffie's wet hole, kissing Saffie as she felt her muscle throb around her.

Eleni removed her pants and lay on top of Saffie, immediately beginning to undulate her sex against Saffie's. She grasped her firmly by the shoulders as she raised herself slightly. Saffie's body responded naturally against the other woman's. Their vulvas pressed and released, pressed and released as Eleni raised her abdomen tantalisingly each time. Saffie held onto the woman's firm bottom, urging her return.

Eleni became wild, and Saffie was affected by this. Eleni squirmed and writhed between her legs, concentrating on achieving her own powerful orgasm. The women moved in unison, clinging to each other, squeezing breasts and buttocks, kissing and biting deeply. Saffie felt her womb glowing hotly and all sensitive nerves awakened. At last, though she tried to control it, her climax overwhelmed her. It burst in her womb and sent waves of delicious joy rippling through her vagina. Her clitoris pulsated against Eleni's. She became aware of the echoing throbbing of the other woman's sex.

Tendrils of acute pleasure extended through Saffie's thighs and belly. A sense of contentment and well-being spread from her stomach to her breasts. Eleni relaxed against her. Saffie kissed her gratefully as she floated into languor. Eleni snuggled closer. As she lapsed into sleep, it flitted through Saffie's mind that this sexual freedom between their new friends was very enjoyable. Because of this obviously long-established intimacy, it was natural for her, and probably Rachel too, to slip into this. That would surely make the filming easier, as Eleni had intimated, and as Constantine hoped.

'Where's he gone?' Constantine asked Yiannis.

'He'll be back soon. He's gone for a ride.'

'You must impress on him that I am not prepared to have my time wasted . . .'

'Look, Constantine . . .' said Yiannis coldly, 'I'm willing to act in your film, for Nikos' sake, but that doesn't mean that I approve of your methods. In fact, I advised him to refuse and face the consequences. Also – I am not your messenger. If you have things to say to Nikos, then you must address him yourself.'

'But, you realise, as he has agreed, that we must now get on with the film.'

'Yes . . . but you should be patient with Nikos. He is a proud man. You can not just bully him. You have a certain hold over him. Perhaps he allows you this? Still, you should respect him. He is the son of your friend. He belongs to an old and valued family.'

'I concede your point. However, though I think that the English women are compliant, it does not mean that they will remain patient indefinitely.'

Yiannis grinned, looking over at Rachel and Georgiou, still engrossed in each other, petting intimately. His sex responded to this overt display.

'I think that they have reason to stay.'

Constantine glanced at the young couple at the far end of the garden, but seemed uninterested. Yiannis smiled secretly.

'I don't think that Nikos should get too involved with Saffron. No, that would not be a good idea.'

Yiannis smiled to himself as he recognised the older man's possessiveness of Nikos, and his obvious jealousy. It echoed his own feelings for the elusive Nikos. He wondered whether, in fact, Constantine's desire to make his erotic film was entirely – or even mainly – to make money. Perhaps the pull of the sexual Nikos was more interesting and desirable. There was no doubt that Constantine had gained much pleasure from the scenes they had filmed so far. In making them, Constantine had wielded significant power over his rich and vulnerable young friend. Yiannis recalled Nikos' violent anger towards Constantine: doubtless this had further fired Constantine's secret lust. Nikos looked very attractive when enraged; his dark eyes flashing fire, his lovely mouth petulant. His entire body filled with controlled rage. Yiannis knew that he had sometimes wanted to strike out at Constantine when, as often, he pushed him too far. Yiannis recalled the producer's sadistic laughter.

Yiannis was also aware that the virile, attractive man was intrigued by his own relationship with the beguiling Nikos. If only . . . he sighed to himself. He shared his thwarted desire with Constantine, though he was not going to confess his own disappointment.

'So . . .' said Constantine moodily, rising and extinguishing his cigar, 'tell Nikos, when he returns, that I invite you all to dinner this evening. Come early. I will outline my proposals for the film and we will discuss them. Tomorrow we will go to Athens. I have arranged for the film crew to be there.'

'So – you assumed the women's compliance?'

Constantine shrugged.

'I knew that they would agree.'

Yiannis laughed to himself as Constantine left, and returned to clear the kitchen and prepare lunch. He himself felt certain that Saffie and Rachel would agree to act in Constantine's film. Yesterday, Saffie had obviously fallen under the older man's spell and last night, she had been with Nikos . . . Yiannis shrugged philosophically. The magnetism between Saffie and Nikos was very powerful. He chuckled to think how that would confuse things for Constantine. He would naturally seek to utilise it for his film, but he would have to control his jealousy.

Nikos scarcely glanced at Constantine's Jaguar as he galloped towards and then past him. Constantine gripped the wheel tightly, and gritted his teeth. An image of the young man, dressed in black, riding hard on his chestnut mare repeated itself maddeningly on his retina.

Constantine railed inwardly against Nikos' arrogant bearing, and his reflex sneer; the cold dislike in his eyes. He pushed aside the beguiling details of his controlled power, his skilful mastery of the powerful animal, the black curls, trembling as he rode. He put his foot down on the accelerator and roared across the island to his home.

Once there, he drank whisky by the tumblerful, but it did not obliterate his passion. Feeling that his perception was jagged, he nevertheless sat at his desk and forced himself to concentrate on the revised scenario of his film.

'Niko . . .' Georgiou came to the stableyard as Nikos swung himself off Calypso.

Nikos merely glanced at him. Then he patted his horse and, taking her reins, led her slowly around the stableyard until her rate of breathing calmed. He was aware of Georgiou, watching him. He took Calypso out of the sun and into her stable. As he attended to her needs, Georgiou hung around the entrance. His presence fretted Nikos, who still needed to be alone.

'Rachel is happy to be in the film.'

Nikos nodded, unsurprised. Georgiou seemed to be looking

forward to the filming; he had actually enjoyed the previous takes. Perhaps everyone had, but he. Though Georgiou enjoyed every opportunity for sex.

'That's good, isn't it? It will be better, with them.' Georgiou was trying to reassure him.

'Perhaps . . .'

Nikos hadn't meant his tone to sound so unfriendly. He was still filled with anger at Constantine; he did not think that his rage would ever subside. He resented the position of helplessness that the man had forced him into. To think that once he had been his father's trusted friend. Nikos shuddered involuntarily at suppressed memories. Georgiou seemed to have moved closer to him. Nikos tried to restrain his annoyance.

'Niko. Are you alright?'

'Yes!' he snapped, then tutted at himself and turned away, hiding his impatience behind Calypso, tempted to go out again on her. The mare snorted, her ears twitching; she was picking up his anxiety. Nikos brushed her coat firmly with a hard brush, soothing her with small familiar words.

Instead of going away, Georgiou had come even closer to him. Nikos felt his eyes on him. He tugged at his curls in an idiosyncratic gesture of discomfort. He lifted each of Calypso's hooves to pick the small stones from them carefully. Then he began to oil them. Lately it seemed to him that everyone wanted to fuck him. Realising the ludicrousness of this, and that he was probably imagining it, Nikos laughed to himself.

Georgiou had gone out into the yard. Nikos watched him as he wandered to the low wall at the edge of the hill and lit a cigarette. He stood looking out at the view and smoking. Nikos wondered why he had not gone to Yiannis. He relented and went over to his friend.

'I think I'll just call and see Dimitris,' Georgiou told him, now scarcely lifting his head to look at him.

'Okay,' said Nikos, sighing.

He stood for a moment, watching Georgiou go down the path towards the house of their young neighbour. He was surprised, in a way, that Georgiou had not returned home with Constantine, but then, he had been with Rachel. Not for the first time, Nikos was filled with consternation at his innate ability to attract

71

people without wanting to, and the feeling of responsibility and confusion this brought. He pushed down the unbidden thought that they recognised something in him that he refused to. He wondered whether Georgiou would return in time for their visit to Constantine's. He continued to attend to the horse.

'Can I help you?' Rachel asked Yiannis.

Yiannis turned to smile at the young woman standing at the garden door. She was very pretty, so different from most of the girls he had known, with her long fair curls bleached by the sun, her clear blue eyes smiling. He had scarcely seen her without Georgiou. He wondered why she was alone. Then he recalled that Nikos had recently returned, and realised that Georgiou had probably gone out to the stable to see him. He liked to alternate his sexual experiences. Poor Nikos. He shook his head affectionately at thoughts of Georgiou. Georgiou refused to accept that everyone was not as willingly bi-sexual as he was. Especially Nikos. Perhaps Georgiou was right. He himself would suffer – or benefit – later.

Rachel was aware of the sensuality of Yiannis' warm brown eyes as she turned back to him. She returned his friendly smile. She was conscious of his silent admiration of her. She reciprocated his attraction. In the liberal milieu of these intimate Greek friends, and the familiarity necessitated by the film, Rachel knew that any sexual experience was acceptable. Beneficial. This freedom was delicious, especially as Yiannis and Nikos were as attractive, in their own way, as Georgiou.

'I would be grateful for your help,' Yiannis quipped. 'They are none too domesticated, my companions . . .'

In companionable silence, spiced with sexual promise, the two worked together, clearing the kitchen and preparing the meal.

'So—' Saffie murmured as she kissed and licked at Eleni's ear-lobe, and caressed her warm body sleepily. 'Where did Nikos go in such a hurry?'

'Oh, he tries to avoid Constantine – going off on Calypso is one way he can retain power.'

'She's a lovely horse.'

'Yes. Do you ride?'

'A little.'

'You must have a go. It's very exhilarating to ride over the island at night.'

They laughed. Saffie imagined riding naked with Nikos in the darkness, a cold breeze whipping at their sweating bodies as she clung to him. Eleni inserted her finger into Saffie, smiling at her arousal.

'There is – something – between the men?' she ventured.

'You sense it? It is an old joke between Yiannis and myself. We believe that Constantine has had his eye on Nikos for many years.'

'And has Nikos—?'

Eleni shook her head.

'No, Nikos is adamant. He says he loves only women – though naturally, he appeals to everyone ... Even Georgiou cannot persuade him.'

'But the photographs of him and Yiannis?' Saffie persisted.

The thought of the two attractive and potent men engaged in sex together turned Saffie on. Her own imagined exclusion added to this enticing image.

'I told you – they were still quite young and the photographs were purely artistic. A friend of theirs – Damianos – he persuaded them.'

'But Yiannis?'

'Ah, Yiannis is more liberal ... But I think he prefers women, no?' Eleni kissed her.

Saffie's body was writhing rapturously at her lascivious thoughts. She recalled her encounter with Yiannis, in the wind-mill, and her night with Nikos, on the deserted island. She was barely conscious of Eleni's accurate touch as she fingered her clitoris, it seemed so natural a part of her self-excitement. The unscrupulous Eleni took advantage of her friend's obvious vicarious arousal.

'And Georgiou ...?' Saffie realised, wondering whether Rachel would mind.

'They are very sexy together, Yiannis and Georgiou,' Eleni confirmed huskily, re-inserting her finger into Saffie's private warmth. 'But they are not exclusive, Saffie, do not worry ...'

Saffie imagined Yiannis fucking Georgiou as she jerked along Eleni's finger. The image excited her enormously. The idea of a man with a man – and here she was, making love with a woman. And somewhere in between was the potent reality, that Yiannis *was* a virile lover; that she enjoyed men. Eleni kissed her as she came.

'You are all very free together, and with others . . .'

'Yes,' Eleni agreed, as though this was nothing out of the ordinary.

'It is very unusual, you know – to sleep together, to have sex, and not be jealous of each other.'

'Oh, I told you before, we are all very good friends,' Eleni laughed. 'We lose nothing by this freedom.'

'I believe you.'

'You don't mind – doing this film?' Yiannis asked Rachel as they prepared salad together.

'No, not at all. I think it will be very instructive . . .' she pondered the dynamics between this libidinous group of people. 'Fascinating . . .'

They laughed.

'You are very – "laid-back" . . .'

'Have a good time, that's what I say. I don't take things too seriously. I see my friends, getting heavy – making difficulties for themselves. Me? I think, why bother? It's not worth it. I'm too lazy.'

'And Saffie – you think she is as free?'

Rachel hesitated, recalling how her passionate friend had suffered when young by falling madly in love with the wrong people.

'Sometimes, I worry that she thinks too much, feels too much . . .'

Yiannis sighed.

'I know what you mean . . . It is the same with Nikos. These serious people . . .'

'We must ensure that they are liberated – have fun,' Rachel decided.

'Yes. Yes, we must,' Yiannis agreed.

Their eyes met and they hugged each other in affection.

'When I first saw you together, I thought how different you looked, and how you complemented each other. You are so fair – so like an angel.'

Rachel laughed.

'And Saffie so dark . . . with her devilish green eyes. How do you feel about her with Eleni?'

Rachel paused in her cutting of the moist cucumber, then said thoughtfully, 'I don't know. If we were at home – it would surprise me . . . But here, well, it's all like a dream.'

'But you have thought of sex with her?'

Rachel turned to meet those candid brown eyes.

'Yes . . . I suppose you are right. But I did not want it to endanger our friendship.'

'Yes . . .' said Yiannis, thinking of Nikos, whom he had known all his life, 'I know what you mean.'

'That will be different. I mean – with any of you . . .' she laughed to cover her sudden shyness, realising that she had voiced her previous assumption – that there would naturally be sexual freedom between them all. She saw the twinkle in Yiannis' eyes. It would be difficult to feel awkward with this sensitive man for long.

'I suppose I've considered it, thought about the film.'

Yiannis nodded. He was standing very close to her. She breathed in the scent of his body.

'So, you will not feel awkward – filming with me, or Nikos?'

Rachel continued to meet his eyes, mesmerised by their languorous mood. As he smiled once more, slowly, he seemed to lift her spirits.

'No,' she whispered, 'I won't feel awkward, Yianni.'

Yiannis pulled her gently to him and kissed her. He felt her yield to him. She smelt of the sun and of some sweet, subtle perfume. He felt his sex stir to life against her. He released her and smiled at her. He saw the acquiescence in her soft eyes. He continued to hold her away for a moment, to drink in her radiance. Then he kissed her again, cupping the firm halves of her bottom, and pulling her towards him, so that her pubis touched his growing penis. Excited, he moved one hand to her full breast and caressed it. He felt Rachel quicken as her kiss became more passionate. He thought of her with Georgiou. Rachel ran her hands down his back to his abdomen and rubbed her palms forcefully over him, then let them go between his thighs. She felt for his imprisoned testicles and fondled them. They were large and heavy. She smiled to herself as Yiannis' rate of breathing increased, his kiss became more urgent, he fingered painfully at her breast. She wanted to be naked. Here in the sunlit kitchen with this gentle man.

'Take my clothes off . . .' she murmured.

Yiannis grinned and began to undress Rachel slowly, smiling in delight at her soft, perfumed body. When she was naked, he played his agile fingers over her golden-white skin.

'Angel . . .' he whispered, lifting a strand of her golden hair to his lips and kissing her as he watched her blue eyes narrow in enjoyment.

She waited with longing for him to touch her quivering sex. He saw this in her eyes, but still he went at his own speed, tracing the fullness of her perfect breasts and the roundness of her bottom, before reaching her hidden bud. He touched her acutely with the tip of his finger, pressing precisely against the delicate, sensitised ridge. Powerful waves of joy rippled out, spreading through her groin, her thighs and belly. Yiannis felt his prick swell even more, trapped in sweet agony under his coarse jeans. He smiled at the pleasured surprise in her soft eyes.

He pressed again, caressing her lovely buttocks with his other hand, touching fleetingly at her ripened anus with his little finger. Rachel was amazed that such tiny, knowing touches could arouse her so deeply. Tender liquid gathered and spread to her vagina. Yiannis kissed her gently parting lips, moving his hand to her thrusting breast and caressing it with infinite sensitivity. Rachel's love-juices flowed down her muscular passage. As his long hot tongue entered her willing mouth, his fingers went into her wet vagina with ease.

He slid in deeper, manipulating her ever-firmer breast, and deepening his heady kiss. Rachel gloried in his beauty, glad to have this wonderful man so very close. The surroundings of the kitchen were hazy and distanced as he continued to slide his fingers artfully up and down her tight passage. He was pressing and grasping her breasts as they urged against his warm body, touching at his shirt. Rachel rode on him, confident in his expertise as he brought her gradually to climax. His administering was generous as he fingered and caressed her. She sucked, eagerly and strongly on his tongue within her mouth, caressing his face

76

with butterfly touches, ruffling and stroking his thick brown curls. He quickened his masturbation as she began to moan softly, gliding easily along his wet finger. Then he stopped and pressed on her clitoris as she came. Pangs of joy flashed through her as the delicious waves of her climax crashed through her contracting body.

Yiannis held her tightly as her excitement gradually subsided, kissing her hair. Her soft body continued to spasm. He opened his eyes to see Nikos, who had just come in from riding. Nikos watched his friend, fully-clothed, holding the naked English girl. Yiannis smiled at Nikos, over Rachel's head. He withdrew his fingers from her vagina, and inserted them into his mouth, closing his eyes and sucking on them deliciously. The taste of her incited him. When he opened his eyes, Nikos was still watching, his face flushed with sexual desire. Yiannis smiled inside and reached for Rachel's dress and helped her to slip it over her head. Nikos had gone. Yiannis released her long hair from under the dress and smoothed it. She smiled happily at him, content in a sexual after-glow. He kissed her, holding her close. Her body was fired again.

'I liked the foreplay . . .' she whispered seductively.

She touched at his swollen denim.

'Later . . .?' he asked, his twinkling eyes full of warmth.

Rachel nodded. That he was suffuse with controlled lust enthralled her and made him infinitely attractive. She eyed his tight buttocks as he turned away to finish preparing lunch. Then she went upstairs to shower.

Lunch was almost ready. Nikos was back in the stable. Yiannis went out to see him, but he did not look up from his grooming. He brushed the animal with strong, repetitive strokes. Yiannis folded his arms, leant against the stable door, one leg crossed over the other, and watched him. Sunlight burnished his bronzed hair. The men had been friends for very many years. They were able to exist for long periods in companionable silence: sometimes, it was as relaxing as being alone. Perhaps more so. Yiannis knew that such restful intimacy was rare. He treasured it.

'They are very beautiful, Rachel and Saffie?'

'Yes . . .' agreed Nikos.

'It will be alright, Niko – to make the film,' Yiannis said comfortingly.

Nikos looked up at him, and met his eyes. He knew that his friend well understood his feelings on this.

'I dread to think what he has dreamed up, Yianni,' he confessed.

'Well, we'll soon find out. He expects us early and intends to reveal his plans. And tomorrow, Athens.'

They glanced across to Georgiou as he returned, and then back to each other. Yiannis raised his arm to their friend.

'*He'll* enjoy it,' Nikos could not keep the tinge of bitterness from his voice.

'He probably will, and why not, Niko?'

Nikos' look became rueful.

'Dimitris was not at home?' he called to Georgiou.

Georgiou shook his head and shrugged. His mouth and eyes betrayed his brooding sensuality. Yiannis laughed, tweaked Georgiou's long curls and kissed his head briefly. Nikos shook his head slowly at the freedom of his friend. Georgiou smiled at Yiannis. Nikos looked away.

After her shower, Rachel went to rouse the women. She opened the bedroom door quietly, and stood looking at Saffie and Eleni. The muted sun came through the muslin blind and warmed their entwined bodies. Rachel saw that her friend's hand was between the Greek girl's thighs. Saffie opened her eyes dreamily and met those of her friend. They smiled. Eleni stirred and stretched sleepily. She turned to kiss Saffie.

Rachel closed the door and went downstairs and out into the garden. The sun began to dry and bleach her long hair. She went round the back of the house to the stable. Yiannis was talking quietly to Nikos as he petted the dark chestnut mare. They did not notice her. Neither did Georgiou, who sat close by, smoking. It was strange, to see Saffie so intimately involved with another woman, to recognise the intimacy between Yiannis and Nikos. Even Georgiou seemed contained in their golden web. And then, as Georgiou stood to leave them, she saw Yiannis caress his long hair with an affection that filled her with amazement. She slipped away, before they caught sight of her, to assess how she felt about this new revelation: the men were bound to be physically attracted to each other. It was obvious. Alone for the first time, she had the opportunity to appreciate the uniqueness of their situation. It was certainly interesting, if a little strange to think that she had recently had sex with two men who were possibly used to having it with each other. Mmmm . . .

She returned to the kitchen. Everything was ready. She smiled at Yiannis' organisation. Her smile broadened as her body recalled the tenderness of his love-making. She poured herself some wine, and sat at the pine table, looking out of the window across the garden. She was content and relaxed. There was a small knot of tremulous excitement in her stomach as she anticipated their making of this film. It was inevitable that Constantine would include all kinds of sex. She certainly enjoyed the company of their new friends, and there was no doubt that they were extremely libidinous – in every way.

Georgiou smiled at her as he came in to pour himself some coffee. He gestured to her, offering her a cup. Rachel nodded. He came and sat beside her with their drinks. He looked out over the garden. Rachel glanced at him; he seemed preoccupied, his pellucid eyes expressing sadness. After a few moments of silence, she asked:

'What's the matter, Georgiou?'

He turned to her, startled out of his reverie. He smiled immediately, shaking off his gloom.

'Georgiou?' she repeated, taking his hand.

'Niko,' he said, 'he drives everyone crazy!'

For a moment, Rachel thought that he was referring to Nikos' unwillingness to do the film, and then it dawned on her that Georgiou was speaking more personally. She thought of his passionate love-making, and wondered whether he felt the same fervour with a man. She used to think that people were attracted either to one sex or the other, but she had learnt that it was not so. She thought of her own private feelings for Saffie. If they had not become involved with these people, she would probably have kept them secret.

'Do you, have you, slept – had sex with Nikos?'

'No!' Georgiou scoffed, finishing his coffee.

'Has Yiannis?'

He shook his head. She was about to ask him whether he had

made love with Yiannis himself when she saw him, with Nikos, coming across the garden. They walked close together, and were deep in private conversation. She shook her head, marvelling.

By the time everyone had showered and changed, or dressed, it was quite late when they began lunch. It was a protracted and enjoyable affair, lasting late into the afternoon. Saffie found it fascinating to gauge the dynamics between members of the group. She noted Rachel's interest in her and Eleni, and Georgiou's speculative observation of Yiannis. She decided that Constantine could make an interesting and libidinous film about the six of them, without recourse to a storyline. She surmised that it would be difficult to find a more sexually liberal, and attractive group of people.

It was liberating to be without Constantine, as though they appreciated this last freedom before coming under his thrall and the demands of the rehearsing and filming. Perhaps because of this, there was little physical contact. They drank a lot of wine and laughed uproariously. Though Saffie noticed that Nikos drank less and seemed slightly detached, watching them. She wondered whether he was dreading his ordeal. Eleni and Yiannis were amusing and entertaining, as though to make up for their friend's preoccupation. Saffie saw that Yiannis often glanced at Nikos in concern, though Eleni made light of his increasing silence.

When Nikos had not returned to the room after a long absence, Saffie went to find him at his desk. He seemed absorbed in the manuscript before him, and did not acknowledge her presence. Saffie took the opportunity to regard him, his face thoughtful, his long curls casting shadows over his narrow face. She considered it possible that his impatience over the film was connected with the demands it made on his time and energy.

He would find little time to write, and less solitude to develop his ideas. She had sufficient in common with him to understand that, though he could be passionate, there was an essential part of him which required peace and loneliness in order to be creative. As if instinctively realising her understanding, Nikos looked up and smiled at her. Saffie returned his gesture and withdrew, to leave him to this last freedom.

As he drove across to the other side of the island, Nikos seemed once more to be smouldering with repressed passion. Eleni tried to cheer him, but he shrugged her off. He did not even enter the house with the rest of them, but hung about the garden, smoking, as if to delay the moment when he would come under Constantine's dominion.

Constantine greeted them all warmly, though Saffie could see that he was looking for Nikos. Perhaps he feared that Nikos had defied him at last, and had not come. Yiannis enlightened him, but prevented him from going out into his garden to talk to Nikos. Constantine began to think that perhaps he had offended Nikos by encouraging Saffie and Rachel to participate in his film; it may have been better to hire new actresses. Nikos had seemed most particular that visitors to his country should not be coerced.

He could even have got the women from the film crew to co-operate. They were attractive enough, and liberated. They had done other films, though more basic than that he planned. In any case, they had all – men and women – agreed to take small parts, already. Also, they knew Nikos and his moods, and had built up affectionate tolerance. This required the kind of humour they possessed, as a team. And they were detached; they would not be drawn in to Nikos' temperamentality. Yiannis, Georgiou and Eleni were even more familiar with the group of young people.

This seemed a sensible idea to Constantine, and he wondered why he had not thought of it before. Doubtless he could hire students, once in Athens, to take over some of the technical jobs. However, when he saw Saffie's expression as Nikos entered, and the young man's instinctive meeting of her eyes, he knew that the film would be better, much better, with Saffie taking part. He smiled keenly to himself as ideas of how he could use the young people raced through his imagination. As if translating his thoughts, Nikos shot him a disdainful look, and then escaped to the bathroom.

Nikos rejoined the others as they sat drinking sherry in Constantine's garden. The man was suave and debonair. He seemed indifferent to Nikos' look of cold dislike, though in reality he was concerned that he had endangered the man's co-operation. He was standing near Saffie, pointing out various landmarks on the horizon. Nikos had no patience with him: he was probably telling her that across the water, on Delos, young men had once

81

danced naked for Apollo. Or perhaps he was referring to lascivious tracts from Aristophanes' 'Lysistrata', which they had recently discussed. He was annoyed that the man should talk of the god or his island with Saffie. He drank his sherry and accepted another from Yiannis.

Eleni came to him and put her arms around his shoulder. She kissed his neck. Her presence was comforting to him. He began to relax. He smiled at her. She looked radiant; her hair, freshly washed, hung over her bare shoulders and back. He took a strand and put it to his mouth, closing his eyes as he kissed it. Eleni took his hand and led him away from Constantine. Saffie seemed engrossed in his tales of ancient Greece. They stood, shielded from the garden by the fragrant hedge, against the old marble wall. Nikos could hear the sea. He closed his eyes. He breathed in the perfume of the bushes, and of jasmine and bougainvillaea, and Eleni. She was very close to him. He opened his eyes to see her smiling tenderly. Her slim body nudged against his. He embraced her, feeling her warmth. He ran his hands over the soft, short dress and lingered on her bottom. He pulled her sharply towards him and let his hands go under her dress to caress her naked flesh. He ran his hands over her small buttocks, and then let the side of his hand go between her parted legs.

She was wet. Nikos tweaked at her clitoris, feeling her pleasure. He pressed her hard against his erection and kissed her passionately, caressing her ripening breasts. Eleni reached for his prick, unzipping his trousers immediately. She pulled strongly on his stiffened cock. Grinning, she lifted her tiny dress, then sat astride him and pushed his prick into her. Nikos pulled her down. Eleni eased herself along his rigid member, feeling it swelling inside her as she descended. She held firmly onto Nikos' shoulders as she moved up and down his penis, squeezing it tightly as she moved. Then she began to writhe and move round and round on him. Nikos held onto her buttocks, supporting her. He began to jerk hard, into her, holding her waist and helping to position her so that her clitoris pressed rhythmically against his pubis. When he knew that she was beginning to concentrate on her incipient climax, he increased his rate of penetration, so that, as she began to writhe and moan, he released his seed into her, feeling her vagina grip tightly and rhythmically around his vibrating penis.

Yiannis smiled at them from the end of the arbour. Eventually becoming aware of him, they turned and smiled back at him. He went towards them. Nikos stood and fastened his trousers, Eleni smoothed down her dress and went to Yiannis. He put his arm around Eleni and kissed her. For a moment, his eyes met Nikos', then he looked away. He bit the inner flesh of his mouth to dispel his fretful desire for his friend. Nikos looked wonderful when he had just made love. His black eyes were as clear as crystal, his olive-dark skin flushed. His aura was tranquil and content. Eleni, understanding, put her arm round Yiannis and hugged him close. An idea had suddenly taken root, whereby she might be able to help Yiannis . . . She would consider it. Nikos glanced towards where Saffie and Constantine were concealed; he was filled with unreasonable jealousy.

Saffie was sitting on the wall, silhouetted against the panoramic backdrop of fields, and young orchards. Constantine stood beside her. She drank old wine and became increasingly enchanted by Constantine and his imaginative ideas for films. He had great interest in the history of his country and its myths, and he wanted to use this knowledge and its appeal in his films. His voice was expressive, hypnotising her as he explained his plans.

Though engrossed in his telling, Constantine was extremely aware of the young woman who listened avidly. He was eager to touch her. She listened to him with wide eyes and parted lips; his words evoked her own love of Greece. It was natural for her to conjure images. He glanced covertly at the shape of her breasts under her thin dress, and ached to touch the slim, shapely thighs next to him, leaning against the wall.

Saffie drained her wine, and noticed Nikos, hands in pockets, watching from a distance. She was shocked by the intensity of his expression. At the back of her mind, she wondered once more at his annoyance of the afternoon and Constantine. It all seemed too complex at present, and she let it go.

Constantine's maid, Marianna, called to them that dinner was served. Saffie jumped down from the wall, Constantine took her arm and they made their way into the house. She was pleased to be seated next to Constantine, as she was eager to continue their conversation. Also, she had to admit to herself, that his presence acted on her like the potent, old wine. It was deep and rich, and stirred her into life. The prospect of sex with this experienced older man was enticing.

However, it was a little discomfiting to be opposite Nikos. She longed for him. His beauty and the knowledge of his sexuality was a heady aphrodisiac. She returned his glances, knowing that he wanted her as she did him. Nikos spoke little during the first course. It was a delicate concoction of artichokes and seafood, aubergines and tomatoes with aromatic spices. Constantine had forbidden discussion of his plans until afterwards. Yiannis, next to her, was chatty, both to her and to Nikos. Eleni, sitting by Nikos, was taken up mainly with talking to Georgiou and Rachel. Saffie saw that Rachel liked Eleni as much as she did, but then she could not imagine anyone being immune to the young woman's warmth. Georgiou was witty and amusing, still inebriate from earlier.

The meal was very good, with several different courses, including seasoned fish and lamb, which they ate slowly, whilst imbibing plenty of Constantine's excellent wine. Constantine joked that he intended to feed them well, as they needed to be fit and full of energy for their future roles. This seemed a signal for serious discussion to begin and they adjourned to the lounge. Saffie noted that the familiar supercilious sneer lingered around Nikos' handsome face. Yiannis sought to encourage him, though she could not hear what he said. Watching them, close together, she could not help but experience a pang of sexual pleasure. How delightful it would be to see them making love. Saffie entertained herself by imagining them, naked and entwined, kissing tenderly – or fucking with wild, masculine abandon. Saffie squirmed in her seat as she aroused herself with her private fantasies.

She happened to catch sight of Constantine, also watching them, and she anticipated that the canny director would seek to utilise the suppressed sexuality between them. At least Yiannis would enjoy this, and she certainly would. Excitement spread from her groin and belly. Now on the threshhold of this venture, she wondered what pleasure and sexual licence it would bring. She looked around the room at her lovely young fellow-participants. She pictured them engaged in scenes of sexual revelry. From her earlier conversation with him in the garden, it seemed that Constantine would pursue his concept of setting the scenario in ancient Greece.

Once they were all settled with drinks and sweets, Constantine began to reveal his plans. Yiannis sat close to Nikos on the settee. Nikos remained stubbornly withdrawn and silent, despite his friend's endeavours to bring him out. Eleni sat by Yiannis, though she would doubtless move freely where she chose. Rachel had her arm around Georgiou, on the couch opposite, though Saffie noticed that Georgiou watched Yiannis, and even Nikos, with lascivious speculation. Saffie smiled, interested. She herself was curled up on a huge comfortable armchair, eating Greek sweets and sipping pernod. Constantine sat on its mate where he could easily address and observe them all. As he began to speak, he seemed a little nervous, perhaps wary of the sullen Nikos. Once embarked, however, his easy confidence returned and Saffie was reminded of his expansiveness, outside in the garden, and the dreaming nature of his ideas. Yiannis played idly with Eleni's long curls. He pulled her down onto his knees and kissed her. Saffie wanted such closeness and regarded the brooding Nikos with longing.

'Well, naturally I would wish to thank you all for agreeing to participate in the film.'

Here, Nikos looked archly away, smirking slightly.

'Especially Saffron and Rachel. First, I propose a toast to its success.' He raised his glass, as they all did, even the reluctant Nikos. 'Of which, I hasten to add, I have no doubt. I have the ideas – you have the talent. I will outline some of the elements tonight, but I have also printed out some of the details for your private perusal. Naturally I will welcome any suggestions you may have.'

Here, he paused to hand round the print-outs. Saffie saw that Nikos' expression conveyed his own basic response to Constantine. The older man sensibly chose not to look at him.

'Obviously it will be beneficial to include as much of our lovely country as possible. I believe it will also be good – healthy – for you all to have changes, journeys, other things to do. So, after Athens, tomorrow, we will go on to Delphi, probably the next day.' Constantine smiled.

Saffie's heart filled with joy. She smiled across the room to Rachel. Saffie loved Delphi. Rachel had not been yet, though Saffie had described it to her. It was an evocative, magical place, filled with ancient memories. She thought of the site, cradled on the lower slope of Mount Parnassos. It resembled a natural ancient theatre. The Phaidriades towered above it and the lovely Pleistos valley spread below. She recollected it vividly.

'And,' Constantine was continuing, '—we will also travel to Crete, and Naxos. It all fits in with our various stories . . .'

Saffie noticed that Nikos had bristled, and that Yiannis sought to console him.

'I'm sure that Nikos will not object to our utilising his house. Niko?'

Nikos merely shrugged dismissively, but Yiannis – and by observation, Saffie – was aware of his acute distaste at this assumption.

'Tomorrow, when we reach Athens, we will meet with the film crew, who are also eminently suitable for doubling as extras where necessary, as most of you know. They are experienced and have no problems with this.' He added the latter comments for the Englishwomen's benefit.

Saffie considered how Nikos would react to this news, though of course, she reminded herself, they had been filmed before. He was probably already familiar with the technical crew. She herself wondered about them with some trepidation. It was one thing, indulging themselves freely with these liberal Greeks, quite another to perform before a strange film-crew. She stretched her mouth in a gesture of uncertainty to Rachel, who sought her response. Rachel smiled reassuringly.

'Now, I will outline, briefly, my concept. Naturally, as I mentioned, I am open to suggestions. We will discuss it later fully. We could travel in my plane, but the journeys will be enjoyable by ship – especially for our guests. Also, I have the idea that I can shoot some footage whilst at sea. My idea has been approved by my London backer. So we have the funds – the rest is up to us. Right . . .'

'How long do you think all this will take?' asked Nikos drearily.

'I'm not entirely sure, Niko. Weeks, months . . .' He raised his arms in his familiar expansive gesture. 'I'm sure the time will pass pleasantly . . . even for you.'

'Tttt . . .'

86

'I must remind you, Niko...' Constantine's voice became hard, 'I have lost much time with your – lack of co-operation. I can not afford to lose more. You understand my position.'

Nikos was silent. Saffie saw that his eyes smouldered. She was excited by his fury. She knew, from Constantine's warning tone, that he was reminding Nikos of his power to destroy him.

'Right. Well, as you know, the stories of the ancient gods of Hellas, as well as her myths and literature, contain much lascivious material. I have decided to utilise and extrapolate some of these for the basis of our film... It will concern a group of young actors, such as you are, travelling from place to place to enact some of the myths and legends. You will play the part of ancient Athenian actors. There will be some historical explanation – the background. I think it will be set in the classical age, that is, in the fifth century B.C. – or B.C.E., as I should perhaps say now... Most of you know something of this glorious time. A time that was important to the whole of European history and development...'

'For God's sake, Constantine – you're making a pornographic film!' sneered Nikos, smiling sarcastically. 'Do you think that your average viewer cares about all this? It may even be a turn off! They just want sex.'

'You are very superior, Niko... People will relate to the storyline. It will add depth and interest. The erotic scenes will be enhanced...'

'You may as well be honest. Why travel? Why not film it all here? I'm sure you could easily set up scenes of depravity; find instruments suitable for sado-masochism, and convince everyone,' he looked round at them all superciliously, 'to participate willingly.'

Nikos drew deeply on his cigarette and exhaled slowly. He appeared arrogant, but Saffie sensed that he was trembling within. She surmised that he was distressed at his beloved history being used for such nefarious purposes. He was afraid that the myths and legends would appear ludicrous. Saffie realised that this was ironical, since the men shared a love of Greek history.

Constantine had hesitated to respond, wishing to pacify, rather than further provoke Nikos. He did not want the familiar trouble before they had even begun. He would have to get him to sign something. A written agreement would prevent him from disappearing. However, he was riled by Nikos' inflammatory accusation that his film was to be merely pornographic. Not that he had anything against such films. In fact, when younger he had been involved in the production of some, and he was well aware that his film crew certainly made them. Theirs were very popular and successful, which was one reason he had decided to engage them. He was proud of the artistic intent of his prospective film, and hurt that it should be summarily dismissed by one to whom it should appeal. It was precisely because Nikos and his friends were familiar with the subject matter that he had decided to use it. He had even, naively, supposed that this approach would placate and interest Nikos.

'You know damned well that I want this to be a good film, with artistic integrity,' Constantine said between clenched teeth.

The room was silent. Nikos looked away. Constantine made a supreme effort to concentrate his thoughts. He drank some of his wine, and then continued in his former train:

'So, there will be enactments of stories, such as those involving Apollo and Narcissus; Theseus and the Minotaur – hence the importance of Naxos, where the abandoned Ariadne meets the god Dionysus. Here, also the genesis of Dionysian, or Bacchanalian, rites and soon . . . Well – time enough for details, hey?' He sipped once more at his wine.

Saffie smiled at the man's attempt to control his enthusiasm. She took the opportunity to regard Nikos, whose face seemed heightened in colour: perhaps he was envisaging the varied sexual roles Constantine had doubtless cast for him. The histories of the Greek gods were wild and hedonistic, with immediate sexual gratification and possessiveness at their very core. They gave much opportunity for sex of every description.

'As well as the mythical aspect, there will be something of the relationships between the actors in between filming.'

Constantine's intelligent eyes filled with sardonic amusement as he surveyed them all in a slow perusal of the room. His incisive look lingered on each individual in turn. Saffie thought that most of them would have experienced his laser-look as though it cut right into their souls, or at least their deeper fantasies.

'So. We will return to Athens tomorrow. By the evening, you

will have familiarised yourself with the plot outline. We will discuss it. You will get to know the crew. Naturally, you will need to know them intimately.' Here, he glanced at Saffie and Rachel, assuring them: 'They are very friendly. So, any questions so far? Niko—?' Constantine prompted.

'I'll read the material,' Nikos decided with unaccustomed control.

Constantine nodded approvingly.

'Well. I will leave you to look through my outlines. You can stay here tonight. I suggest that you all get as much rest as possible from now on. Also, it would be a pity if you squandered your natural talent.'

Here, Constantine directed a significant look at Nikos. Saffie thought that he was certainly far more interested in what Nikos got up to than he was in Yiannis or Georgiou.

Rachel and Georgiou began to look through their pages together, immediately engrossed. They mused together on sexual possibilities and roles. Georgiou would not have any difficulty, whatever was demanded of him. Naturally enough, their libidinous talk soon led to like actions. Saffie thought that there was little chance that they would be camera-shy. She was impressed with her friend's sang-froid. Eleni went to make them all coffee, and Nikos merely placed his copy of the notes on the table, and lit another cigarette. Yiannis flipped through his, relieved that Nikos was now demonstrating restraint. Constantine certainly intended to get his mileage out of his captive actor. He looked up, caught Saffie's eye and whistled silently through his teeth, looking comically up into the air as he did so. Saffie wanted to laugh.

'I'm just going to get some fresh air,' she said, leaving the intensity of the room with difficulty.

Yiannis was quickly behind her. They went to the edge of the garden, and looked eagerly through the pages.

'There's not much Nikos won't be doing in this . . .' Yiannis said. 'It's not developed yet – or, rather, not written down – but I'm sure it's all there in Constantine's mind . . . Nikos seems to get all the "god-parts", which means he'll get everyone else, I expect . . .'

'How will he feel about that?' asked Saffie, thrilled by this prospect.

'I wonder if he would back out? I should think we will not get detailed scripts before we are well into the film.'

'He can guess though . . . Apollo . . . Hyacinthus . . . Marsyas – there's a lot of sadism.' Saffie smiled dirtily at Yiannis, who returned this almost shyly. Saffie thought that he was about to kiss her, and she was about to reach out to test his physical reaction when suddenly, Constantine was upon them.

'I'll go and see Nikos . . .' Yiannis whispered as Constantine arrived. Saffie nodded.

'So, do you like the idea – and what you have read so far?' asked Constantine.

'Yes. I think it could be very good, Constantine. Do you think that Nikos will agree to all you have planned for him?'

'He has agreed, in essence, though he is not too keen, I admit. He will be fine – you will all be fine – all possible sexual adventures are permissible under the auspices of the film. He will lose his inhibitions – scruples – once he is living in that life . . . He is an extremely talented man . . . And very attractive, you would agree? You have seen the cuts from previous filming, he is a natural.'

Saffie saw Constantine's eyes narrow – in memory, or anticipation?

'So, you will enjoy the journey? Athens tomorrow . . . We will relax, have fun . . . perhaps discuss the film, then Delphi.'

'You will film there?'

'A little. We will develop the ideas together as we go along.'

Saffie interpreted this as Yiannis had suggested: Constantine was wisely not going to reveal the scenes too far in advance. Therefore Nikos had no material with which to argue.

'Where are the photographs? Of Yiannis and Nikos . . .?' she asked suddenly. It was worth a try.

Constantine looked suspiciously at her, perhaps believing that she intended to steal them for Nikos. Then, a slow knowing smile spread across his face, from his eyes.

'I promise you, Saffron, you will most certainly enjoy some of the scenes I have devised.'

'What are the photographs like?'

'Yiannis hasn't told you? They are very beautiful, Saffron. If you saw them, you would not believe that there is nothing between those two young men.'

Constantine cupped her chin in his palm, and lifted her face to look into her inviting green eyes.

'Elfin creature . . .' He smiled as he took in her high cheek-bones and narrow chin.

Saffie blushed under the seriousness of his look, her body aroused by his closeness. He leant to kiss her, taking her lip firmly between his. Saffie's hungry body responded immediately. His tongue went roughly into her mouth and he pulled her strongly towards him. Saffie clung to him eagerly. Constantine's body surged with desire, denied for too long. He had certainly wanted this lovely young English woman since he had first seen her.

Saffie was aware of his strong masculine power. Her body burned to be possessed by him. Her darker self was in thrall to his cruelty. She felt his hands moving quickly and roughly all over her receptive body, stirring her into profound sexual life. Her sex throbbed in anticipation. His impatience seared through her. She would even have him here.

'Saffie.'

Saffie was jerked back to reality as Nikos called imperatively to her across the garden. Constantine released her reluctantly, enraged by Nikos.

'Rachel wants to speak with you,' Nikos continued calmly, looking coldly at Constantine.

'I'll see you later,' Saffie said to Constantine.

He nodded, unsmiling. Still in a sexual haze, Saffie passed Nikos, who lingered, a look of cold triumph in his dark eyes as he regarded Constantine. Saffie was aware of the powerful waves of agitation between the two men.

Saffie looked into the lounge, where Yiannis was with Eleni on the settee. They smiled at her. Eleni was more or less naked, and Yiannis was caressing her ripe breast.

'Where's Rachel?'

Eleni shrugged.

'With Georgiou? Upstairs?' she pointed upwards and smiled.

Yiannis pulled Eleni to him, and continued to caress her, stroking her thigh tenderly, and licking at her extended tongue as she turned back to him. Saffie's sexual readiness increased wildly. She wanted to be in Eleni's place. Her own breasts tightened.

'Rachel?' she called, going upstairs. She was feeling a little annoyed that she had been summoned away from her own lascivious enjoyment.

'Saffie?'

Following the sound of her friend's voice, Saffie found her in one of the many bedrooms. Surprisingly, she was alone.

'So, what do you think?' Saffie asked, her eye lighting on Constantine's crumpled notes on the bed.

'I reckon it'll be exciting.' Rachel smiled, putting her arms around her knees and hugging them to her body.

'Yes . . .'

Saffie obviously sounded uncertain to her friend, who sought to assure her:

'We don't have to do anything we don't want to, Saffie . . .'

'Except for Nikos,' said Saffie thoughtfully. 'And there's certainly lots of opportunity for sado-masochistic scenes . . . The gods could be most cruel.'

'Marsyas flayed alive?'

'By Apollo – Nikos . . . And Hyacinthus, the first mortal man to be loved by a god – Apollo?' And then she added, remembering: 'Nikos said you wanted me?'

Rachel looked puzzled.

'Did he?'

Saffie suddenly realised that Nikos had merely wanted to get her away from the libidinous Constantine. She was torn between being flattered by and angry with him.

'Anyway, it's nice to see you,' Rachel was saying. 'We've hardly spoken since all this began.'

Saffie smiled in agreement and squeezed her friend's hand. A flash of sensuality sparked between them. Saffie withdrew her hand, and smiled again, shyly. Rachel got up and wandered over to the window. She pulled the drape to one side, and looked down to see Nikos, standing alone. Constantine was walking away; she had the feeling that they had been arguing.

'He's very beautiful, Saffie . . .' she said wistfully.

'Anything goes, Rachel. We can't afford to be possessive. Anyway, then he won't worry about me with Constantine tonight.'

The friends exchanged conspiratorial looks.

'It occurred to me today,' Rachel began, hesitantly, 'when I saw the men together . . . Well, have you thought, Saffie, that they probably screw each other?'

Saffie laughed.

'I'd be surprised if they didn't, considering . . . But, from what Eleni says, I don't think Nikos is too keen.'

'I'm sure Georgiou is.'

'I find it exciting, don't you?'

'I'm not sure.'

'Does it bother you, though?'

'I'm not worried that it makes them less interested in us, if that's what you mean.'

'I'm sure it doesn't. They just allow what many people suppress.'

'Yes . . .' agreed Rachel, looking thoughtfully at her old friend.

Nikos was sitting on the wall, one knee raised and his chin cupped in his hand. He was deep in thought, and seemed unaware of Rachel as she approached. She handed him a glass of wine, and he smiled graciously as he took it.

'I really do not want to do this, Rachel,' he confessed with a sigh, anticipating her question.

'I know . . .' she said sympathetically, grasping his arm warmly.

They drank in silence for a few moments, engrossed in their own thoughts: Nikos filled with dread at the weeks to come, and the ignominy of being under Constantine's power; Rachel regarding him, and thinking how very lovely he was, and how this very quality was causing him such pain. All around them was the sound of cicadas, and the sweet scent of night-flowers.

'Are *you* certain about all this, Rachel . . .' he asked, turning to her, '—this film?'

'Yes. I'm fine.'

Nikos was aware of the confidence in her blue eyes, and relaxed a little in the calmness of her presence.

'You are very pretty,' he said softly.

'Let's go for a walk, shall we – out of here and down to the beach?' she suggested.

'Alright . . .' he agreed after a moment's thought. Then he smiled, getting down from the wall.

They left the walled garden, and climbed down the steep path which led directly to the shore. They took off their shoes and walked hand in hand along the beach. They spoke little, each easy in the other's company.

'We should swim . . .' Rachel suggested laughingly.

'Okay!'

Nikos' eyes gleamed in amusement. They undressed and ran down to the moonlit sea. It was refreshing and invigorating to be immersed in the pure, cool water. After swimming strongly for a while, racing each other and proving equally strong, they became playful, grasping and ducking each other, yelling and screeching with laughter. Then Nikos held Rachel and they became silent, aware of the desire in each other's eyes and their bodies cleaved naturally together as they exchanged their first kiss. It lasted a long time, whilst they explored each other's nakedness. Rachel was excited by the jutting of Nikos' engorged penis against her crotch.

She gasped as Nikos touched her expertly, teasing her body into a flame of desire. They left the water and lay on the sand. Nikos lay next to Rachel, supporting himself with his left elbow on the sand, his hand cradling his head as he looked admiringly down at her. Her pale body seemed to gleam in the moonlight, her soft golden hair spread around her head like a halo as she lay, very still, one leg raised. Her firm breasts pointed up to the star-filled sky. Slowly, Nikos reached out his hand and, beginning at her inner thigh, he began to ripple his fingers up her body, across her softly rounded belly to her generous breast. This he cupped tenderly, echoing her gentle smile as he caressed it. Rachel's body quivered all over. He took her enlarged nipple between finger and thumb and rolled it repeatedly, causing small spasms of sensitivity to race to her sex as he squeezed tightly. The nerves of her vagina leapt into expectant life and a little moan escaped her lips.

Nikos leant to kiss her breast. He began to lick and tease at her large nipple. He moved his hand to its twin and fondled it lovingly. Then, taking her erect teat into his hot mouth, he began to suckle it strongly. The bond between breast and vulva burned like steel. Nikos trailed his elegant hand languidly over her body to her pubis, where he fingered her clitoris delicately. Expertly, he raised her pitch of sexual excitement. Rachel began to writhe deliciously on the warm sand. Nikos sucked more strongly on her teat, nipping at it with his teeth. He inserted his fingers deeply into her moist vagina. Rachel tightened her muscle strongly around his thrusting fingers. She felt his thumb pressing rhythmically on her raw clitoris. She lifted her abdomen high, urging him to jerk more powerfully. Nikos did so, biting with increased hunger at her breast and manipulating her sex with hard, powerful movements. His remaining fingers teased at her anus, touching acutely at the tight centre of dark pleasure. Soon, he had brought her to a first slow orgasm, easing his rate of masturbation as she began to beat strongly around his hand, remaining still as she controlled its pitch. Then he held her close and kissed her.

He lay back on the sand. His expression was infinitely lascivious. As she raised herself to look at him, she felt something stir deeply within her. He had an amazing faculty to move others. She was almost shy in the face of such raw passion. She looked quietly down into his beautiful black eyes, now smouldering with need. She touched his full, passionate mouth. A surge of glorious power filled her. She had this wonderful man entirely in her control. He gasped as she grasped his standing penis strongly. The intensity of his arousal was transmitted in his deep eyes. She regarded him in wonder as she began to pull on his swollen member, squeezing it tightly.

Nikos' eyes closed in sensual pleasure, his mouth parted invitingly, the tip of his red tongue coming between his lips. All he could think of was the naked girl administering to him; the swell of her white breasts in the moonlight and the sensitive touch of her hand as she moved it up and down his cock, pulling his foreskin over his bulb, and then down to his root. Her pace of movement, and pressure of squeeze was exactly right as she masturbated him, agonisingly slowly at first and then steadily increasing as she responded to his expression, and the response of his body. His entire body glowed with joy. He could exist in this delicious moment for ever. He relaxed in the expert hands of this woman, eschewing all responsibility except for his own enjoyment.

His testicles, sometimes roughly fondled, tightened pleasurably. He basked in the knowledge of imminent orgasm. He relished her ability to prolong and extend his experience as she wanked him tirelessly. He followed the pressure of her hand with his mind, feeling the tightness move up and down his prick. It was lovely, it was a release just to lie here and have this done to him. His groin and thighs glowed with increased sensation. It spread outwards, filling his belly and making him suffuse with enjoyment. Rachel knew that she brought him almost to orgasm, and deliberately slowed her rate of manipulation, to delay this, pinching the end of his penis to aid her, feeling the leaking juice from his hot cock on her fingers.

Rachel smiled as she watched the changing expressions of extreme pleasure fleet over Nikos' beautiful face. She was filled with peace and stillness to thus regard him. She quickened her rate of masturbation again, knowing that he would soon reach his release. But, she wanted him. The thought of his spunk shooting over her hand and arm, and him lying back in repletion caused her vagina to burn with longing.

When she released him, Nikos opened his eyes wide. She smiled at the sudden wildness reflected in them. She took his balls tenderly in her hand and squeezed on them. She traced his sensitive perineum, finding the thickened vein and following its route to the tip of his penis.

He lay still, though she knew that this was with immense control. Keeping his sultry eyes, she moved her fingers to his anus and inserted one, deeply. Nikos felt the heat spread over his body. He closed his eyes against his anguished pleasure, and bit strongly at his lower lip until it bled. His sexual capacity was violently increased, but he shook his head from side to side. Narrowing her eyes, Rachel pushed more deeply into the tight muscular hole. Nikos moaned, almost sobbed, his breathing coming rapidly now.

Rachel began to move her finger up and down this forbidden passage, seeing his cock rear angrily. She knew that she could make him come like this, but he would not like it. He would be angry – wild at such exposure. Or he would release himself, force her down and ravish her. She withdrew her finger, meeting his eyes in shared secret knowledge. Then she went down on him, taking his lovely prick deeply into her mouth. Nikos reached out for her, touching her breasts fleetingly. Rachel ridged her tongue and pressed it down on his shaft as she sucked him hard, moving her mouth strongly up and down its length. She thought that he wanted to fuck her but she worked on him until she felt his pre-come against her tongue. She licked at his hole. Nikos was lost in her powerful manipulation of his prick.

As she withdrew, he pulled her up and eased her onto his cock. He groaned in relief to feel the hot muscle gripping him securely. He felt at Rachel's bouncing breasts as she rocked and ground on him, then he moved her on to her back, raised her legs high and thrust his phallus deeply into her. Bending her legs at the knees, and holding them down, he rammed powerfully, banging against her clitoris until she cried out loudly in unbearable pleasure. Her sexual contractions caused his cock to erupt with violent jerks. She watched him as he ejaculated, seeing his face transfixed in pleasure and pain as he came gloriously, at last shuddering in his powerful release. He remained within her, his prick throbbing as she reached another simultaneous crescendo. Then he lay and caressed her gently.

Later, arms around each other, they climbed back up to Constantine's house.

'We'll have a bath . . .' Rachel suggested as they entered the garden.

'Alright,' Nikos agreed, squeezing her tightly and kissing the top of her golden head.

They lay opposite each other in the deep foam bath, its soporific perfume filling the air. Rachel was relaxed and content, very happy that she had had this man. She knew that there would be more sex with him in the days ahead, and looked forward to Constantine's imaginative scenarios for the film. Nikos gave her his slow, lazy smile. He was ready for more. Rachel's body glowed in anticipation. Nikos raised himself, and, holding on to the sides of the bath he positioned himself so that he kissed Rachel's red clitoris with the end of his penis.

This tender touch was thrilling. He then trailed his dripping member up from her crotch, over her belly and up to her breasts. His cock sent waves of arousal along her nerves everywhere it touched on its luxurious journey. She raised her lower body, inviting him to enter her. Nikos knelt and pulled her abdomen from the water and inserted himself slowly into her. It was already good to have him back within her as they made love gradually, this new element a challenge.

Four

Saffie had watched her friend go off with Nikos, and then gone in search of Constantine. Yiannis was alone in the study, working on the computer.

'Are you writing the script for Constantine?' Saffie teased, thinking how he could take the opportunity to add in some lewd scenes for himself and Nikos.

Yiannis smiled.

'As Constantine is so keen to be authentic, I thought he could use some of Aristophanes' "Lysistrata" . . .'

'You don't think you'll be getting just a little too intellectual?' Saffie jested.

'No, it's very bawdy stuff. They used phalluses – everything – in the "Comedies" . . . This is very rude, promiscuous.'

'Yes. I see . . .' said Saffie thoughtfully. 'And plenty of homosexual love?'

Yiannis smiled to himself without looking up. Then he told her:

'In Plato's "Symposium", Aristophanes believed that there were three kinds of person – heterosexuals, and male and female homosexuals. Originally, human beings had four legs and double the amount of all other organs, and there were three sexes, male, female and hermaphrodite. Zeus punished them for fighting against the gods by slicing them all in half. Therefore, forever after, people looked for their other half – this is what we came to call love, so Plato says.'

'Or sex?' suggested Saffie.

'Right,' he grinned, returning to the screen.

Saffie ruffled his hair, tempted to remain, but she knew that she would definitely have sex with him again and so moved on to find Constantine. She was beginning to understand the ease with which the friends took up with each other. Confidently, she went up to Constantine's room and pushed open the door. She was so ready for sex that she hoped he was already in bed. It was good to have sex so simply, without complications. She was sure that he wanted her.

'Oh . . .' she backed away in confusion as she saw him with Eleni, lying naked in his arms. He was still big, so she knew that they had not finished. In fact, they could not have been together long, she realised.

'No . . . Saffie, come . . .' Eleni urged, smiling encouragement and gesturing with her bare arm.

Saffie hesitated, her questioning eyes locking with Constantine's. The Greek man nodded and widened his eyes invitingly. He smiled at her. As she entered the bedroom, and closed the door, Saffie saw that Constantine was stroking Eleni caressingly. Saffie felt the warmth of sexual arousal increase as she watched Eleni respond to his gentle massaging of her breast. She saw the woman's enlarged nipple held tightly between his finger and thumb.

'We must make her feel welcome,' Eleni murmured, rising generously from Constantine's hold to go to Saffie.

She took her hand and led her to the end of the bed. Standing behind the English girl, and meeting Constantine's avid gaze, she ran her hands over Saffie's body, caressing her breasts and pressing right on her clitoris. Saffie was assailed by conflicting reactions. This was a most unusual beginning, yet she could not move from Eleni's attentions. Eleni began to undress her. She touched her as she divested her of her clothes, kissing her neck and tweaking at her breasts and sex. Then, she stood close behind her and ran her hands rapidly over her body, bringing her to purring, receptive life. Constantine watched the two lovely young women, naked before him. Eleni opened Saffie's labia to Constantine, who suppressed the vital urge to go and thrust in his pulsating phallus. Saffie turned to Eleni and embraced and kissed her. Their breasts and vulvas touched. Constantine's manhood reared uncontrollably. His artistic self longed to reach for his camera and film them. There would be time enough for that, he told himself.

The women kissed and fondled, seemingly engrossed, but

100

actually very aware of Constantine. Eleni urged Saffie to the bed. Constantine received her, kissing her hungrily. Saffie sensed the animal power in him. His prick moved greedily against her thigh. Her vagina seemed consumed by liquid fire as she yearned to invaginate his big cock. Both man and woman concentrated on Saffie, touching and kissing her everywhere, teasing and playing with her until she was a mass of desire and did not care who did what to her as long as they did not abandon her for each other. She knew that Eleni was deeply aroused and glimpsed, through the heat of her sexual frenzy, Constantine's angry, rearing prick.

Eleni lay back and pulled Saffie onto her. The women jerked strongly against each other, knowing exactly how to give pleasure as their pussies rubbed and pressed. Saffie raised herself, and descended hard, slamming her sex hard against Eleni's, seeing that the woman was as close to orgasm as she was as she felt the gathering sensation threaten to burst within her. Eleni squeezed at Saffie's engorged breasts, jerking her nipples rapidly, repeating this almost to the point of pain and grunting as she felt her orgasm begin to break.

Constantine grasped her strongly by her slender waist and raised her. Eleni parted her legs, so that Saffie's knees were between them. Saffie gasped as she felt Constantine's enormous prick between her legs, and Eleni fingering at her sex. Eleni's fingers went deeply into her vagina. Saffie prayed that Constantine would bugger her; her forbidden hole glowed hot for him. But as Eleni dragged out her fingers, he thrust his cock deeply into her dripping vagina.

He held her hard by her waist as he fucked her, doggy-fashion, supporting her against his deep thrusts. Each sexual surge rammed her whole body forward, sending shudders through her. She was very aware of the strength of his body and the power of his mind. Eleni smiled lasciviously at her, sucking on the fingers trailing with Saffie's juices. She felt at her own breasts and then began to bounce under Saffie's rapidly moving body, masturbating in time. She fondled Saffie's juddering teats, raising herself to suckle deliciously on them, beginning to moan as she brought herself to orgasm, tossing wildly along her hand and crying in anguish. Her rising cries took Saffie to a state of pure lust.

Constantine held Saffie very tightly as he rammed home

against her abdomen, jerking her slim body hard. Eleni now squeezed very very tightly on Saffie's nipples, laughing cruelly into her eyes as Saffie yelled out. Her swelling orgasm was held back and controlled by Constantine's urgent animal thrusting as the man sweated and grunted, his powerful body wracking Saffie's. She felt she could bear no more. But Constantine's savage jerking showed no sign of abating. He was able to keep this up for hours if necessary. He was lost but to the feel of his thick wet cock as it penetrated repeatedly into Saffie. He was suffuse with the glory of his power, his entire body filled with raw sex. He was also possessed of sadistic satisfaction – Nikos did not have her.

Saffie moaned and complained, panted rapidly and swore at his savage mastery. Her body was more and more aroused. She wanted him to handle her breasts, to possess her entirely. Soon, her climax would engulf her.

'Feel my tits, you bastard.'

Constantine teased at them, dandling them deliciously in his hands. Eleni held on to Saffie. Constantine squeezed her breasts very hard, kneading and pulling them. Saffie felt her anus burning with dark pleasure as he hit it repeatedly. She decided then that she would have anal sex at the next opportunity. She thought of Nikos buggering her. This, together with the knowledge of the exciting frisson between these two equally dominant men took her even higher. Eleni began to tweak at Saffie's suffuse clitoris. Saffie shook her head, feeling her belly begin to contract. Possession of her breasts speeded Constantine. He should release them in order to hold out. But he wanted the sweet delight of handling them. So, to punish Saffie for this, he tore and squeezed, feeling the hot joy wrung unwillingly from him. Torn between rage and dark pleasure, Saffie felt her orgasm fill her body, spreading out, wave after wave, making her body tingle. Constantine stopped moving, feeling only his own tremendous pleasure as his spunk rushed violently from his balls and through his aching prick into Saffie. He throbbed hugely within her, her muscle contracting in unison. He released her and rolled away, exhausted. Eleni continued to finger Saffie's clitoris, now pressing on it as Saffie arched and then collapsed. Saffie held her and kissed her as she pumped against her, experiencing wave after wave on Eleni's eager vulva.

'Are you alright?'

'Yes, swine . . .'

Eleni caressed her friend, holding her close and stroking her breast and bottom lovingly. She kissed her and rocked her until she slept. Constantine got up and left them. He passed Nikos on the stairs and threw him an arrogant smirk of triumph. Nikos guessed what he had been up to and his hand automatically went into a fist, wanting to punch him.

'You're working in the dark,' Georgiou addressed Yiannis from the door, having watched him for several minutes in silence. Yiannis had not noticed his presence, so engrossed had he been in his personal computer.

Yiannis turned to him and grinned.

'I'm not in the dark as far as knowing what you're here for,' he commented, saving his file on disk and rising. He crossed the room to where Georgiou waited. He smiled indulgently at Georgiou's moody vulnerability. Yiannis stood in front of him for a moment, his eyes containing friendly humour. Then he moved closer and kissed him fiercely, feeling the savageness of Georgiou's desire as he grabbed at him. His cock became rigid as Georgiou seized it.

'Okay,' he laughed, pushing Georgiou away, 'but not here. Upstairs. Otherwise we run the risk of Constantine standing over us with his video-recorder.' This thought amused him greatly. Georgiou wouldn't give a damn, he realised.

It was difficult to restrain the desperate youth as they climbed the stairs. Yiannis was filled with mirth, admiring his companion's acting skills. It was really only hours – if that – since he had had the passionate Rachel, yet he was acting like he was sex-starved. It was a pity Constantine was so single-minded in his concentration on Nikos. Georgiou had absolutely no hang-ups and would agree to anything as long as it involved another.

They reached Yiannis' room and Yiannis pushed Georgiou onto his bed: he could play at this game. He grasped Georgiou's arms and pushed them above his head, against the bed, and pinned down his legs by the thighs with his knees. Georgiou did not wince; in fact his sultry eyes expressed expectation. Yiannis smiled again and pushed his thighs apart and went between his legs. He brought his mouth down hard on his friend's as he positioned his crotch on top of Georgiou's. Beneath the denim of his jeans, and through Georgiou's, he felt the rigidity of his cock. He pressed down firmly with his own erection. A violent thrill shot through his prick and into his groins. He tensed his buttocks as he jerked powerfully against Georgiou. He knew that this was too little for his impatient lover, and that it frustrated him, but he continued. He tensed his buttocks, experiencing a rod-like glow up his anal passage.

Georgiou bit brutally at his tongue. He threw his body about as though it was wracked with uncontrollable urges. He flung Yiannis off him and was immediately over him, holding him down. Without finesse, he ripped off Yiannis' clothes, and then his own. Then with fevered energy, he played with Yiannis' naked cock, sucked strongly at it. The adaptable Yiannis was infected by Georgiou's frenzied sex. He fingered teasingly between his legs, pulling and squeezing at his balls, poking with his finger at the entrance to his sphincter.

'You're a fuckin' whore, Georgiou . . .' Yiannis said into his ear, feeling himself wanked wildly by this man.

Georgiou pushed Yiannis over onto his belly and slapped lubricant haphazardly over his abdomen.

'I should save the rape scenes for the film,' Yiannis suggested lightly, his body forced upwards as Georgiou pushed several fingers into him.

'Ha! Constantine, he is a bastard . . . Anyway, he only wants our little Nikos.'

Pain and desire seared through Yiannis. Georgiou was immediately aware of this as Yiannis disengaged himself.

'Ah! And you too, Yianni . . .' he laughed.

He continued to pull on Yiannis' cock. He was very business-like and precise, with none of the exciting tentativeness of a woman. He jerked on Yiannis' prick violently. His efficiency was too precise for Yiannis.

'Georgiou, I'll come,' Yiannis warned him, a plea in his voice.

'And we can't have that, can we, Yianni?'

Georgiou took a handful of Yiannis' luxuriant chestnut curls and tugged on them. Then he leant and bit savagely at Yiannis' mouth. Yiannis yielded for a while, willing his pitch of excitement to subside. Georgiou lay along him. His body was muscular and hard. Yiannis' consciousness went to where their naked cocks met, enjoying the feel of Georgiou's erect phallus against his own. Then he got out from under Georgiou, turned him over and held him down by his arms again, his eyes flaming. Unable to move, Georgiou spat up at him, his eyes wild. Yiannis smirked. Then he leant and kissed Georgiou, deliberately trailing the tip of his prick against Georgiou's.

'Fuck me, Yianni.'

'No!'

'Come on, you bastard.'

'Why should I?'

'You know you want to. Look at you.'

Yiannis lay on him, grasping his straining muscular buttocks firmly, digging his nails sharply into them. He encircled Georgiou's yearning hole with his index finger, and kissed him roughly. Then he made his hand into a fist and stuffed this hard into him. Georgiou cried out dramatically, grasping Yiannis' cock and piercing his nails into him. Yiannis remained quiet at some cost. He continued to ram his fist into Georgiou, then released him and drew him close, holding him. He kissed his hair, his shoulder, his neck. Then he sucked like a vampire at his neck.

'Yianni?'

Yiannis stopped and looked at Georgiou, bit his lip and nodded. He turned Georgiou onto his side and lavished oil from the bedside table on to his prick, and around the man's anus. Then, holding on to him, he inserted his cock carefully, slowly pushing deeper. He felt the sphincter muscle grip him tightly. Georgiou moaned in abandon, encouraging Yiannis to hold on to his prick as he sodomised him strongly.

'Come on, Yianni, give it to me, man!' demanded Georgiou imperatively.

Finding it difficult to control himself, Yiannis moved his friend over on to his stomach and began to fuck him hard. With masochistic self-control he moved up, so that he was almost released, the tip of his prick pinched, then, he banged down into Georgiou, making his body shudder with his force. Each time he felt the strong muscle gripping him tightly. He was lost in the decadent indulgence of this when Georgiou suddenly threw him off and held him down on his back, kissing him wildly, tearing

105

and biting at his flesh. Yiannis' arousal was extreme.

He had no idea that Saffie was watching them, entranced, by the door. She had passed, on her way from the bathroom, herself in a state of sexual languor. She had been drawn to them. Their unfamiliar masculine passion was wild, almost frightening in its rage and intensity. But she could not take her eyes from them. They fought as much as they made love. Georgiou tore at Yiannis' writhing body, teasing and pulling at his prick, poking into his back passage with his fingers. They were strong, fit men, aware only of each other, though Saffie knew that each was a generous and expert heterosexual lover. This secret, exclusive aspect thrilled and intrigued her.

They wrestled and thrashed about, frantic in their sexual fighting. Saffie wondered whether Constantine would be able to catch something so intimate and personal on screen. She felt her fanny burn with renewed desire as she watched them. Georgiou held Yiannis down and, lavishing cream on his prick, he rammed it between Yiannis' clenched buttocks, despite Yiannis' writhing. Saffie saw the deep sexual flush spread over Yiannis' face and neck. She saw the suffuse head of his prick squashed under his restrained body.

Caring only for himself, Georgiou screwed Yiannis. But, before he was allowed release, Yiannis tossed him off and straddled him. Breathing hard and unsteadily, he applied cream carelessly, too far gone to concentrate. Drunk on sex. Saffie smiled affectionately at his state of abandon, his face sensual, his hair tousled. Her vagina throbbed as he rammed his prick into Georgiou's welcoming hole. Georgiou raised his abdomen, and Yiannis seized his long prick and began to jerk on it.

Saffie watched them, surprised at how long Yiannis lasted. When he came at last, after straining and teasing, and restraining, it was with violence. He swore and cursed and thrust selfishly into Georgiou until the last few spasmodic jerks. She backed away instinctively, seeing that Georgiou's prick shot its creamy load as Yiannis sank onto him. Yiannis groaned in exhaustion and fell away from Georgiou, back on to the bed. As he collapsed he saw Saffie through a crimson haze. He smiled wonderfully at her, raised his hand to his lips. She smiled as his eyes closed.

'You like to watch?' asked Nikos, making Saffie jump. She had not realised he was there, she had been so engrossed.

106

'Gay sex, it turns me on . . . Men together . . .' she confessed.

'As much as our lord and master Constantine?' he asked jealously.

Saffie smiled, seeing the wildness in his expressive eyes.

'I want you, Niko . . .' she did not tell him that he turned her on more than anyone she had ever known; that he was more potent than any fantasy.

'Ha!'

He turned away. She followed him downstairs.

'You promised to come to me . . .'

'Yes.'

Nikos entered the darkened lounge and lit a cigarette. Saffie was fascinated by his moodiness and possessiveness.

'Niko, we cannot afford to be possessive. The film . . .'

'Constantine, he thinks only of himself!'

Nikos dragged on his cigarette, then pressed it vehemently into the ashtray. Had he been watching them, Saffie wondered. Why was he not bothered about Eleni?

'How do you feel about the scenario?' she risked, unable to fathom his restlessness.

'Do you think I have a choice?' he challenged. His black eyes swept her coldly.

'But – afterwards, you will be free . . .' she reasoned.

'Ha! Do you think that man will *ever* let me go?'

'Come to bed with me, Niko.'

He looked across at her and then nodded, spent, passing his hand wearily across his eyes.

Saffie bathed and then lay on her front on Nikos' bed as he massaged aromatic oil into her. His touch was intimate and caring. Saffie turned languidly over, smiling at him. Joy unfurled in her belly as she surveyed his lovely features, the tenderness of his mouth and the limpidity of his beautiful dark eyes. She reached up to take tight, springy curls between finger and thumb. Nikos was held still by her admiration of him. He saw the wonder in her laughing eyes.

He looked down at her voluptuous body. He poured more of the fragrant oil into his palm and began to massage her breasts. She saw that his eyes became hooded in lascivious recognition of their firmness.

107

'I only have to look at you – think of you – to be turned on, Niko . . .' she said softly. 'You are the most perfectly beautiful man I have ever seen. You are my artistic ideal. No-one has ever reached me as you can.'

The black eyes dilated and met hers. She wondered what he was thinking. He put down the oil and leant to kiss her.

'Let me do it to you now. Take off your clothes . . .'

Nikos stood, and, as gracefully as a prince, he slowly disrobed. Saffie relished every long moment. He lay on the bed and she poured oil lavishly over his hard, muscular body, smoothing it into his flesh in small circular motions. She enjoyed the feel of him beneath her sentient fingers.

She made him turn over, and continued to smooth in the cream. He was placid and still. She bent to kiss his firm prick. She moved to smile, and was touched by the naked longing in his narrowed eyes. She wanted him to do what Constantine had not, to fill her tight, yearning hole with his wonderful prick, but instead she said to him,

'Make love to me, Niko.'

Niko nodded in assent. She lay beside him, as ever deeply thrilled by his intimate caresses. His intrinsic knowledge and imagination filled her with delight. She rose to embrace him as he entered her. As he fucked her slowly, he encircled her anus with penetrative fingers, extending her joy. Sensing her wish, he withdrew and lubricated her, and then himself, jerking his cock languidly whilst caressing her raised abdomen. Then he entered her anus with infinite care. Sweet invasion. She loved the fullness of her secret passage, loaded with his prick. He withheld his weight from her with generosity as he buggered her. Saffie's body beat with pleasure. She knew that Yiannis would enjoy this. She smiled smuttishly to herself. Nikos lowered himself and caressed her breasts. Now he slid his penis more rapidly along her muscle. He closed his dark eyes in supreme enjoyment at this tensile gripping of his sensitive member. He felt his phallus gripped spasmodically by Saffie as she undulated frantically against the bed. He stimulated her clitoris, and fingered at her wet labia, infiltrating her vagina and moving his fingers up and down in rhythm with his anal fucking. Saffie began to tense and gasp. He felt her hole squeeze his fingers as she came. Her abdomen beat in echo. Nikos let himself go, ramming his impatient prick into her tight hole as he slapped against her. His senses gathered in his testicles and groins, and his own anus burned with denied longing. Saffie continued to groan with pleasure, whispering his name over and over as repeated spasms gripped her.

'Come on, come, Niko . . .'

Nikos lay along her back, holding her breasts, and then worked himself up until he was possessed with the compulsive need to ejaculate into her arse. With a few sharp, rapid final thrusts, he gave way to the elevating feeling from his sex as his spunk gathered to be ejected rapidly through that tight duct. The euphoria filled his warm body and he seemed to be lifted into lightness . . .

He came to to feel Saffie fingering gently at his anus. He seemed to recall that she had been doing that for a long time. Had she smiled to witness his re-arousal at this stimulus, and whilst he was most vulnerable and incapable of dissimulation? He saw her recoil as he opened his eyes. He knew that they expressed his animosity. He moved her head down gently, so that she could no longer look into his eyes, and kissed the top of her head.

'What is it, Niko?'

'Nothing.'

Memories of early personal awakening, shattered cruelly, filled his mind. Saffie removed her fingers from between his buttocks. She was moved by the sadness in his voice. She held his slackening penis in her palm. Was he thinking of Constantine's plans for him? Was he afraid of what he would be made to do? She raised her head and met his avid kiss. He had closed his eyes against her intuition. Saffie slithered down to his penis and began to coax it back to stiffness with her mouth, gripping his buttocks to force him to respond.

Nikos smiled at her care, and reached down to fondle her breasts. They lay on their sides, looking deeply into each other's eyes as they touched and stroked in silence. Nikos was glad that she did not question him. He relaxed. Saffie took him back into her vagina, seeing his eyes close in pleasure. She held him tightly between her thighs as they made love, kissing and embracing as, after a long time of slow pleasure, their mutual orgasm possessed their bodies. They were deeply aware of each other's joy. After a time, replete, they slept.

In the early morning, Saffie awoke and went to retrieve her small sketch-book from her bag. She then spent a peaceful time drawing the naked Nikos as he slept. It was good, afterwards, to hold the body she had been scrutinising so closely.

'Back to Athens, today, Niko,' Yiannis smiled at them, placing a jug of fresh orange juice on the cabinet.

Saffie regarded him, recalling him and Georgiou. She wondered if he thought of screwing Nikos.

'Breakfast is nearly ready,' he added.

'You're such a wonderful cook, Yianni . . .' Nikos joked.

Yiannis shook his head and said seriously:

'No, it's Marianna. We will go on Constantine's boat. Do you have to fetch anything, Saffie, from your lodgings?'

'Oh, yes . . . It's easy to forget!'

'We are going to meet the film crew in Athens this afternoon.'

'All very exciting,' said Nikos coldly, drinking juice and getting out of bed to go to the en-suite shower.

Saffie watched Yiannis' reflex appraisal of his friend's naked body. He grinned broadly at her as he left. She went to join Nikos in an enjoyable shower.

Rachel was alone in the garden as Saffie strolled out to drink in the view. Rachel smiled to see her friend.

'I think I would have forgotten to collect our things, if Yiannis hadn't said,' Saffie told her.

'I know what you mean,' agreed Rachel. 'It's all a bit unreal.'

'A wonderful dream . . .' sighed Saffie.

'He's very good – Nikos,' Rachel said.

'Yes, he is.' Saffie nodded. 'A Greek god?' She laughed, recalling Rachel's first sight of Nikos, thinking, if her friend had not called her attention to him, they might have missed all this.

'Veritably,' was Rachel's emphatic rejoinder.

'They are all wonderful lovers, though I haven't had the pleasure of Georgiou – yet . . .'

'Oh, he is too . . .' Rachel assured Saffie.

'He's pretty good with Yiannis.'

Rachel was silent for a moment, then she smiled and shrugged at Saffie.

110

'I imagine he would be.'

'It doesn't bother you, then?'

'There's no point in letting it. They've known each other for ever. I suppose we should be honoured that we've been allowed in.'

They looked at each other and burst into laughter.

'It's a bonus, to be able to go to Delphi and Crete and Naxos,' Saffie said dreamily at last.

'Yes,' Rachel agreed, 'And of course it means that we won't have to invent travels to relate to our envious friends when we get home.'

'I think our friends would be even more envious – and interested – in what we have really been doing.'

'I reckon you're right there, Saffie . . .'

They laughed again together.

'Come and eat!' called Yiannis from the kitchen door, 'We have to go back to Nikos' house, to pack a few things.'

'Clothes?' Rachel's tone was risqué.

Yiannis grinned.

'We will collect your things too.'

The women went in to partake of Marianna's excellent breakfast. Saffie for one found that she was inordinately hungry lately and thoroughly enjoyed the various delectable meals that were laid on for them. She chuckled inwardly to think why she needed so much more sustenance. Constantine did not eat with them, which was a relief really, as there was always constraint between him and Nikos. Constantine was to meet them at the quay when they had got their luggage together. Nikos planned to ride Calypso whilst Yiannis took Saffie and Rachel back to their apartment. Then he was to take her to their neighbour, Dimitris, and her usual stable. Yiannis had told Saffie that Nikos had several horses on Naxos, and she looked forward to riding with him. She expected Constantine would try to incorporate them into his film, but doubted Nikos would agree.

The voyage was relaxing. Constantine spent most of his time making notes for discussion with the technical crew. Nikos and Yiannis steered the magnificent vessel. They reached Pireaus in the late afternoon. The port was very busy, packed with travellers and tourists awaiting ferry-ships or family and friends. Saffie always found this aspect of travelling exciting. Constantine's limousine was awaiting them, so that they could drive immediately to Athens. The plan was that they would go on to Delphi on the following day. Constantine had arranged a luxury minibus and driver for the journey. The film crew had its own transport and would travel with them.

Saffie and Nikos stood in silence, each immersed in their own imaginative reconstruction of ancient history as they stood beneath the tiny temple of Athene Nike, on the Acropolis. Saffie imagined the scent of incense, wafting from the front of the temple as sacrifices were made. She thought of the young men, preparing to fight the Persians; their triremes awaiting them at the port of Pireaus. The whole of Athens was lit up below them. The marble temples: the Parthenon, and the Erechtheion gleamed white in the artificial lights trained on them. The night was warm and tender, laced with magic. Other devotees strolled quietly around them, caught in the spell of place and time. Below, in the Theatre of Dionysus, a play was being rehearsed in ancient Greek. Nikos said it was Sophocles' 'Electra'.

It was magical to Saffie, to stand here with this beautiful Athenian. She thought of Nikos growing up here, this exotic land as familiar to him as London was to her. His mind was as fascinating to her as his wonderful body. She would like to read his work.

'Have you been to England, Niko?' she asked.

'Yes. Of course. I have been several times . . . and to see the Parthenon marbles . . .'

'They plan to build a museum to house them here . . .'

'Yes.'

'You think they should come back?'

'I don't know . . .' he said, surprisingly.

'Sometimes, I think we are losing everything in England.'

'Post-imperial depression?' Nikos joked, then added quietly that things were more stable politically for her than for the Hellenes.

He lit a cigarette, leaned back against the wall, relaxed, at home. In an hotel room below, the others waited, discussing the content of the film, planning the shooting with the film crew.

Saffie knew that Nikos deliberately delayed returning.

'When I first saw you . . .' Saffie recalled, taking his cigarette and inhaling briefly, then returning it, 'you reminded me of an ephebe, from the Parthenon frieze . . . half naked on your glorious horse . . .'

Nikos smiled, beginning to laugh at himself.

'You are just like the young knights who came here, two and a half thousand years ago, swearing allegiance to each other before Athene. They could love each other, make love, Niko . . .'

Nikos' eyes narrowed suspiciously.

'Has Constantine asked you to persuade me?'

'No, I'm just trying to make it easier for you.'

'It isn't necessary, Saffie. All that he plans . . . I have agreed to participate. He will just write in these scenes to humiliate me.'

'Why humiliate? You might enjoy it . . .'

'Oh, yes. I might. But it is him. *He* wants me.' Nikos' voice was bitter. 'From being young, he always has.'

Saffie nodded in understanding.

'Yiannis and Georgiou . . .' she began, aroused by memories of their savage love-making of the previous night.

'Yes, I know . . .' said Nikos, impatiently, almost pettishly. 'They would more naturally enjoy the scenes he will make me do.'

Saffie looked at him with interest, thinking of his unconscious arousal of last night. She suspected that he recalled it too, and thought that she would misinterpret.

'Come. I suppose we ought to join the others,' he said reluctantly.

He took Saffie's hand as they descended the modern walkway, passed the Roman Agora, and made their way to the Plaka below. The night was filled with music and laughter. Bazouki music came from all quarters and tourists attempted to join in the dance. Saffie lingered to enjoy one display of Greek men in national costume linked in a fast-moving circle.

'Can you do that?'

'But of course – and come, so can you, Saffie,' he said as he caught her eye. 'You have been here many times . . .'

'Go on, Niko – I want to see you dance.'

Nikos' handsome face filled with amusement, and then he nodded slowly.

'Alright. But not here. I know where to go . . .' he pulled her quickly through the throngs, 'And then, of course, you must also dance, Saffie . . .'

She laughed as they began to run down the steps, past the Agora and through the crowded streets until they reached Nikos' Taverna. It was just a small place, in the middle of a narrow street. They went downstairs and into a room of mainly Hellenic people, mostly men. They all seemed to greet Nikos in unison. Saffie was included in their warmth. People crowded round Nikos, who was kissed and hugged. They were given ouzo and sweets. Nikos addressed them in Greek, calling them by name and enquiring after their families and work. Saffie was enchanted by his popularity.

'I cannot stay long, but I have come here to dance.'

'Dance, Niko . . .'

'Nikos will dance!'

'I come to dance for my friend, Saffie . . .'

Nikos held out his arm to her and smiled. Saffie was flooded with warmth. She watched, eager to retain every second of this unusual hour. Nikos nodded at the bazouki player, who could have been his cousin. The men joined in a circle and began to dance, slowly at first, with complex repetitive footwork. They went to the left and to the right, in perfect step, gradually becoming faster and faster. The music rose in crescendo. The men danced together with expert, long-practised movements, turning their lower bodies one way, and then their heads the other, consummately, full of grace. Their steps gradually quickened. After a time, they released Nikos to dance at their centre, clapping as he did so. He was wonderful, dancing with grace and style, perfectly at home as his lithe body rose and fell on the invisible crests of the music. He danced for a long time, tireless. They clapped and tapped their feet to his rhythm, caught up in an atavistic spell which seemed never to end.

Saffie imagined him calling her to him, and she would dance in response. But she was glad that he did not, that she had the freedom to watch him, spellbound, until at last he finished, going down on one knee and stretching out his arms, throwing back his dark head. Then he rose, his long curls damp over his laughing black eyes, his friends crowding round, embracing him and kissing him. He looked across the room to her, their gaze extended in understanding. At last he came to her, his breathing still not quite steady. She wanted to kiss him; she breathed in the fresh scent of musk and sweat.

'This is your place, Niko. Another time, I will dance for you.'

Nikos nodded, taking up his jacket. He waved to his old friends, explaining that they must leave; that they would return. He shook his head laughingly, held out his hand in a gesture of farewell. Loud protestations of disappointment followed them as they went upstairs.

'That was incredible, Niko. It was like, a gift . . .'

'Ah, you are the artist, Saffie. I suppose we had better get back to Constantine's damned meeting. I trust that we have missed most of it.'

Saffie was thinking that she would much rather go somewhere and fuck him.

'Tomorrow, Saffie, in Delphi . . .' he said, as if telepathic.

He stopped walking, grasped her and kissed her fiercely. His power shot through her body. She could let him go only with extreme reluctance.

Constantine shot an impatient glance at Nikos as he and Saffie joined the meeting. Saffie was introduced to the film crew. They all shook hands. There were six: three men and three women. They were all quite attractive, especially the cameraman, Mike, who had shaggy grey-blond hair and beard and expressive blue eyes, which rested on their object with perception. Saffie was immediately drawn to him. His smile crinkled his face, and was very appealing. His arms and torso were muscular and strong. He had a tattoo of a dragon on his right upper arm. Constantine reiterated some of the details he had been through with the others, though Saffie thought that he might have saved his breath as far as Nikos was concerned, as he demonstrated not the slightest interest. Later, they would try on the clothes Constantine had ordered; chitons, himations, chlamyses and peploses.

Constantine and Mike had decided that the crew could get on with filming background material, whilst the cast rehearsed. Already, they had taken shots of Athens that day. Saffie thought that Mike, who appeared to be in charge, was confident and at ease with his work. He radiated an aura of peace. She surmised that he was old enough to have been a hippy, and certainly possessed a sixties relaxed attitude. It seemed that nothing would 'faze' him. Perhaps it would not be so difficult to work with him.

All of the team knew the others; they had been employed in the aborted film. They seemed to Saffie to be tolerant of the silent Nikos, some of the young women, especially, stealing affectionate glances at him. They laughed and joked with Yiannis, Eleni and Georgiou as if they were old friends. Saffie noted that Georgiou seemed to eye all of them up with sexual intent in his sleazy eyes and she found it hard to stifle a giggle.

Before going to Delphi the next evening, they were to record some footage in Athens. Dressed in their Grecian robes, the actors would be filmed on the Acropolis, and in the Theatre of Dionysus. They were to be ready very early the next morning, so as to be there before the crowds. Saffie and Rachel had very little to say, and the others seemed confident about what they had to do, so Saffie tried not to become worried about it.

The film was to begin with them leaving Athens, after the festival of Dionysus, or 'Dionysia', (during which many plays were seen for the first time). Then, en route to Delphi, they would stop at several significant places and be shot against the unchanged scenery. Still, here they would be mainly discussing the plays, and various bits of contemporary news: the idea was really, at this point, to give a sense of time and place. Later, they would have more lines to learn.

Filming in Delphi would begin on the following day. Saffie understood that their time would at first be divided between the external locations and the internal ones. In the former, they would merely speak rehearsed lines: comment on progress and political events, or display the complex relationships between them all by various arguments. The latter would involve the shooting of erotic scenes.

They tried on their various costumes; the long himations, and shorter chlamyses (which would sometimes be worn without the tunic beneath, as was usually the case in ancient Greece). The crew were also adept at make-up and would help them with this, and with their hair and garlands.

When Saffie was dressed, in her long tunic and with her hair coiled elaborately, she paused to look around at the others and was struck with how it seemed that by donning these clothes, they had entered another world: Constantine's world of make-believe and sexual fantasy for which he had prepared them. Though they were not yet due to film sex-scenes, and only had to walk about the Acropolis and say some simple phrases, she knew that they had advanced from their uncomplicated sexual indulgences with each other, into a more complex, and perhaps potentially dangerous era.

Saffie slept alone that night, as Constantine was adamant that they should all get some rest before their early start. She dreamt of Nikos and Yiannis as members of the 'Sacred Band', an elite group of ancient Athenian knights; homosexual lovers, who defended each other in battle. She woke, extremely aroused and spent an enjoyable time masturbating and indulging her fantasies of Yiannis and Nikos together. She employed her vivid memories of Yiannis with Georgiou to aid her. Even when she had come, she was still turned on: she needed a man. She laughed at herself and rose to shower. When she went to breakfast, she looked around at her companions and wondered how many had had to revert to onanism. She doubted they had all obeyed Constantine's strictures.

The filming of the first scenes went extremely well. They were all imbued with high spirits, and it was a lovely morning, not too hot yet. Saffie and Rachel thoroughly enjoyed themselves. They were able to indulge their play-acting even further at the isolated areas at which they stopped en route to Delphi. Saffie found the film crew very friendly and light, and was glad that they had been given this opportunity to get to know each other before the filming or rehearsing of the sexual content.

Mike was especially warm and dependable. He had the ability to get on with everyone, and worked well with Constantine, who obviously relied on him a great deal.

Nikos and Saffie walked along the road from the hotel, with the ruins of Delphi on their left, the Phaidriades towering above, and the extensive plains of the Pleistos valley, covered with ancient olive trees, on their right. Plaintive music came evocatively, wafting across to them as a group of young people playing pan-pipes rounded the road, coming towards them. Nikos told

Saffie that music was forbidden within the sacred precinct of Apollo, and how strange this was, as he was the god of music. They crossed the road and went to the ancient Kastallian Fountain.

'Pilgrims used to purify themselves by washing in this water, and the Delphic Priestess washed her hair. Then, chewing on bay leaves, she would go up to the Delphic oracle, through there to the precinct of Apollo—' he pointed up through thick undergrowth, 'and translated the words of the god . . . into verse, of course,' he laughed, 'for those who sought help or guidance. Individuals or states. The advice was fairly ambiguous.'

They re-crossed the road, and continued on, to Marmaria, where they descended to the circular temple, the Tholos. Saffie wondered whether the stream descending from beneath the road was the Kastallian stream, from the fountain. After wandering quietly around these ruins, they ascended and went into the small café, to drink freshly-squeezed orange juice.

They could see the film crew, taking shots of the ruins. They would spend the afternoon gathering filmic material in readiness. Saffie contemplated the team; they were all, as Constantine had said, easily able to double up as extras. In getting to know them, she had become aware of the individual appeal of each. They had permission to go into the sacred precinct early the next morning, before the official opening time, to begin to film them acting.

Tonight, they would rehearse the first of Constantine's sex-scenes. Saffie had to admit to a little tremulousness at the prospect of this. Even now, back in the luxury hotel, the others were discussing content and approach. Last night, in Athens, Constantine had tried to talk to Nikos, but the young man had treated him with contempt. However, Saffie was aware that he was drawing the others into his rich fabrication, luring them with his tales and inventions. The presence of the vivacious technicians had brought new life, and a reduction of intensity. They seemed liberal and enlightened: a willing bunch, prepared to join in and have fun. They were being well-paid, and had none of Nikos' hang-ups. The filming in Athens, and on the way to Delphi had been good fun. Saffie felt that everything was taken care of, and all she had to do was as instructed. Nikos also complied, but without enthusiasm. Saffie was aware that Constantine regarded him in concern but, wisely, he left him alone. It did not matter, for now, that he looked moody on film. He looked beautiful, and that was sufficient at present. Already, the camera lingered often on him.

They went over to Delphi, climbing up through the temples, past the theatre to the stadium. The area was dotted with groups of cypress trees. Saffie looked across to Mount Parnassos, from where criminals were once thrown. She imagined the ancient theatre to Apollo, where ingenious machinery had made the god descend. Here, ancient myth had it, the god Apollo had fought with the Python and won – a triumph of reason over chaos? The philosophy of the 'civilised' god had been discovered here inscribed on marble, during excavations at the end of the nine-teenth century, when the modern village of Kastri had been removed to its present location. 'Know thyself' proclaimed the inscriptions and 'moderation in all things'. In winter, Apollo's wilder brother, Dionysus (more appropriate to their project, as Nikos had said), returned to the site, whilst Apollo was on his island of birth, Delos,

Saffie sighed happily. She loved Delphi. It was a transcenden-tally beautiful site. Once considered the 'omphallos', or centre of the world: she could easily believe it so still. They stood by the ancient Temple of Apollo, and surveyed the magnificent view over the low-lying area of the sanctuary and the whole of the vale of the Pleistos to the distant bay of Itea. The sea glimmered in the glorious light, so special to Greece. It was good to have this silent time with Nikos.

Saffie was already dressed in her long, simple robe, or chiton, a yellow rectangle of fine cloth arranged around her slim body by Carrie – one of the technical crew – and wanted to be distanced from the rest of the cast's nervous arguments and pre-recording anxiety. So she sat on the balcony and sketched the delightful scene below, the broad valley surrounding the deep ravine of the Pleistos: vineyards, olive-groves and orchards. Voices were raised peevishly within. Saffie thought that her friends were naturally nervous in front of the film crew, partly because of Nikos, and that it would be wise for Constantine to allow them to become familiar again. Then, she decided, he probably relished the tension caused by this new factor. Perhaps he thought that they were all too familiar – blasé or even 'incestuous'.

Her mind wandered over the scenery she was drawing, lost to the present. And, when she was suddenly recalled to a sense of her surroundings, it was as if she was still encaptured in that imagined past as Nikos stood before her, dressed in a short white tunic, and leather sandals. The familiar Greek key was embroidered in gold around its border. One shoulder was bare. A short circular scarlet cloak; the chlamys, was slung across one shoulder. On his head was a garland of laurel leaves. Saffie gasped in astonishment. She let her eyes slowly trace this vision, from his strong calves, to his crisp curls, entwining the fresh leaves. She reached out to the hem of his short skirt but he stopped her, his eyes teasing, enticing. Nikos looked as natural in these clothes as he did in his usual smart black trousers and loose white shirt.

'Constantine has gone to a lot of trouble with the costumes,' said Saffie, fingering the fine stuff of her own robe. 'It's exquisite material.'

'A bit of a waste, since we'll scarcely be wearing them,' responded Nikos bitterly.

Saffie realised that, whatever was proved to the contrary, Nikos was not going to admit Constantine's higher motives.

'I'm a poet,' he said cynically, raising the small harp to show her. He sounded a couple of notes.

'They think that the poets recited, occasionally twanging a couple of strings. No-one really knows what the ancient music sounded like.'

Still entranced, Saffie nodded.

'Apollo was not more beautiful,' she said.

Nikos' beautiful dark eyes were stilled at her expression. It was easy to believe that he was a bona fide ancient Greek, especially against the marvellous backdrop of the Pleistos Valley. Saffie wanted to lift the short skirt and lick at his penis. Her constant desire for him was enhanced by his costume and its romantic connotations. She was suddenly angry that she had not had sex with him for too long. Her need for him was so constant that an hour was too long.

'Constantine wants us to save the sex . . .' Nikos said, translating her smouldering expression.

'Fuck Constantine.'

120

'I believe you have,' he recalled coldly.

Saffie saw with wonder the jealousy in the black eyes. She smiled secretly. Nikos looked idly over the landscape, feigning carelessness.

'I told you, I'd rather have you, Niko.' She had thought she had assured him, and sensed that his mood was mostly as a result of his annoyance at being under Constantine's command.

She rose and grasped his arm. He looked down at her hand coldly. Saffie removed it. She sighed at the unnecessarily complicating affect the older man had on Nikos. Yiannis appeared, alleviating the tension and summoning them to attend Constantine's directions.

Constantine sat in a large chair at the front of the huge ballroom. His jacket sleeves were rolled neatly back over his crisp white shirt. He had a file of notes in his hands, to which he was referring – more for effect, Saffie considered, than from necessity. They were arranged in various groups around the hall; some sitting, some standing or leaning against the wall – all dressed in their ancient Greek garb. Saffie smiled at Eleni, who looked particularly enchanting in her short white chiton, with her long black curls encircled with a wreath of white silk flowers.

Yiannis wore a short tunic and chlamys and Georgiou merely the longer cloak, or himation, at present wrapped around his nakedness. Some of the crew were chatting quietly. Mike, the head cameraman, and his assistant, Nicola, a very pretty red-head, were by the camera. Saffie considered that they would wisely film rehearsals too, so that they could discuss them, with a view to improvement. She felt the slight nervousness in her stomach increase. They would of course retain any suitable sexual performances, which may be better than during 'real' filming. One never knew. As she had sensed when they had first all donned their new clothes, in Athens, they had certainly entered a new phase of their relationships. Perhaps Constantine was right, and this experience would liberate them all, sexually. She smiled across at Rachel, standing close to Yiannis. Rachel wore a gown like her own, but pale blue. This suited her fair colouring very well.

Constantine was ready to address them all. He looked up a

couple of times, as though waiting for them all to attend, cleared his throat, and then began:

'Right, so you have come, as a group of actors, to Delphi, to enact a play for the Pythian Festival. For Pythian Apollo. This is a great honour, and you are all eager to perform to the best of your ability.' Constantine's keen gaze wandered, as if by accident, casually across to Nikos, who stood by Saffie. 'There were also games and dances, so I thought that we would incorporate a taste of these. We'll film them tomorrow evening, when the site is again closed to the public. The on-location filming will be of a minimal and symbolic nature. Especially on sacred sites. It will give a taste of authenticity. Mike will get the background. You will be filmed there in your role as fifth-century B.C.E. actors. Most of the erotic scenes will be in the countryside – say, in Nikos' grounds on Naxos, or indoors. You have read through your instructions; there are few lines to learn for the erotic scenes, but I would like you to practise the scenes between the actors – arguments, petty spites and jealousies. When slotted in, it will be good build up to the sexual encounters. A bit of fire and spice.' Constantine seemed to relish this, his eyes sparkling as he rubbed his hands together. 'Now, tonight's run-through. It is a piece of mythology – Apollo and Daphne. A brief explanation will be spoken before each scene, for the benefit of the audience – maybe in the form of poetry. Niko, you can help us there. Nikos is Apollo. Naturally, you only have a little to learn and speak. Here, in Delphi, as I was explaining in Athens, to most of you—' Here, Constantine shot an accusing glance at Nikos and Saffie, 'You are actors, with your own private lives also . . . as the film moves on, you appear to lose your real selves and become more and more creatures of legend and myth – so that, by the time we have gone from Crete, to Naxos, you are completely gods or ancient Greeks or whatever . . .'

'I've had a better idea—' said Constantine enthusiastically. 'We'll try this. It may be more effective to have the scenes – or tableaux – silent, mimed, and dialogue when the actors are chatting amongst themselves. Now we will do Apollo – Nikos – with Daphne – Saffie.'

'Since Daphne was rescued from the lecherousness of the god, by being transformed into a laurel, there won't be much sex,' intervened Yiannis humorously.

The others laughed.

'In this case . . .' Constantine continued unabashed, 'the actors playing Apollo and Daphne have been arguing, so it's especially difficult for them to do the sex scene.'

Nikos and Saffie exchanged cold glances.

'So Saffie gets to be a tree after all?' asked Georgiou.

'Right, Niko, Saffron,' their director called, regardless of the renewed buzz of laughter.

Nikos and Saffie took their places on the 'stage'.

'You, Saffron, are a mountain nymph, so trip amongst the cypresses and olive trees and look beguiling – the god is watching you. You are unconsciously provocative. I think you will wear something flimsier, or perhaps nothing . . . You, Niko, watch her avidly, full of lust, from between the trees . . .'

'Lust, Niko . . . Not difficult, hey?' laughed Georgiou, standing and feeling at his crotch, his erect prick scarcely hidden by his cloak.

Saffie felt that he was playing up for the sake of their new audience: the film crew, who indeed found him amusing. She saw Georgiou eyeing up the blond, deeply-tanned Andy and his assistant, the petite Lyndsay, speculatively. She knew that he was not fussy which he had first.

Despite their jibes, and his own reluctance, Nikos acted seriously, stalking Daphne, and watching her as she wandered lasciviously amongst the imagined scenery. Then, with a rapidity which made them all gasp, and which genuinely startled the mountain nymph, he seemed to fly across the bare boards and grasp her.

'Cry out to Gaia – Mother Earth – Daphne. She'll transport you to Crete, and you'll be "Pasiphae",' advised the garrulous Georgiou.

The god was full of arrogance and enchantment. His dark eyes were suffuse with Olympian desire. He paused to charm her with the sweet music of his lyre. Daphne was bewitched and could not flee from the wondrous Apollo. Then Apollo-Nikos grasped her by the waist, dropped his lyre, and fell with her down to the ground.

'I do think that a nymph should be naked in the first place,' observed Georgiou as he watched Apollo struggling with Daphne's robe.

123

'They're actors, Georgiou . . .' explained Eleni, with exaggerated patience.

Saffie felt Nikos' rough handling of her sex. With a rush of adrenalin – fear, she was Daphne, and then longing, she was herself. She realised that he was really going to – pretend to – take her by force. She saw the challenge in his eyes, and thought that it was because of her with Constantine. Or perhaps he was really getting into the authenticity of the film. Anyway, this was just a rehearsal: no-one was expecting this.

'What are you doing?' she whispered as he forced his fist into her vulva. Saffie gasped as desire flooded her body. This was a different Nikos. She could really believe he was this most beautiful of the gods. Her body thrilled at his brutality.

'Gods don't go in much for foreplay,' he whispered.

Nikos threw her to the ground, lifted her robe and penetrated her. Saffie was filled with dark delight. It seemed to her that he was even bigger as his penis filled her tight vagina. She pretended to struggle: her unwillingness added to their ardour. Apollo-Nikos squeezed at her breasts, and then with god-like energy, continued to thrust wildly into her, lifting his bare abdomen high, and then slamming home with gusto. Their friends began to chant and roar, repeating the monkey-chant from Fellini's 'Satyricon'. Daphne-Saffie clung to the god's buttocks, digging her nails deeply into him. Nikos did not flinch, and did not pause from his rapid fucking.

Saffie raised her knees, arched her back, and clenched him between her strong thighs. She forced him to kiss her, and he massaged and squeezed at her breasts until she cried out. She urged him over, desiring mastery over this arrogant deity. The audience cheered at her dominion, as she forced him to slow his pace, so that she could take him long and slowly. He pulled her robe from her to expose her to them, and she tore off his tunic.

The crew were now watching with amused enjoyment. Nicola, with foresight, had even started to film them when she realised what they were up to. Naturally, Constantine was delighted with this. Instead of chasing orgasm, they concentrated on raising each other to an ever higher pitch of arousal. It was actually very exciting, Saffie discovered, to make love in public with a man who turned her on so deeply. She was dimly aware of their small audience clapping and cheering, and issuing lewd calls of encouragement. Saffie felt that she was drunk on sex, on Nikos, her own Greek god. They rolled on the hard floor, exchanging priority, swapping roles, until at last, Saffie conceded the part – allowing Apollo to play his allotted role. Nikos took his cue and ravished her with selfish abandon. When it came, their mutual orgasm was powerful and all-consuming, lasting for very many minutes. Saffie held Nikos close, kissing him and feeling him continue to throb dramatically within her.

'Thank you, Apollo – and Daphne . . .' said Constantine in a business-like tone.

Nikos sat and retrieved his tattered tunic, fastening it around his waist. Saffie slipped her chiton over her head, adjusting her belt, and put Nikos' fillet crookedly back on his curls. He smiled at her, and took her hand as they stood. Saffie stooped to pick up his harp. They bowed laughingly to the small audience, which applauded, and went from the room, and on to the balcony.

'I reckon you took us all by surprise, there, Niko.'

'Do you mind?'

'Do you think I did?'

Nikos shook his head, grinning. Mike brought them a glass of wine each. He raised his eyebrows to Saffie, who laughed. She was relieved to have accomplished her first public sexual display so easily – without the tension of anticipation. That Mike had watched and filmed her was a bonus.

Constantine came out.

'It was gratifying to have an early display of your prowess, Niko,' he said dryly, adding: 'It bodes well for future liberation.'

Saffie saw that Nikos stretched his tender mouth in distaste. Constantine narrowed his eyes at the young man.

'I think you should loosen up, Niko . . . Time is of the essence.'

Nikos said nothing in reply. Constantine left. Saffie wondered with foreboding what on earth Constantine was expecting of Nikos, if he could advise a man who had just performed a spontaneous sexual act very successfully in public to 'loosen up'.

Nikos drew Saffie onto his knee. They drank their wine whilst silently surveying the lovely view. Saffie wondered what the others were doing. In fact, Saffie and Nikos' public performance had served to turn them all on, and Mike was now busy filming

125

various clips of their random sexual acts with whoever was handy. It was all good fun, and the wine flowed freely. In time, Yiannis joined them, bringing his glass and a bottle of wine. He re-filled their glasses.

'Constantine was as jealous as hell, Niko,' Yiannis grinned at them. 'You should have seen him.'

'Fuck the man.'

'I think that's his intention,' agreed Yiannis, though scarcely audibly enough for his preoccupied friend.

Saffie looked up at Yiannis in enquiry. Yiannis shrugged his shoulders.

'I ought to warn you, Niko . . .' he began hesitatingly. 'He intends to bring forward the Apollo-Hyacinthus scene. In retaliation, perhaps?'

Nikos flushed. He looked away from Yiannis.

'Georgiou can take the part. He's had enough practice.'

'You are Constantine's star, Niko. His Apollo.'

'And Dionysus,' Nikos added coldly, in resignation.

Saffie wondered whether she imagined that she could detect a hint of sarcasm in Nikos' tone. She rose from his knee as he pushed her gently. Nikos went to the edge of the balcony, as far away from them as possible. Saffie and Yiannis exchanged concerned glances.

'He intended to spring it on you.'

Nikos turned to him, anger in his eyes.

'Was that your idea?' he hissed at Yiannis.

'Mine, Niko—?' asked Yiannis in bewilderment.

Saffie was shocked at the vehemence in Nikos' tone. She pitied Yiannis, who shook his head miserably.

'Niko, you knew what all this Greek history stuff entailed,' she intervened, reasonably. 'It was there – in the notes . . . implicit at least . . .'

'You won't complain though?' Nikos continued to address Yiannis.

Despite his hurt, Yiannis was heartened by the definite future tense.

'No,' he replied, simply. 'I won't complain, Niko.'

'Perhaps . . .' Nikos suggested, cruelly, 'you put the whole idea into his mind. Maybe you gave him the photographs, Yianni? I seem to recall that it was your friend who was so keen to take them . . . I expect you suggested it to him?'

'Niko, that is unfair . . .' Yiannis tried, but failed to grasp Nikos' arm as he left. 'You didn't complain, Niko . . . Damianos asked you, discussed it with you.'

'Damianos was your lover!' Nikos threw at him.

'So was Anna . . .' Yiannis responded meaningfully.

Nikos gave him a look of pure hatred as he left them.

'Oh, Yianni . . .' Saffie said sympathetically, going to him and holding him close. 'He's just worried . . . Why is he so against it?'

'Possibly because he wants it?' suggested Yiannis significantly.

'And he thinks it's wrong?'

Yiannis seemed to take a deep breath and hesitate before telling her:

'When he was young, he was raped . . .'

'Not by Constantine?' asked Saffie, shocked.

'No, by another friend of his father's, who had taken him away on a sailing holiday with his sister.'

'Poor Nikos. He told you this?'

'No, Anna – his sister, his twin – told me. It devastated him. The loss of control – trust. He felt humiliated. His family, honour, history were very important to him. This had been his father's friend. I do not think he would even have told Anna, but she found him in great distress. He told her that if it had been her, he would have killed the man. I believe he would have. His mother had warned him to keep care of his beautiful sister. And he did – they are very close, Saffie . . . No-one ever dreamed that he was in more danger. He was very beautiful, Saffie . . . Untouched. I believe that it was at an age when he was considering sex with men. He was vulnerable . . . I don't think he has faced the rage in him. He tries not to remember . . .'

'If Constantine knows this . . .'

'No. No! You must promise not to tell him, Saffie. Nikos does not even know that Anna told me. She told me because she knew how I felt for her brother. It helped me to accept the impossibility . . .'

'Constantine may be sympathetic . . .'

'But then Nikos would know that I had told him – he would guess. He must have suspicions that Anna has told me. I was very

127

close to her. Anyway – I do not think that Constantine would necessarily have sympathy – he wouldn't let it prevent him, believe me, Saffie . . .'

No, thought Saffie, recalling the man's cruel selfishness with a shudder, he would probably find it a turn on. Perhaps, she thought, he already knew. It made sense that he was a mutual friend of Nikos' attacker. It may be an additional – very cruel – hold Constantine had over Nikos. He would not want this to be made public, or even for his family to know. Saffie went cold; suddenly Constantine seemed very sinister. She pulled herself together.

'Is Anna as beautiful as Nikos?' she asked Yiannis.

'Yes . . .' Yiannis smiled, 'but she has long straight black hair. She is bright, not so serious as Nikos. She is very good for him. She is married now and has babies – a little boy, Yiannis, and a little girl, Sophia. You see, Nikos has many responsibilities, to keep the family property. I truly think that Stavros would give it to his daughter, if Constantine showed him the pictures.'

'Are they that damaging?'

'It is true,' Yiannis confessed, 'I got Damianos to take them.'

He was silent for a moment, before adding quietly:

'They look very convincing.'

'But – you see – that is not so bad, if what you say is true. Perhaps, before the take, we can help Nikos . . . free him . . .'

'Poor Nikos. Everyone has designs on him.'

'Does Eleni know?'

'Yes.'

'He trusts her. Perhaps you and she—?'

Yiannis turned and met her eyes.

'You are very generous, Saffie . . . I know what you feel for Nikos. I agree it is an idea. Eleni herself has mentioned it. I think she feels sorry for me.'

'You love him, Yianni . . .' Saffie said, in wonder.

She took his hand.

'That's not so bad, Saffie. I'll always be his friend. In fact, it's better this way . . . or I could lose that. His friendship is very precious to me.'

'But, this way, Yianni – with the film – you can have him.'

'Maybe – but, Saffie, if he has begun to suspect me . . . Well, wasn't I just as bad as Constantine? Exploiting him, lying to him . . .'

'No, no, Yianni, you are nothing like Constantine . . . never think that. Anyway Constantine is doing it for gain.'

'Is he, Saffie?'

'You must never tell Nikos. You did it, because you loved him, and wanted something of him.'

'I do not think that Constantine and I are so different, Saffie . . .' he said sadly, going over to the rail where Nikos had stood, unconsciously echoing his dejected posture.

Saffie went to him, and put her arm around him. She kissed his head softly. The door opened and, to her surprise, Nikos returned. She wondered whether he had come to reiterate or extend his accusations of Yiannis. She met his eyes, continuing to stroke Yiannis tenderly. Nikos was an extremely sensitive man; she wondered what he had picked up.

'Constantine wants you, Yianni,' he said, his voice a little hoarse.

'Okay.'

'I'm sorry, Yianni.' Nikos grasped his arm and looked into his eyes. 'I was wrong to accuse you.'

Yiannis remained a moment, and then left. Nikos frowned. Saffie realised that one day, Yiannis would confess to his friend. She hoped that it would not be too soon. One day, it might not matter to Nikos: he may even be moved by Yiannis' romantic deceit. She longed, more than ever, to see these mysterious photographs. After all, Nikos had complied willingly . . . Perhaps that should be significant to Yiannis?

Eleni was bare, lying on the wide bed, watching Yiannis. She gloried in her sexuality, taking every opportunity to enjoy it – alone, or with others. Now, Yiannis seemed preoccupied, worriedly pacing around the room, so she felt languidly at her breasts. Always slightly aroused, she stirred herself lazily, taking her clitoris between the edges of finger and thumb, entwining her long silken curls idly in her fingers. She moved the tip of her long red tongue over her lips, and inserted her right index finger into her moist vagina. She narrowed her eyes at Yiannis, wondering what Saffie was doing, and whether Yiannis would notice if she abandoned herself in frenzied masturbation. The door opened and Nikos entered. He looked immediately at Eleni, scarcely seeming to notice Yiannis. He smiled at her, his sex unfurling at the sight of her, lying, ready. He looked at the deep, wet crimson of her parted labia, and her finger, going between.

He saw her teasing at her clitoris. Eleni returned his smile. It was then that Nikos noticed Yiannis. He made no response. He sat on the bed by Eleni and leant to kiss her, and caress her, as intimately as if they were alone. He slipped his hand between her parted thighs and cupped her breast. Yiannis felt his prick spring further into life as he saw Nikos administering to Eleni. She reached up to embrace his neck, entangling her long fingers in his tight curls. Yiannis saw his friend's penis, huge and swollen under his light, soft trousers. He saw Eleni's legs fall further apart to reveal to him her sex, swollen, scarlet and glistening with her juices. He watched Nikos' fingers go into her. His cock rose further and his body raged with desire.

Eleni was helping Nikos to undress. She gestured to Yiannis, opening her dark eyes wide in command and promise. With some trepidation, Yiannis went back to the bed, untying his robe. He lay beside Eleni, who welcomed him with a kiss and a caress. She grasped his prick and he turned on his side to run his hand over her warm body. Sometimes, he encountered Nikos, similarly engaged. This gave an added frisson. Eleni moved the loose skin of his penis up and down whilst squeezing it tightly. She thrilled at the increased enjoyment given by having two men caressing her. She luxuriated in this pampering. It was most delightful.

Yiannis and Nikos caressed her breasts, which were yearning with pleasure, thrusting into their hands. Yiannis caught Nikos' eyes, seeing that he was extremely turned on. This knowledge aroused Yiannis even further. They were both familiar lovers to Eleni. They exchanged a mutual look of affection at the woman's obvious joy as she tossed and writhed beneath their knowing hands. With tacit accord they began to concentrate solely on this; on exciting her to a frenzied pitch. Yiannis was fired by Nikos' participation, stealing longing looks at his friend's generous prick as he worked on Eleni.

Eleni abandoned herself to their sensual caresses, thinking only of herself as each man kneaded at her breasts and stimulated her sex. She did not care who was who, or what they did to her. As long as they did not forget her and turn to each other, though this had been their plan: to accustom the unwilling Nikos to the gay sex he would have to engage in in Constantine's scheme for him. This prospect lent an added excitement to the session for Eleni. It was exciting to feel so many unexpected touches. Everywhere. All at once.

Nikos creamed his fingers and inserted them deeply into her anus, his deep fingering sending spasms of sexual electricity surging through her squirming body. Yiannis applied himself to her vagina, moving rhythmically in time with Nikos. Like twins, they sucked at her heaving breasts, chewing at her teats. She moaned and writhed in ecstasy. Yiannis squeezed painfully at her clitoris. She knew of his impatience, and that his need was becoming uncontrollable. Fleetingly, he grasped at Nikos' lovely cock, thrilling with dark passion to feel it respond to his pressure. He chose to ignore the warning in Nikos' liquid eyes. He moved his leg over Eleni's thigh, lying across her body to kiss Nikos. Before the man moved away, Yiannis felt the hard kiss of his passionate lips. Yiannis was filled with intense relief.

Eleni moved on to her side, and took Yiannis' prick into her grasp, pulling it to her open legs. Yiannis pressed its head against her sex, rubbing the tip of his penis urgently against her ridge. He watched Nikos as he lavished cream on to his stiff rod and thrust it into Eleni's tighter hole. Eleni cried out, and opened her eyes wide to Yiannis. She was beautiful. Yiannis pulled her into his close embrace, against his chest and belly and kissed her. He felt her eager teats pushing against his chest. But he watched Nikos close his eyes in extreme pleasure as his cock went deeply into Eleni's tight hole. And Yiannis wished he was doing it to him.

Nikos' red mouth parted as he panted. Yiannis saw his tongue between his white teeth as he thrust rhythmically, sending Eleni's body repeatedly against Yiannis. Yiannis supported her. He squeezed very hard at her engorged breasts, so that she cried out again. He put out his finger to Nikos' tender mouth, and Nikos licked, sucked and then bit hard on it. Yiannis' pain fired his lust. He wanted to hurt Nikos; to claw at his hot flesh. He positioned himself so that he could enter Eleni's dripping vagina. Nikos

131

paced himself to aid him, opening his eyes to recognise the lascivious rage in Yiannis.

Yiannis concentrated on the enhanced feeling in his swollen prick as he was taken deeply into Eleni's tightened muscular passage. She slid easily along his stiffened cock, welcoming him. Yiannis gasped, he was so close to Nikos. He could feel his prick. They moved perfectly in time. Eleni was in a delirium of excessive joy. She swore and groaned, warning them not to release her. They smiled at her animal lust as they fucked her. She had her arms around Yiannis, holding him so tightly that he could scarcely breathe.

Yiannis reached out to move his hand over Nikos' clenched, pumping buttocks. He ran his palm over them, and – scarcely daring to breathe – slowly let the outstretched tip of his index finger go between the sweaty hemispheres to that glorious place. Nikos was sucking and biting Eleni's neck and shoulder, her breasts tightly in his kneading hands. Yiannis encircled the tender hole, feeling his own surge with sensation. Biting the tip of his tongue, he pushed into Nikos, feeling the tight muscle grip him.

Nikos' heart beat rapidly. A surge of darkness overwhelmed him. He opened his eyes to Yiannis, who almost recoiled at the dislike – and fear there. But, he pushed his finger deeper, jerking it in time to Nikos' anal ravishment of the girl between them. Yiannis moved to lean over Eleni and kissed Nikos, holding him close to Eleni so that he could not free himself.

To Yiannis' pure joy, Nikos returned his kiss with passion, taking a fistful of his hair and pulling painfully on it. Yiannis automatically quickened his fucking of Eleni, and his manipulation of Nikos's anus. He felt Nikos become wilder. Nikos began to pump into Eleni very quickly now, biting savagely at Yiannis' mouth, yanking on his hair and squeezing so hard on Eleni's nipple that she yelled out in anguish. Yiannis matched Nikos' rapid fucking. Their straining, sweating bodies slapped unceasingly against each other. They concentrated on maintaining their constant rhythm. Nikos released Yiannis, moved his hand to hold on to Eleni's waist and moved even more quickly in and out of her. Yiannis saw and felt his muscular abdomen jerking powerfully as he continued to pump and thrust. Nikos threw back his dark head. Yiannis knew that his own pleasure was now paramount. Eleni smiled at Yiannis, and he kissed her, caressing her breasts as she mounted her ascending orgasm and rode it energetically.

He felt her muscle grip his full prick tightly, milking him of his love-juice as his creamy spunk shot into her. He knew that Nikos ejaculated at the same time, and watched him as he strained and shuddered, emptying himself into Eleni's secret passage.

Gradually, their rapid breathing slowed, and they returned to normal. Yiannis watched in affection as Nikos kissed Eleni's neck tenderly, his extended tongue licking her. His hands touched Yiannis incidentally as he stroked at her flaccid breasts, and moved his hand down between them to her pubis. Joy shot through Yiannis as the root of his penis was touched fleetingly, accidentally.

Nikos did not open his lovely eyes. Yiannis continued to watch his friend as he lapsed into a deep, contented sleep. He was thankful at least that Nikos did not go sullenly off. He closed his eyes against his anguished need, as his greedy prick began to swell again inside Eleni. She smiled lasciviously at him, her dark eyes dreamy. He kissed her. As she moved towards him, Nikos was released, and rolled on to his back.

'I want him,' Yiannis confessed to the sympathetic Eleni.

'I know, my darling . . .' she murmured. 'Be patient, Yianni . . .'

Unexpectedly, she released his prick and moved down to kiss it. She licked and sucked it back into slow life, and then, smiling wickedly, she placed the jar of cream in his hand. Yiannis opened his eyes wide as he returned her smile. Eleni rolled on to her belly, and began to move her small, smooth abdomen up and down invitingly, parting her legs as she did so. Yiannis slapped the cream over his cock, and then filled her hot, wet hole with it.

He entered her immediately, ramming his prick home, and making a fist of his hand to place under her vulva. Eleni masturbated against his clenched knuckles, her red bud caught perfectly between his fingers, feeling his other hand going from breast to breast, pinching and squeezing at her dangling teats. Then he removed his hands, using them to support himself as he slammed viciously in to her abdomen. Eleni squirmed and wriggled in response, tightening her sphincter muscle against his invasion.

Yiannis began to moan and sob, lost. This was good, but it was not Nikos. Nikos watched him, seeing Yiannis' lithe, strong body, tense with strain. He reached out to stroke his friend's straining abdomen tenderly. Yiannis looked at him in astonishment. Nikos moved his palm slowly up his friend's back, and then held his face in both hands and raised his head to kiss him. Eleni felt Yiannis' increased sexual excitement as Nikos kissed him deeply. With a sudden surge, Yiannis rammed hard and ejaculated. Nikos released him and moved his hand under Eleni's pubis, fingering and pressing her sex until she came.

Yiannis reached out longingly for Nikos' engorged prick.

'Shhh . . . now, Yianni, go to sleep . . .' Eleni said, lulling him as she cradled him in her arms.

She looked at Nikos as she felt the exhausted Yiannis relax. His eyes were serious. She touched his lips and smiled tenderly.

'You can take him to heaven, Niko . . .'

Distant fear flashed swiftly at the back of his black eyes. Eleni brushed his delicate cheekbone with the back of her hand.

'You know it will be better – to be familiar before Constantine gets you in public.'

Nikos imagined the ignominy of any kind of failure before this powerful, sardonic man. He nodded, and Eleni smiled sleepily, taking his hand and cuddling the sleeping Yiannis as she closed her eyes.

Five

Constantine sat and began to watch the film of Nikos and Saffie for the third time. After all his secret fantasies, seeing Nikos suddenly fucking Saffie worked on him like madness. He had sat there, unable to move, he was so aroused. His cock had immediately stuck out, so conditioned was it to stimuli concerning this extremely sexual young man. Constantine had always been aware of the effect Nikos had on almost everyone who encountered him. His sexuality was like a gift attracting everyone to him. A rare quality he himself could scarcely be unaware of. And he fucked like an angel.

Constantine watched now as his muscular arse jerked rapidly up and down, his long cock deep into Saffie's ripe hole. And he could see how much the woman was enjoying it as she growled and moaned. Constantine was filled with the rage of frustration. He was angry with Saffie for getting Nikos so easily. There was patently something very special between these two. Not just sexual chemistry either, though that was powerful enough. No, they had much in common. They were intelligent and well-educated people, as well as being creative, and having a deep interest in Greece and her history.

Saffie was now dominating Nikos, and he was loving every minute as she bounced and ground on him, her ripe tits exposed and moving in time to their screwing. Constantine lit a cigarette, but put it out, it tasted foul. He drank the vintage wine, but it could as well have been cola. Desire to possess Nikos filled him completely. He realised that he had been handling his heavy cock in response to Nikos' frenzied fucking; his supposed enravishment of Saffie.

Nikos was tearing at Saffie's breasts savagely as he bucked and

135

groaned. Constantine's wild arousal was complicated by a sudden surge of desire for the randy Saffie. He turned as the door opened, darkness in his eyes. Rachel recoiled, seeing how Constantine was still drawn to the screen, where Nikos and Saffie were reaching their all-consuming orgasm. At first, he scarcely seemed able to see her, or realise who she was or why she was here. Then, a strange light of possibility came into his eyes and he smiled and reached for her.

Rachel was torn between flight and acquiescence. This man was extremely attractive, his sexuality enhanced by his aura of power and his control of their sexual partnering, in his film. He would imagine what they would do, and then order them to do it, and make them do it again, if he did not approve. His dominion fired her. As he rose to grasp her, she knew that she wanted to experience his powerful sexuality.

Constantine put out his elegant palm and cupped Rachel's small chin. Her blue eyes were huge as she stared back into his appreciative gaze. He detected a hint of apprehension in her. He wanted her. She was lovely, her long blonde hair over her bare shoulders, her small black dress clinging tightly to the rounded contours of her voluptuous body. His immediate need for her concentrated all his fretful thoughts of Nikos, and Saffie. This was real.

He rubbed his thumb firmly over her soft mouth, seeing her eyes soften. Rachel felt her panties moisten with the sexual fluid of sudden excitement. She felt that the liberty offered by her agreement to participate in Constantine's film could easily be extended to include the man himself. Constantine saw the woman's mouth open in invitation as he removed his thumb. He kissed her passionately. Rachel was aware of the strength of his desire as it transmitted itself through her flesh. Constantine ran his palms strongly all over her soft, lightly-clad form. She seemed to ripple under his strong touch, her entire body undulating in response to his urgent need.

His hand went between her thighs, forcing them apart. Rachel quivered, collapsing into his hold. Constantine scraped at her vulva with his thumb. Shocks of intense feeling originated from this rough stimulation of her clitoris as he pressed and then sped on to her hidden vagina, there repeating the movement. Rachel was a mass of longing. She wanted this man to handle her roughly, her breasts swelled in anticipation of his certain touch. Constantine thrilled as his hand fingered her sex, hot beneath her soaking silken panties.

He moved his hand to the lacy elastic of the legs, dappled at her firm, moist thigh with his fingers, then inserted them under the soft material. He felt first the intense intimate heat of her, and then the wetness of her gusset. He delighted in the feminine, sexual smell released by his handling. He rubbed at her sex-lips, pressed her suffuse ridge, and then opened her labia wide. Rachel gasped as he stuck his hand savagely into her gaping hole. He stretched her wide. Constantine smiled in satisfaction and reached to knead her ample breasts powerfully. For luxurious moments, impaled on his hand and supported by his firm handling, Rachel slid up and down, grunting in response to the unusual pressure he inflicted on vagina and anus. Very soon, her excitement exploded around his hand, and she quivered as her first impatient orgasm shook her.

She withdrew from Constantine's hand, seeing his hooded eyes, his sensual mouth. Her eyes laughed at him. His cock reared to fuck her and he caught her back, yanking down her dripping panties. Rachel grabbed at his crotch, seeing his eyes narrow as she squeezed his stiff rod tightly. She relished the thought of it up her vagina. He felt big. She moved away from his fingers.

'What will you do to me,' she asked provocatively, 'if I don't let you have me? Will you punish me?' she added the last invitingly, enjoying teasing this potent man.

'I will,' he promised huskily as she stepped over his fiddling hand.

Rachel laughed and moved away, looking enticingly back over her shoulder at him, lifting her dress to reveal her round, soft bottom to him. Constantine followed her. He grasped her dress and tore it off. He whipped off her bra with a deft pull. Rachel lay on her belly over the chair, opening her legs and sticking her behind into the air. Constantine smacked her bottom very hard with the palm of his hand. Hardly had the smarting begun before his hand had ripped through the air and met with her hot, stinging flesh once more.

Rachel's skin tingled and then glowed. The heat spread to her sex as she rocked it against the chair-seat. As Constantine smacked her harder and harder, his rigid rod burned for release. Constantine looked lasciviously at her undulating abdomen. He saw the inviting red between her legs. He saw her enlarged breasts, pressed against the chair. He pulled her up and slapped at her breasts. They shook as he did so. Rachel smirked at him, her blue eyes semi-closed in her sexual haze. Constantine continued to smack her tits and arse until his cock could wait no longer.

He shoved her onto the floor. He re-set the video of Nikos fucking Saffie. Then he lifted her legs high, so that she could not move, and unzipped his trousers. Rachel was distantly conscious of the film of Saffie and Nikos, and that he had paused it. Then she faded away as Constantine pressed down on her bent legs with his arms and penetrated her violently. When he was deeply in, his huge cock swelling her vagina, he also rammed half his hand up her arse. For a moment he was still, Rachel saw that he was looking at the screen, and wondered vaguely which bit it was. This man certainly did not require any artificial stimulus! Then she was lost as he began to ram hugely into her, jerking into her anus at the same time.

Rachel was soon taken into a realm of dark pleasure, on the edge of pain, but just this side of loss of control. The possibility of danger added to her deep excitement as Constantine continued to jerk his long, wet rod very hard and fast into her. Rachel was aware of her anus, extended by his hand as he fisted her. Her abdomen was filled with him as he banged down on her, only sometimes hitting her clitoris. He began to tear at her breasts savagely. She had the idea that he sought to punish her as he fucked her wildly.

He removed his hand and began to massage cruelly at both teats, squeezing them tightly and yanking at her nipples. Then he concentrated on screwing her. She knew that he did not really care about her and she was torn between a perverse thrill, and violent anger. She could not honestly say that she wanted him to stop, nor that she did not derive intense pleasure from his fucking, but it sent her to the edge of orgasm, and she knew that she might miss it in his selfish quest. He rocked around, ramming his prick in any way he fancied, to give it maximum pleasure within her muscular passage. It was merely a convenient sheath for him. Soon, he raised his big arse, supported himself on his elbows, and looked with pleasure down at her breasts. She wanted him to feel them, but he did not. He was just going to ram his cock home until he came. Bastard. Although her wet muscle loved every second of his strong penetration, she wanted him to hit on her clitoris. He seemed deliberately to avoid this. Of this she was certain as he raised her legs further and pushed them towards her. His balls tickled at her aching anus.

He speeded suddenly, fucking Rachel faster and harder than she had ever experienced before. She cried out for him to continue as her body shuddered at his rapid and powerful jerking. Spasms of intense sexual arousal shot through her legs and belly. Her breasts jutted at him longingly. Constantine had closed his eyes, and was thrusting, his abdomen contracting spasmodically with each shuddering jerk. He was a mass of sexuality. His anus burnt, his balls tightened, his prick shot along this woman's clenching muscle.

He thought of her full breasts with their big red nipples; he thought of Nikos erect on the screen. He clenched Rachel's quivering buttocks, emitting a long, low guttural moan as his balls tightened and his prick filled and pumped his spunk into her.

'You bastard!'

Constantine withdrew, made his hand into a fist, and began to pummel accurately against Rachel's quim. Though satiated, he knew what to do. Despite her anger towards him, Rachel could not help but respond to the man's dexterous handling of her sex as he thumped against her engorged clitoris.

He began to manipulate her breasts, pulling at the larger dark area around her nipples, as well as the teats themselves. All of his touches demonstrated his knowledge and supreme self-confidence.

Rachel was in agony as he fought off her orgasm with his knowing touch, taking her higher and higher, so that she thought she would explode if she didn't get release. At last, he took pity on her, slowing down and pressing sensitively on her bud and massaging her suffuse breasts until her climax crashed in power-ful jerking throbs, which made her entire body tremble. The deep glow of euphoria after such energetic screwing then slid through her veins, reaching all of her and making her languid and replete.

She noticed that the clip on the screen was of Nikos, gloriously erect, about to ram it home to Saffie. She smiled at Constantine as if she knew his innermost secrets. Constantine flipped off the switch and said, in an off-hand manner:

'You can have the shower first.'

'Can't you sleep?' Mike asked as he came out to Saffie on the balcony.

She smiled at him, admiring his physique, and responding to the curiosity in his perceptive eyes. She sighed happily.

'I just want to make the most of every second here in Delphi. I think it's my favourite place on earth . . .' Then she thought of Delos, and added, laughingly, 'Well, one of them . . .'

'What do you like about it?'

'It's beautiful. Its natural site is breathtaking – and then, there's the history, and mythology. The atmosphere is so rich – magical.'

Mike nodded.

'You're an artist?' he asked, seeing her sketch-pad and pencils on the table beside her.

'Yes . . . It would take a long time though, to capture even some of all this,' she laughed. 'Plenty of excuses to return?'

'You were good, earlier tonight. Have you done this kind of thing before?'

'No.'

'This film is different from the usual ones we make. More arty.' Mike laughed.

'Have you made many?' Saffie asked.

'Quite a few, yes – there's a growing market.'

Saffie hesitated for a moment, before venturing:

'You know Constantine expects the film crew sometimes to participate?'

'That's no problem. I've done it before. How did you come to take part?'

'By chance – Rachel and I are travelling around Greece on holiday.'

'Captivated by the Greek men, hey? Charm, and looks, and money . . .'

'You reckon?'

'Have you ever seen a real porno flick?'

'No, I haven't. I suppose I've always been contented with my own imagination.'

They both laughed at the implications of this. Mike imagined the attractive woman naked and masturbating on top of her bed. She would caress her small breasts tenderly, and finger her sex languidly as she wove sexual fantasies in her mind. Judging by her performance with Nikos earlier, Mike wouldn't have minded betting that at least some of them had involved dark handsome Greeks. At least Nikos was being less temperamental than last time, so far. Perhaps this level-headed English woman was having a calming effect on him. He wondered whether Saffie could read his mind as her naked image played on. He smiled.

'We're watching some up in my room. Come and join us. Georgiou's there.'

'Alright. Why not?'

She took Mike's hand as he stretched it out to her, picked up her materials and went up to his room with him. The rest of the crew, Andy, Carrie, Nicola, Lyndsay and Jaspar greeted her with friendly waves and words. Nicola sat lasciviously on Georgiou's knee, her arms around his neck as she looked across at Saffie and Mike entering. Saffie noticed that Georgiou's hand was inside Nicola's panties. She wondered where the others were. Perhaps they were asleep. It was late, and they had another early start on the following day.

'We've watched you and Nikos – purely to edit . . .' Andy told her. 'Very successful. Let's hope the rest goes as well, hey?'

'This is nothing like your film,' Mike said, leading her to a seat. 'It's much rawer stuff, but it's quite a turn on. I expect your boys would like it, lots of role-swapping and ambiguity of the sexes.'

He exchanged a look of intelligence with Andy. Georgiou was too occupied with Nicola to hear them.

'You have to like rock to appreciate this,' Carolyn warned.

'Oh, yeah, that's okay,' said Saffie, settling down. Andy handed her a lager.

'Cheers.'

They were plunged into darkness as the room was suddenly filled with wild and raucous heavy metal music. Onto the screen leapt an agile male singer, dressed in tight black leather. His long permed black hair flew as he danced energetically around the stage to each of the musicians in turn, caressing and fondling them intimately. They responded with lascivious smiles, sensual movements and kisses. The lead singer thrust his face towards the camera, singing with gusto, his muscles taut. He stared with feigned innocence through kohl-rimmed brown eyes. He was very fit. He danced with tremendous energy, though he was obviously no longer very young.

The rest of the band looked on in tolerant affection as he ground and thrust his firm body, slithering his leather-gloved palms over his chest and thighs. Saffie felt her body liven to his overt sexual movements. He began to thrust his lower abdomen rapidly back and forth, fingering his crotch yearningly. Saffie noted the small tattoo on his muscular upper arm. It was a flower.

The singer turned his back to them, and wriggled his tight arse, looking back at them over his shoulder and caressing his buttocks lovingly. The lead guitarist came to him, and the singer kissed him passionately. They held each other, front to front, rubbing their leather-swathed crotches against each other, pressing tightly as they moved in rhythm to the music.

'I've seen this band,' Saffie said to Mike.

'Watch, you won't see this on MTV . . .'

The lead singer was ripping off his black vest, teasing at his flies, and shaking his head, wagging his finger at his supposed audience; perhaps this was where the mass-released film ended. For now, as the music changed, he began to undress the lascivious guitarist, fondling his crotch and seeming always to address the invisible audience to seek their approval; knowing it was freely given. The guitarist was naked, his prick standing out magnificently. The singer knelt and began to suck him, and then moved behind him, rapidly unfastened his own leather trousers and stuck his rampant cock into him. The other musicians continued their raucous music, speeding up to respond to the thrusting of their members. Saffie was extremely aroused as the attractive lead bit hard at his guitarist's neck, then held him tight as he sodomised him. The clip ended with spunk shooting over the camera lens, amidst orgiastic cries from the band.

'Now watch this,' Mike said.

The next extract showed a glamorously dressed woman strutting and preening, watched by a man. To the sensual strains of a rising saxophone, she began to strip seductively, holding the spectator's avid gaze. With a pang of realisation, Saffie saw the flower tattoo on 'her' arm. It was the male lead singer from the heavy metal band!

'Convincing, isn't he?' asked Mike, as the man stripped off his scarlet basque to reveal his true nature.

Saffie smiled. Next, the same man was leading a seemingly unwilling woman towards a bed. He was now clad in tight denim jeans, which fondled his erection, and shaped his tight muscular buttocks. His eyes were huge and sexy, his mouth passionate. He was full of directed sexual energy. Saffie thought that the blonde girl, who looked a bit like Rachel, must find it hard to pretend she did not want him. Her own sex yearned already with vicarious longing. The man was masculine, forceful and bewitching.

He threw the woman on to the bed and ripped off his own clothes. His huge cock reared in greedy expectation. Saffie swallowed hard. He eyed the camera sleazily with his black-encircled eyes and pulled up the woman's legs to expose her naked sex. Saffie throbbed in desire. Mike pulled her on to his knee. She could feel his bulge under his denim. She rocked on him, positioning her vulva over his straining masculinity. The actor ripped off the struggling woman's scanty clothes, pulled up her legs and entered her. Selfishly, he screwed her, his behind ramming and contracting.

Mike began to finger Saffie's quim as she squirmed on him. He squeezed at her breasts. Saffie turned to kiss him.

Now the singer had the woman on all fours and was buggering her, whilst pulling on her hanging breasts.

Saffie wondered whether Constantine was with Rachel. Mike still had his hand on her breast, and was caressing it. She fondled his crotch. The film finished with the woman whipping the naked singer until he was re-erect and then forcing him to fuck her. Mike smiled ruefully, and went to put in another film. Whilst he was at the machine, Andy asked him something, which led to a lengthy conversation. Saffie glanced across to see that Nicola was sitting, facing Georgiou, and easing herself up and down along his hidden prick. Saffie smiled. On screen, the tireless singer was strutting around in a black military uniform, complete with peaked cap, restraining his abundant curls, and black thigh-length leather boots. In his hand, he held a whip. The woman, now dressed in a skin-tight leopardskin body suit, unseen by him, came from behind and grabbed the whip. The performer feigned astonishment and stepped away from her. The woman raised the whip and gestured for him to strip. With a flamboyant gesture, the singer took off his hat. His long black hair cascaded down his back. He shook it, backing away from his advancing adversary defiantly.

She cracked the whip over his thighs and indicated that he should continue to take off his clothes. Teasingly, turning to the audience, he began to undo the buttons of his jacket.

Saffie squirmed on her chair, wondering whether Mike would return, and then decided that when she could tear herself away from the sexy singer, she would go and find Nikos or Yiannis.

The woman whipped violently across the singer's back. Sleazily, he unfastened his shirt buttons, beginning at the waist. Then, he tugged out his shirt tail, wiggling his tight behind at them. He ripped off his trousers quickly. When he was naked, his thick short penis standing proudly before him, the woman, still clad in her leopardskin, whipped him furiously, concentrating especially on his groins and prick. The singer seemed to give in to her. Then, suddenly, he rose and grasped the whip and turned it on his attacker, ordering her to strip. She wriggled out of her tight suit. His cock reared visibly. Once she was bare, he dropped the whip and went to fuck her.

Saffie left the film room. There was no-one in the bar. She went up to her own room, and there encountered Rachel, who appeared to have been waiting for her.

'Are you alright, Rachel?' Saffie frowned: something had happened to her friend.

'Yeah, I'm fine. Shall I make some tea?' asked Rachel, going over to the cupboard where a kettle had been left, along with the other items necessary for private tea- and coffee-making.

'If you like. I've been watching some of Mike's films.'

'Oh. Any good?'

'Kind of. A turn on, in a seedy kind of way. What is it, Rachel?'

Rachel turned to face her friend, leaning against the cupboard and folding her arms.

'I've been with Constantine. I'm feeling a bit . . . shaken?'

144

Saffie sighed and nodded.

'I know what you mean. It's very good sex. But—'

'The man's a complete megalomaniac,' said Rachel.

'Selfish bugger!' agreed Saffie.

The friends laughed. Saffie went to hug Rachel.

'He's like a drug,' Rachel decided. 'You have to have more of him.'

Saffie, already made ready for sex by the film, was rendered even more so by memories of Constantine's prowess. She moved self-consciously away from Rachel. Rachel looked after her in speculation. She felt that she needed a woman's tenderness after Constantine's rough handling. She made them tea, and went to sit on Saffie's double bed. Saffie joined her. For a few minutes they flicked channels on the television, and then they fell to talking about their recent experiences, and the relative merits of their various lovers. They drank more tea, and ate all the sweets on the tray, left for them by the manager.

Rachel snuggled down against Saffie. It was quiet and peaceful, and outside, an owl hooted occasionally. Saffie switched off the bedside lamp. It seemed comforting and natural to have her friend so close. Just to be alone together was an oasis in the recent rapidly-moving events. It was easy. Saffie felt drowsy. Rachel was warm and somnolent in her arms. Her head on her breast.

They slumbered peacefully, though Saffie was aware that she did not sleep fully. Vivid images of Nikos and Constantine came to her. The decadent singer danced and stripped. Her gentle arousal increased. When Rachel woke and turned to her with a smile, it was natural to kiss her. Rachel responded positively to Saffie's kiss. Saffie was relieved. It was strange to be in such a position with someone she had known for so long.

When they kissed again, Saffie's pent-up sexual tension seemed to explode throughout her body. She had not expected to feel so aroused with Rachel. She merely thought that something was bound to happen between them as a spin-off from the atmosphere of sexual indulgence they were living in. Her breasts tingled, her vagina throbbed, but still she was a little reticent, unsure of how Rachel felt and unwilling to jeopardise their friendship. She kissed the top of her head and tried to relax.

'I reckon that Constantine is into Nikos something rotten.'

'What do you mean?' asked Saffie, having sudden images of the two men having been long involved in a sexual relationship. Her ideas somersaulted as she tried to square this with Nikos' seeming reluctance. Had Rachel seen them together, or (here Saffie felt a rush of envy) had she been with them both together?

'When I went to his room—'

'Why did you go to his room? Did he ask you?'

'Kind of, we were going to discuss something, to do with the film. But I think that he'd forgotten about me.'

'Charming . . .'

'He was watching the film of you and Nikos. He was in a strange, wild, animal kind of state . . . I was just an object to him. He was very turned on. He froze the film on Nikos.'

'So it wasn't me who turned him on?' joked Saffie, very interested in this secret admission of Constantine's need for Nikos. Perhaps Nikos was right in believing that the older man would never leave him alone?

'There's something – I dunno – dangerous about him,' said Rachel after some consideration.

'I know what you mean.'

'He doesn't really care, in the way Georgiou, or Nikos do.'

'Or Yiannis . . .' agreed Saffie.

'Right.'

The women lay in silence for a few minutes, Rachel recalling Constantine's attitude towards her with a mixture of anger and arousal, and Saffie further excited by thinking of Constantine with Nikos. They therefore reacted to each other impulsively, transmitting their feelings as they moved closer.

'Are you alright with this, Rachel?' asked Saffie.

Rachel reached up to kiss her friend.

'It's less strange than some of the things that have happened lately.'

'Yes . . .' Saffie had to concede.

The women began a long, slow, almost shy discovery of each others' bodies. Their reticence lent gentleness, and to Rachel at least, this respect and consideration was welcome after Constantine. It was healing. They lay down on the bed and, like virgin-lovers, pressed and caressed each others' breasts, bottoms and vulvas. They smiled into each others' eyes as they responded in like

146

manner to each delicate stimulus. They took off their clothes and entwined comfortably, dozing for a time in the weariness of the night.

They awoke, refreshed and relaxed and began to kiss urgently, exploring mouths with tongues, and breasts and crotches with gentle hands. Their arousal was exquisite, seeming to touch far more acutely than the powerful caresses they were used to. They were certainly learning many different ways of making love. They moved very close, lying on their sides so that their bellies pressed together, thus flattening breasts against each other, and fannies.

They ran their hands down each other's back, and lingered on buttocks, enjoying the firm but soft yielding feel. They intertwined legs, positioning their pussies very close so that each could stimulate her clitoris whilst undulating gently against the other. This languid, leisurely pace was satisfying, like being naked out in warm sunshine and being taken up by the life-giving properties of the element.

There was no panic, or need to achieve. They expected what they gave. They smiled as the small gentle waves of sex filled them, now and again, drifting over their warm bodies.

It was lovely to feel no urgency, but simply to caress and fondle idly, kissing and pressing, as though very young and expecting no more. Each felt rejuvenating waves of relaxed pleasure. Eventually they lapsed into a deep, contented sleep.

Nikos got out of bed. He glanced at Eleni and Yiannis. They were deeply asleep, entwined in each others' arms. He looked particularly at Yiannis, whose strong thigh was over Eleni's. His hand was on her breast, caught in her long hair. Nikos pulled his trousers on, still regarding him. He knew his friend's body so well. He thought that his trepidation was unnecessary and over-emotional. There was no escape now from Constantine's designs. Anyway, if he backed out, he felt he may seem to appear churlish to the others, especially Saffie and Rachel, whom he admired, and who were willing to participate in the film for his sake. Even to him, his reticence seemed bewildering. He was surely a modern, liberated man, despite his ancient family ties? He repressed a dark shadow at the back of his brain.

He sat by the window, sometimes glancing out into the night, and sometimes making himself imagine sex with Yiannis. He could probably fuck him: after all, he had fucked Eleni anally many times. He had to admit that he had often admired Yiannis' muscular, strong body. His hair was rich and lovely, and his eyes intelligent and perspicacious. His lips were full and passionate. Nikos was close to him – he knew him very well, and delighted in his sharp mind, his wit and perception. Also, Yiannis was a kind, compassionate, sensitive and generous man. They had known each other well since school. They had gone to university together. Nikos liked him. A lot. He was an integral part of his life. His closest friend.

Nikos sighed. Would it be easier if it was Georgiou? Or even Constantine? He shuddered. Cold, he put on his shirt. He hoped that they would stay asleep. But, then, tomorrow – he would be cold, and he did not know how he would react. Doubtless Constantine would have rewritten mythology, re-casting the gods, symbols of ancient Greek history and philosophy, as rampant whores.

Yiannis moaned softly in his sleep and turned over, away from Eleni, who turned away, into the space that Nikos had left, and curled up. Nikos went to cover Eleni. Yiannis sprawled widely over the bed, his limbs stretched luxuriously. His thick, flaccid penis lay against his thigh. Nikos smiled at him. Very slowly, he reached out his outstretched fingers towards his phallus. He did not think that he would actually touch Yiannis, and wake him. In this silent peacefulness, Nikos relaxed. He told himself that it would be no different from touching himself. His penis began to uncoil from its tight home in response. It was not as though he had not seen Yiannis naked, often. He had even touched him. He recalled images of Yiannis glancing at him, his expression sometimes one of naked desire, rapidly concealed as Yiannis smiled and looked away. Nikos was filled with tenderness for his generous friend.

So far, he had thought only of himself. Suddenly, especially with Eleni so near, with memories of sultry nights, he realised the pleasure he could give Yiannis. Someone may as well benefit from Constantine's perversity. His hand hovered near Yiannis' penis, which (through instinctive animal knowledge, or as a result of his lascivious dreams) began to grow. Nikos became uncomfortably aware of his own extending erection.

Yiannis opened his eyes wide. Nikos was sure that he was aware of the proximity of his hand, as his eyes seemed to challenge him. But then, he closed his eyes. Nikos forced himself to think of Constantine, coming up with some sudden change of plan – well, for him, Nikos, to be buggered by someone. Knowing Constantine, he would be perverse enough for it not even to be Yiannis, but Georgiou, or one of the crew-men. Mike. Andy. Jaspar. Even, Nikos shuddered, Constantine himself!

Nikos knelt beside Yiannis and kissed his mouth. His heart beat rapidly. But, he told himself, he had done this before. He felt alone without Eleni. He wished Eleni would awaken. Yiannis turned to embrace him. Nikos had thought he was still asleep.

'Niko . . .'

Yiannis smiled wonderfully and pulled Nikos closer. Nikos felt the dynamic electricity of Yiannis' response zest his blood. He lay beside Yiannis, trailing his fingers slowly down and merely feathering his cock with soft touches. Yiannis pulled him roughly on top of him and kissed him hard. Nikos was reminded of Yiannis' strength. He could take him by force if he chose. Nikos shuddered. He thought of the veneer of civilised behaviour merely restraining men. Yiannis felt Nikos' swollen prick against him through the expensive material of his trousers. He pushed down firmly on his buttocks, so that Nikos pressed on his cock. Nikos looked towards the sleeping Eleni.

'You don't need her. Don't wake her, Niko,' Yiannis almost pleaded.

'Don't hurt me.'

Yiannis squeezed him tightly. Nikos undressed. Yiannis reached out to take him in his arms.

'I just need to get it over,' Nikos told him.

'Very romantic,' Yiannis joked, concealing his disappointment. He moved so that Nikos could lie on the bed.

'Do you want to put this on yourself?' he asked flippantly.

'You do it.'

Yiannis dipped his hand into the soft, rich cream and looked at Nikos' abdomen. He narrowed his eyes lasciviously. He smoothed his palm lightly over the muscular buttocks feeling the standing hair. Nikos tightened his buttocks instinctively. Yiannis creamed

149

the soft white stuff into his crack, feeling Nikos' abdomen clench in repulsion.

'Look, Niko, I can't do it to you this cold. It will be like rape.'

'For God's sake . . .'

'It will hurt you . . . Can't you relax?'

Yiannis urged Nikos over and kissed him. He took his stiff prick and began to wank him very strongly. He knew that Nikos felt he had to go through with this now and was willing to comply: however he had Nikos would be Elysian to him now. Yiannis encircled Nikos' ring, then urged his sphincter muscle to open. Nikos had to admit to a feeling of pleasure in Yiannis' capable hands. Yiannis moved to straddle his buttocks. He wanted to make love to Nikos, to take him slowly, to kiss and caress him. Maybe next time? If there was one! Yiannis took his own prick into his hand and rubbed the head against Nikos' anus. At the same time, he fingered Nikos' lovely prick. Yiannis closed his eyes in enjoyment. It was exciting to be allowed thus close to his beautiful friend. With infinite care, and a lot more gently than he himself needed, he pushed his way carefully into Nikos, continuing to pull on his penis to keep him aroused.

Nikos felt the unnatural load inserted into him. Ancient pain shot up his spine, as a weight, heavier than Yiannis, seemed to push his younger body into the ground. He felt that he could not breathe. His head was filled with blackness. As Yiannis penetrated more deeply, Nikos' jagged brain was filled with memories of sex and violence; savage pain and fear and humiliation.

Yiannis wanted to let go. It was exquisite pain to maintain so much control. He had waited so long for this. Nikos felt sick. Suppressed rage welled up inside him as he vividly relived that time of terror. He threw Yiannis off and belted him hard across his face. Yiannis fell to the floor with the unexpected impact of this blow. He looked up at Nikos, who was shaking; full of rage.

Eleni woke up suddenly and went to Yiannis.

'I'm alright.'

He inclined his head towards Nikos, meaning that she should go to him. Nikos was dressing. He was still trembling. He wanted to go and hit Constantine until he left him alone.

He shook his head at Eleni as she reached out to comfort him. He returned to Yiannis, and put his hand on Yiannis' arm.

'Please forgive me, Yianni – it isn't you.'

'I know, Niko . . .'

'Apollo was the aggressor – the gods were dominant – insist on doing the screwing. You can do that to Yiannis, or Georgiou?' suggested Eleni.

'Just pretend it's you?' said Nikos with a sarcastic smile.

He went down to the lounge, where Carrie was smoking and drinking wine.

'Hi, Niko . . .' She turned to him, pleased, offering him a drink and a cigarette.

Nikos accepted both.

'Do you think you'll stay the course this time?' she asked.

Nikos sneered. Carrie smiled at his petulance. She watched him as he drank and smoked nervously. Something had upset him. Carrie reckoned that she could capitalise on his state. She found him very desirable (as indeed everyone else also seemed to), though he was not her usual type. She did not take him too seriously, and was sometimes amused by his temperamental behaviour. He seemed vulnerable at present, and, Carrie (being somewhat familiar with the penchants of their director, and the complexities of the relationships between this group of rich, epicurean friends) surmised that he would welcome a woman. Especially an outsider, who would confirm his heterosexual attractiveness. However, she was far too independent to play games with him.

'I'm off to bed, Niko,' she told him, standing and taking up her drink. 'Do you want to join me?'

To her surprise, Nikos merely said, 'Yes. I'd like that.'

Smiling happily to herself, Carrie led the way to her room. She had had sex with Yiannis in the past, and of course, with the insatiable Georgiou, but Nikos had so far preserved a distance between himself and the crew. He had limited his off-screen love-life to Eleni, who looked so like him she could almost have been his sister.

Nikos was relieved to be offered this opportunity for uncomplicated sex. He spent the rest of the night re-affirming his heterosexuality with Carrie.

Early the next morning, they were all gathered at the sacred site of

Delphi. Mike had, on the previous day, recorded a lot of background scenery which Constantine seemed satisfied with. Now they were to record a few scenes from a Greek play at the ancient open theatre. This was to be Aristophanes' 'Frogs'. Nikos was Dionysus. The recording went quite well. Those not participating at present watched.

They then went up to the remains of the Gymnasium, where all of the men, except Mike and Constantine, had to strip and be filmed racing around, being awarded with ribbons for their feats. The women were required to sit and cheer, and thoroughly enjoyed the spectacle.

'So,' said Constantine, addressing them from the head of the table at lunch time, 'I think I have worked out the dynamics between you,' he surveyed them all keenly, 'as classical-age actors, of course.'

Nikos regarded him with disdain.

'You – Rachel and Georgiou – you will be new and passionate lovers, so much opportunity there for titillation. Sometimes, you will argue in passion and there will be cause for jealousy, from other quarters . . .' His eyes rested meaningfully on Yiannis and then Eleni. 'You will take on all transgressors, Georgiou . . .'

'I'm a pacifist.'

'It's a film, Georgiou.'

'Eleni, you will be pleased to have sex with everyone.'

Eleni grinned.

'Saffie, you will be wild about Nikos. You will follow him around, longing for his attention. Nikos, you will be, if you can manage it,' Constantine smirked, 'arrogant and dismissive. You do not want sex with her, for you are in love with Yiannis.'

Saffie saw Nikos' deep flush of anger. He went from the room. She herself was not too enamoured with her subservient role of submission.

'Yianni . . .' Constantine said wearily, 'go and tell Nikos that it will only take longer if he insists in behaving so petulantly.'

'You should not push him, Constantine,' reasoned Yiannis. 'Why do we need all this other stuff, anyway? Why not just the myths? There's sufficient sex there – especially with your interpolations.'

'Perhaps. As you've seen, we will use some of the plays as well. But, I think it could get a little inaccessible – ludicrous if extended. This way, we will have more "ordinary" episodes which will lend interest . . .'

'Widening the market?' asked Eleni.

Saffie wondered whether Constantine had been influenced by his conversations with Mike.

Yiannis went out to his friend. Nikos was standing looking over the valley.

'Come on, Niko . . .' Yiannis pulled at his arm.

Nikos shook him off.

'The whole thing will drag out indefinitely if we don't comply.'

'I can't do it, Yianni . . .' Nikos shook his head. 'Definitely not.'

'Come on, Niko . . . he's waiting. Decide later . . . We will try and work something out. Come back for the sake of the others.'

Nikos nodded and followed Yiannis back into the dining room.

'Also—' Constantine continued, in the tone of one adding yet another well-considered dictum, 'there are two, perhaps seemingly contradictory things. You, Yianni, you must impress this upon Nikos. One is that you cannot continue to squander sexual energy whilst we are filming. However tireless you think you are it will show.'

Saffie noticed that Georgiou looked disbelievingly at Constantine. She suppressed a snigger at his open-mouthed consternation.

'There will be plenty of opportunity – rehearsals and re-takes,' Constantine assured them.

He looked thoughtfully around at them.

'On the other hand, you should – to start with, at least – you should learn to be completely at ease with each other and experiment with all types of sex in front of the camera. We will have no time for shyness. So, you can get together with the others tonight, to start with. I will be interested to watch you, to see where I need to direct you.'

Yes, I bet you will, thought Saffie, as she met his confident, self-congratulatory gaze. Then – an orgy! she thought. She looked at Nikos. He met her glance with one which recalled to her his warning on Delos: that she would be subjected to all kinds of sexual humiliation at the hands of this man.

They spent the afternoon re-taking some of the morning scenes and adding a few more, including some which were to demonstrate the relationships between the 'actors'. Rachel and Georgiou staged an argument, which drew many spectators. Saffie thought it was strange to act in front of these interested passers-by, who were perhaps impressed by their costumes and authenticity of their ancient Greek, but who had no idea of the more decadent content of their film. She decided that this was quite amusing. It was a little wearing to work in the hot sun. They were all relieved when, after this, they returned to the hotel to shower and change in preparation for their dinner, and – as Saffie suspected – the 'orgy'.

They met in the dining room, admiring each others' fresh chitons, and chlamyses, which were of all colours and intricately embroidered at the hem. They were treated to a veritable feast, of delicate and unusual foods, which Constantine apparently considered would enhance their amorousness. Perhaps, Saffie thought, the fare was what he thought was eaten by the ancient Greek actors! The wine flowed freely. Sweet music from harp or lyre added authenticity. Constantine's guests laughed and joked, enjoying the refreshing company of the film crew. Saffie saw that Nikos ate little, but seemed to drink copiously. The Dionysus in him, she decided, thinking of the decadent god of wine and ecstasy. Perhaps the ideal of Apollo was Nikos at his most civilised. An Artist. She thought of him dancing in the basement taverna in Athens. After dinner, they all went down to the baths, (which were surely, thought Saffie, more Roman than Greek?) in the basement. The surroundings reminded Saffie of one of Alma-Tadema's colourful and decadent paintings. There were several different baths in the large hall, which was decorated with bawdy pictures of nymphs and satyrs be-sporting themselves. Aromatic fragrances mingled with the steam, and eastern music filled the air. The atmosphere, especially after the wine, induced relaxation. Already, Saffie felt the heady intoxication of sexual licence.

She looked around at the others. She smiled to see that Rachel and Georgiou were first to disrobe, and were soon shrieking, laughing and playing, in the hot water pool. Yiannis was showering, naked and alone in a small pool. She noticed that he glanced in concern at Nikos, who sat on a wooden bench at the side, lingering over discarding his leather sandals. This tableau would, in itself, have made a convincing neo-classical subject for a painting. The crew were together at the side, gradually undressing, whilst Mike alone was immersed in a serious conversation with Constantine, manning the camera. He was obviously explaining a few details to him. Saffie stifled an hysterical snigger, wondering whether Constantine intended to address them through a megaphone, in order to command various couplings.

Eleni, unashamedly naked, had gone over to Nikos. Saffie let her robe slide to the tiled floor and went to join Yiannis, who smiled happily and pulled her under the foaming shower with him. Carrie had joined Nikos and Eleni. Jaspar, Lyndsay, Andy and Nicola joined in good-naturedly.

Constantine did indeed attempt to oversee their couplings, though he could not really maintain control over them as they began to lose themselves in their orgiastic sex, and Saffie noticed that Nikos managed to avoid any possible homosexual involvement despite Constantine's machinations. Throughout the session, they engaged in some kind of sex with whomsoever they encountered. It was liberating and, Saffie thought, good fun.

Six

The voyage to Crete was to be a respite. Nikos was cloistered away for most of the time in his cabin, writing on his word processor. Saffie and Rachel took the opportunity to spend some time together, and so sat chatting on deck. Georgiou played cards (cheating outrageously) with Andy and Jaspar. Mike and Carrie worked on the film-tape, while Eleni introduced Nicola and Lyndsay to the delights of lesbian love. Yiannis steered the yacht. He smiled at Saffie when she went to see him. He had even dressed up in one of Constantine's white 'Captain's' uniforms, complete with peaked cap. He looked very endearing.

'Where is Constantine?' asked Saffie.

'Filming the girls?' Yiannis slid her a sideways glance and grinned.

Part of the yacht had been prepared for some filming later, somehow contriving to resemble, or suggest, an ancient craft. Saffie imagined the clever artwork which would be required to convince. She marvelled at the lengths Constantine was going to to prepare what was after all, to be fundamentally a sex film. She had been glad of a little break as her body ached, her thighs and sex sore after their wild night of communal sex. However, she had soon recovered and now thought how pleasant it would be to make love to Yiannis. As if reading her mind, Yiannis looked thoughtfully at her.

'It's Georgiou's turn to take command,' he said.

'I'll go and find him,' Saffie laughed.

Georgiou was reluctant to leave his game of poker. In fact, Saffie thought, he was probably trying to convince the other men to change to 'strip poker'. He was persuaded to take over manning the yacht only with the inducement of wearing one of Constantine's uniforms.

'This is Nikos' cabin,' Saffie said, mystified, as they stopped.

'Yes.'

'He won't want us to disturb him from his writing.'

'He's expecting us,' Yiannis looked at her with a twinkle in his warm eyes.

Saffie's stomach lurched, her body flooded instantly with increased sexual receptivity. Yiannis drew her against his body and kissed her. Then, he turned the handle of Nikos' cabin and pushed it open. Nikos was not sitting at the table, as Saffie had expected. He was lying, naked and languid on his bed under the port-hole. Saffie was moved by the vulnerability of his posture, and captured by his absolute beauty. She breathed in the essence of spilled semen in the air, and wondered whether Nikos had been masturbating, and had brought himself off, in order now to appear semi-flaccid.

His lovely cock lay against his thigh. She looked, in question at Yiannis, who smiled. Already, he appeared more sensual, his pupils dilated, his eyelids hooded, his passionate lips fuller. Saffie felt a surge of sexuality shoot up her vagina. Sex with these two infinitely desirable men would be close to paradise! She didn't care about their motives, or that they had obviously planned this and taken her co-operation for granted. Yiannis took off his hat and jacket. Saffie wanted to go to Nikos and take his generous organ into her mouth. Her vagina secreted hot fluid at the prospect of this being so easily achievable. She knew that he would like it, and that he would respond. There would be added frisson too, with Yiannis watching. However, though it was difficult, she decided to remain passive, to see what they had devised. With a sexual pang, she recalled the film Constantine had showed her, of Eleni with Yiannis and Georgiou. Eleni as a captured slave-girl, prey to Nikos' whims as the other men did what they pleased to her.

'Will you help me to turn him on?' Yiannis said urgently into her ear.

Saffie was suffuse with sexual anticipation. Nikos turned his head languidly to look at them through his drooping eyes. Saffie wanted to kiss his full lips. Yiannis stood behind her and pulled her hard against him, so that her bottom was against the rock-hard of his cock. She wondered whether it was Nikos or she who had aroused him. She felt the violence in him, and a tremor of fear spiced her arousal. She saw that Nikos' eyes met Yiannis'.

Yiannis pressed firmly at her breasts and then hard at her crotch, sending a spasm of awareness through her groins as he hit on her clitoris.

Saffie was hot and wet, and needed one of them to fuck her now. She saw Nikos recognise her readiness. He held out his hand to her, but Yiannis pulled her away and shook his head at Nikos. Saffie watched as Nikos' prick filled. His hand went to it.

'Niko!' Yiannis shouted in a tone that made Saffie jump and Nikos respond. He moved his hand away from his penis reluctantly.

Yiannis began to strip Saffie's clothes from her. She was naked against his uniform as he manipulated her roughly. He squeezed her breasts and shot his fingers fiercely up her. Nikos' eyes were full of longing. Yiannis undressed quickly.

'Keep him hot for me, Saffie . . .' he said, biting and sucking at her neck. 'No, don't touch him – touch yourself . . .'

Obediently, Saffie felt at her breasts and sex, all the more aroused for being denied. Her vagina burned in desperate longing. With a gasp, she felt Yiannis' extended cock nudging at her anus. A thrill of excitement impaled her as he pushed. He caressed her breasts painfully, and smirked at Nikos. He lowered his cock, so that it jutted between her clammy thighs, and Nikos could see the end of it. He saw the glistening hole amongst the taut purple. Saffie began to slide along it, her eyes closing in pleasure.

Suddenly, Yiannis forced his prick into her vagina. Saffie opened her eyes wide to Nikos. He saw that they were flooded with lust. Yiannis withdrew, and Saffie was filled with violent rage. Nikos saw the anger in her green eyes. Yiannis went to Nikos.

'See how much she needs it, Niko . . . It's up to you!'

Saffie frowned. She was in a sexual haze and somewhat bewildered.

Nikos bit his lower lip and nodded. Yiannis smiled in triumph to Saffie, and urged Nikos over. Saffie's heart beat rapidly in sadistic anticipation. She fingered her clitoris and breasts as Yiannis plastered his greedy cock with oil, and then tipped it liberally over Nikos' abdomen. He inserted fingers, coated with the lubrication, very deeply into his forbidden hole. Saffie watched as Nikos closed his eyes. His lips stretched sideways in protest against this act. Yiannis sat astride Nikos and trailed his cock teasingly over Nikos' crack, holding the end tightly and rubbing it, with obvious enjoyment, on his ring.

Saffie knew how much Yiannis wanted this. She realised that his mixture of light-heartedness and bossiness belied his acute desire for Nikos.

She thought that Nikos wanted to throw him off. But when Yiannis raised himself to position his prick, and thrust it slowly into Nikos, she was moved by the dark pleasure in his eyes. Saffie continued to touch herself piquantly as Yiannis began to fuck Nikos. The pain ripped through Nikos like fire, igniting his entire body in a mixture of extreme violence and decadent joy.

Saffie smiled sleazily at Yiannis' bliss as he took Nikos slowly. He felt his prick nursed and rocked in Nikos' intimate place. Wave after wave of joy coursed through him, in growing frequency. He concentrated on his prick moving deeply within that treasured place, gripped tightly by Nikos. He lost control and began to screw him wildly, holding him down strongly, groaning and grunting, working his own pleasure to a magnificent crescendo. He held himself still and cried out in ecstasy as he ejaculated into Nikos. Saffie wondered just how many years Yiannis had waited for that. He fell away from Nikos, smiling and satiated. Drunk with joy.

To Saffie's surprise, Nikos suddenly rose, furious and still erect. He pulled the belt from Yiannis' trousers and turned back to whack it down powerfully on Yiannis' buttocks. Yiannis winced but remained on the narrow bed. Nikos repeated this. The belt sang as it whizzed through the air and down onto various parts of Yiannis' body. His rage showed no sign of abating. His dark hair flew with each sudden movement; his black eyes burned.

Saffie grasped his arm, preventing him from continuing, partly by surprise. He whirled round to her, with the belt raised high in his arm. She waited, excited, her flesh tingling. In a fraction of a second he seemed to Saffie to challenge her darkly. Saffie inclined her head, possessed by excitement. Nikos' moved his head in acceptance and the belt whipped through the air to impact with her buttock. The shock was electric, though Saffie was sure that Nikos had controlled the belt, taken some of the force out of its speed, and it hadn't hit her as hard as it had hit Yiannis. Still her flesh tingled and burned. After the impact however, and while he was lifting the belt to strike her again, the heat was dynamic, spreading through her body and making her flesh tingle.

Saffie's sex burned at the fire in his wild eyes. Once more he struck her reddened bottom. Then he began to trail the belt over her breasts, flicking at her nipples, and dragging it between her dripping vulva. Saffie held her head back proudly, trying not to let him see the effect he had on her.

She knew that Yiannis watched from the bed, and would intervene if Nikos should lose control. She kept Nikos' haughty gaze challengingly, letting him see, by a flicker of her eyes, that she was aware of his powerful arousal. Nikos dropped the belt, pushed her to the floor and rammed his erect cock deeply into her. Saffie felt her randy sex begin to throb in climax immediately. With immense control, Nikos raised himself high and jerked back into her very powerfully, several times.

Then he clung to her as their bodies writhed together, out of control, sweating and slamming. They were most aware of the place where their bodies met and joined, feeling the intense shared enjoyment their pressure and jerking gave them.

Yiannis watched, his cock re-erect as he saw them through narrowed eyes. Their primaeval lust touched something deep within him as they rolled around the cabin floor, grunting and straining. Then Nikos held Saffie down forcefully by her arms and proceeded once more to raise himself high, and then ram himself hard into her. Saffie's legs were spread wide to accommodate him.

Yiannis watched in agony as Nikos' arse went up and down. His prick stiffened unbearably: he needed release. His balls tightened. He met Saffie's eyes, and looked at her shaking breasts. Unable to contain himself, he knelt beside them and began to knead Saffie's breast. He kissed her, and then pushed Nikos from her. Taken completely by surprise, Nikos fell back, catching a glimpse of Saffie's open sex just before Yiannis rammed his own stiff purple rod into her.

Yiannis sighed with relief. Saffie smiled at him, and kissed him as he moved slowly along her tight muscle, which gripped him powerfully as he glided. This could be fun, she thought wildly to herself, thinking that this was what they had planned. She could be in for a long, enjoyable session if they took turns!

She was a bit fed up when Yiannis was pulled from her, as Nikos fought to regain his former position. However, her disappointment was alleviated as she watched the naked men begin to wrestle and fight, rolling around on the tilting floor, each gaining dominance in turn. This was fascinating, thought Saffie, idly fingering herself as she saw the mens' sweating, glistening bodies cling together in their fight. They were very close, and, Saffie saw, they had by no means lost their erections as their fit bodies pressed against each other.

Yiannis seemed determined to regain Saffie, or at least beat Nikos to her. Saffie swung her legs far apart, her knees reaching the floor as she reminded them (as if they needed reminding) of her delights. Yiannis was under Nikos. He smiled across to Saffie. Saffie returned this; Yiannis was obviously enjoying himself immensely. She began not to worry so much at present about one of them screwing her, and soon. After all, she knew she could not go short of sex for long. She immersed herself in enjoying them, and wondering at the enigmatic Nikos.

Yiannis made a move to squirm out from under Nikos' body towards Saffie, eyeing her ready sex with pleasure. But without warning, Nikos suddenly took Yiannis' head between his palms and kissed him deeply. Saffie watched as Yiannis responded to Nikos, embracing him and caressing his back, running his palms over his buttocks, pressing Nikos' crotch hard against his.

Yiannis was undulating his lithe body, rubbing his hot, glistening muscle against Nikos'. Saffie rubbed at her clitoris, excitement welling as she saw the mens' cocks together, pressed close. For a glorious moment, Nikos gave in, raised himself onto his hands, raised his abdomen high into the air and then descended and pressed his prick against Yiannis' over and over, moaning and straining, his eyes keeping Yiannis'. Saffie smiled at Yiannis. Nikos moved away and Yiannis went to Saffie and inserted his longing prick deeply into her.

Nikos saw that Saffie responded passionately, her waiting at its limit of endurance. Nikos watched Yiannis' powerful abdomen moving up and down between Saffie's legs. His penis pulsed, needing to be where Yiannis was. He throbbed as he saw the muscular buttocks clench and unclench spasmodically. He saw the dark, hairy crack, and closed his eyes as he thought of his tight red ring. His head swam. Yiannis met his eyes and urged Saffie on to her side.

Nikos lay behind him, and put his arm round his waist. He bit painfully at Yiannis' shoulder, and then took the head of his prick in his hand and rammed it into Yiannis' slowly yielding ring. Yiannis thrilled, his happiness transmitting to Saffie as his prick stiffened even further, and he moved more rapidly along her gripping muscle. Saffie smiled at Nikos, whom she felt looked as though he would come to bugger her instead of Yiannis.

'No . . .' she mouthed silently: don't spoil his pleasure.

Nikos closed his eyes and held Yiannis tightly by the waist and then let himself go, pumping hard into his arse, as if intent on punishing his friend for this forbidden pleasure. His prick was gripped very tightly by Yiannis' anus. Saffie and Yiannis held each other close against Nikos' increased rate. Saffie delighted as Nikos' thrusts echoed through to her, and she determined that next, these two potent men could both fuck her. They all strained together, in accord, writhing and jerking, increasing their mutual enjoyment. Yiannis smiled into Saffie's eyes as Nikos came dramatically, swearing and cursing loudly in Greek. Yiannis felt his cock contract and throb within him. Pure, unadulterated joy filtered through Yiannis. And a tremendous peace. Saffie was aware that Nikos' orgasm was making Yiannis reach his. She hugged him close as they cleaved together, working towards their inevitable shared orgasm.

Nikos smiled ruefully at Yiannis.

Constantine had borrowed an authentic-looking 'ancient' boat from a Cretan friend who was an historian, and also specialised in such reconstruction. They were once more clad in their classical Grecian garb, including short cloaks (or chlamyses for the men, and peploses for the women), and longer ones, himations, which they wrapped around them 'against the voyage'. They were given instructions on how to react to each other, in order to portray the particular phase of their supposed stormy relationships. So Yiannis had to be fawning towards Nikos, which he did with sardonic humour, especially considering his recent conquest. Nikos was suitably distant and disdainful. Saffie thought of the sexual congress she had witnessed between them. She wondered how far Constantine was aware of this. He did appear to watch them with some speculative interest. Rachel and Georgiou were to be in amatory mood and had to be almost copulating at every take. Saffie was at present dismissed by Nikos, and seen to be suffering, at times hysterically. Eleni offered herself freely and light-heartedly to everyone.

They filmed a snatch of the supposed sea-voyage, and of them disembarking at Heraklion. A few takes were made of their various conversations, as actors, and also of them discussing their next play, which was based on the story of 'Theseus and the Minotaur'. Yiannis was to be the Athenian King, Theseus, taking the annual sacrificial victims to placate the Minotaur, Georgiou, who was half-bull and half-man. They were to be depicted as bull-baiters and dancers. Acrobats on bull-back really, though as Eleni was the only one who could even pretend to such skills, this was to be cleverly filmed, with Mike enhancing the movements, using computer graphics. However, they were given some complex, semi-acrobatic steps to learn, and were to convey an atmosphere of threat. It was to be a fairly short sequence, merely to explain the story of Theseus, and Ariadne (Saffie) who fell in love with Theseus, and helped him to escape, only to be later abandoned by him on Naxos. After filming the 'actors' around the site of Knossos, the main action – of them dancing and performing for the Minotaur – was to be recorded in a studio in Heraklion, which Constantine had booked through a friend who was also in the business. The Minotaur was to be portrayed as a man-bull at times, but this was more symbolic than real, and he was to emerge amongst the dancers to participate in their sexual games as a highly-sexed male human. Andy, Jaspar, Lyndsay and Carrie were to participate as dancers and performers. This added interest and complexity to their encounters.

There were no other visitors at the re-built site of Knossos. The actors were filmed wandering around the site, discussing with fear their impending confrontation with the Minotaur. Eleni told them that she had learnt that he has a huge sexual hunger, and that this knowledge could help in their release. Yiannis and Nikos had to stage a passionate argument, and Georgiou and Rachel had to make love, 'hidden' in the undergrowth at the base of the ruins.

Saffie recalled her first visit to the site. She had already been to many of the other sacred ruins of Greece, and had been surprised that Knossos had been reconstructed, and contained elements of colour. The site seemed to possess a drifting quality, by reason of the light, and the various differing heights of the re-built storeys. Saffie recalled that she had almost stepped off the upper one by mistake. There were lemon groves below, and the dense sound of cicadas filled the air.

Constantine directed them where to group or act. They were dressed as dancers – in very little – and followed Theseus (Yiannis), their king, who planned to save them from the Minotaur, who was lonely and frustrated in his unnatural shape. Constantine had some novel ideas on interpreting the legend. Their actions on-site, and to some extent in the studio, were sometimes to be symbolic as he had explained before, and minimal, merely to add depth and substance to the lavish erotic scenes.

They had also learnt various scenes, the dialogue of which was provided by Constantine, which involved jealous arguments between Saffie and Yiannis over Nikos. These were fired by sessions in which Constantine goaded them; this 'play' carried over by him into real-life, for added verisimilitude. Saffie thought it interesting how affected they became by these inventions. It was as if they had been induced into another life. Eleni seemed to have fun behaving as the high-class haetara, or prostitute, she had been cast as, and complied by making advances towards everyone. Naturally, everyone – including the film crew – responded positively. Saffie smiled to think that there must be far too much footage of Eleni fucking them all.

Nikos' smouldering rage increased as did Constantine's hold over them. As time went on, and with physical journeys as well as imaginative ones, they seemed more and more drawn into Constantine's unreal world, where anything was possible. Sometimes, Saffie was shocked by the intensity of Nikos' hateful looks towards Constantine. He for one was certainly not enveloped entirely by excitement.

They spent the day on the site of the Minoan palace site of Knossos. They were enchanted with the frescoes, especially with the 'Prince of Lilies'. After dinner, they began to rehearse the scenes where Theseus and his dancers performed for the Minotaur. Georgiou enjoyed his costume, which was minimal, but endowed him with a large phallus. From deep in his labyrinth, he was to watch the sensuous erotic-dancers, becoming more and more restless in his prison. Ariadne (Saffie), King Minos' daughter, was to show Theseus (Yiannis) the way to the centre of the labyrinth. However, instead of destroying the creature, Theseus was to be struck by his now human attractiveness, as well as the size of his phallus, and be tricked into releasing him. Georgiou was then to fling himself discordantly into the centre of their wild dances and whip them into sexual frenzy.

These scenes were to be silent and exaggeratedly acted for dramatic effect. There was to be strange, evocative music depicting deep tunnels, the cry of a trapped monster-human, and sexual longing. Saffie thought that it would be interesting to make a full-length film along these lines. She was quite impressed by the studio-set, which was to be enhanced by Mike's clever lighting of crimson, deep blue and green.

As Nikos was to be Dionysus, who rescued the abandoned Ariadne (Saffie) on Naxos, and as images of the dancers could be later technically multiplied, he did not take part in the film sequences at the Herakleon studio. He stood apart, smoking and watching as the dancers leapt in and out of the flashing lights, and the sound of the trapped Minotaur roared. The dancers' costumes were scanty; flimsy streams of silk or diaphanous tunics, and the dancers were lithe and fit as they fulfilled Constantine's scenario. Yiannis was particularly good as the Athenian King. Nikos watched him with affection.

Saffie was ready to go on, as Ariadne, but first Yiannis-Theseus was to attempt to penetrate the labyrinth alone.

'It *is* good, isn't it?' she asked Nikos as she went to stand beside him.

'It's okay,' he said grudgingly, shrugging carelessly.

'I think it's an imaginative interpretation.'

'Hmmm . . .'

Their dances were to wild, discordant music, intended to

arouse them, especially with the 'accidental' sexual touches. They turned somersaults, and balanced along 'bull-shapes'. They appeared to beckon to and goad the bull-king. Yiannis followed the noise of the Minotaur, but could not reach it. Saffie went to help him. She was moved by their liberated dancing as she went through them. By now, they were high on the dance and their fleeting touches were charged with sexuality. Increasingly, they lingered, drawn to each other in intimate embraces.

Ariadne-Saffie took Theseus-Yiannis by the hand and kissed him. She was helping him because she found him so physically attractive. Yiannis responded hotly and then allowed Saffie to race with him through the labyrinth of lights and strings until they reached the Minotaur – Georgiou. He was chained to a post and was pulling wildly on this. Theseus turned to Ariadne in gratitude, and she pulled him to the ground, reaching for his penis, loose under his short tunic.

Forcefully, she caressed him all over, bringing him to instant sexual arousal. Georgiou-Minotaur shook madly at his restraints as he watched them. Yiannis had been turned on by taking part in the frenzied dance with the others. As he was now touched adroitly by Saffie, his cock sprang immediately into greedy life. His balls tensed with pleasure and he was ready to screw her. He ripped off her fine gown and penetrated her immediately, demonstrating his future treatment of her by his rough selfishness. He closed his eyes in joy as he felt his prick gripped by her tight muscle; that she had not been quite ready excited him further. Saffie was soon fully aroused by his rapid fucking. Constantine was giving them directions: Yiannis was to indulge himself fully, leaving Saffie as the abandoned Ariadne.

Saffie was annoyed at this, though she knew the scene, and realised that Constantine was merely reminding them. Despite instructions, she strove to come, gliding along Yiannis' stiff cock. Yiannis felt he had to beat her to it for the sake of Art and allowed the gathered, burning fluid to rush unimpeded from his testicles and out in a joyous spurt and into Saffie, who gave a few last jerks and then subsided, managing to look despondent and trying to pull Yiannis back as he went to release the Minotaur.

The ever-libidinous Georgiou had been fully aroused within his big, artificial phallus, and so was therefore more than ready to rush amongst the dancers and incite them to sex. Ariadne watched sadly before going off-set. Yiannis followed the randy 'Minotaur', smiling inwardly at how aptly Constantine had chosen him for this part of unrestrained sexual indulgence. Georgiou grasped the near-naked Eleni and grappling at her breasts, he parted her buttocks and moved his phallus around her ripe anus. Eleni bent obligingly, and, still holding her breasts, Georgiou rammed the phallus deeply into her tight hole. He fiddled with her dangling labia as he thrust, and pressed on her jutting pink clit. Georgiou 'came' dramatically, and then moved on to Rachel, whom he penetrated vaginally.

Rachel was tremendously excited by the size of Georgiou's artificial phallus as he worked it up and down her, extending the walls of her vaginal passage. His extended pubic bone hit hard on her clitoris as he moved. He grabbed at her large breasts and squeezed them unbearably as he rammed into her. Her flesh seemed alive with spasms of sexual electricity as he jerked her high. The other dancers were fired by the 'Minotaur' and began to engage in various sexual acts.

Fretted by Theseus-Yiannis' swift penetration, Saffie watched the performers with envy, feeling herself become ever more aroused. As often, because she had had some sex, Saffie's need was even greater. She saw Eleni, buggered by Jaspar and fucked by Andy, as they supported her between them. Their agile bodies moved eagerly together. Saffie was riveted as the men handled Eleni with knowledge. She seemed able to glide along their pricks lightly. Saffie's own breasts swelled as Eleni's were caressed by Jaspar; her fanny secreted juices as she imagined the feel of being fucked both anally and vaginally. She really fancied this with Yiannis and Nikos. She looked for Yiannis, who was now being penetrated by Georgiou's phallus, whilst Rachel sucked on his own extended cock. Saffie squirmed in her seat and glanced over to where Mike and Constantine were engaged in the filming.

Suddenly, as if by magic, fulfilling her unbearable longing, her breasts were grasped and a powerful body pulled her to him. Joy coursed through her veins.

'Niko,' she whispered hoarsely as she felt his bulge nudge against her crack.

Nikos let his hands run down, over her belly to her pubis. He nibbled at her neck.

'Come on,' he said urgently, releasing his tight grip and taking her hand.

Saffie glanced across to Constantine, who appeared to notice them going, through the corner of his eye, though he was seemingly engrossed in the scene he was helping to shoot. His mouth stretched in annoyance; he could not really prevent them from leaving, thought Saffie, despite his repeated instructions for them to curb their extra-film sex. Saffie sniggered to herself as they left, suffuse with the prospect of intense sexual arousal soon to be fulfilled.

They could not make it back to the hotel, and so went through the upper floor of the studio, looking for somewhere suitable. They did not care at all that they ended up seedily in a toilet, especially as they had had to decide on somewhere quickly when they heard footsteps behind them and had no intention of letting Constantine stop them. Nikos stripped in the small space. He had never looked more alluring to Saffie as she gazed at his sensuous black eyes; his slim, brown, strong body and his luscious lips.

She knew that she must seem incredibly sleazy to him as she leant against the closed toilet door. Nikos sat on the toilet and smiled lasciviously at her, drawing her down onto his erect penis. Saffie parted her legs and sat astride him, lowering herself onto his hot rod. It went right up into her, and her muscle contracted in response. Nikos gripped her around the waist and began to urge her up and down his length. They smiled at their freedom, and kissed in relief. It was very good to be away from Constantine's intensity. Their kiss deepened, exploring the familiar heat of each others' mouths. Saffie held onto Nikos' shoulders to support her as she raised and lowered herself along his penis, her belly pushing against his. They took it very slowly. Nikos suckled at Saffie's nipples as he urged his penis deeply into her. Saffie undertook most of the movement, raising herself to the tip of Nikos' phallus, so that she almost released him. She smiled to see his apprehension, lest she did, demonstrated in his narrowed eyes, his teeth against his lower lip. She felt his relief as she descended. Gradually, their bodies straining as they concentrated on their sexual growth, they moved faster, so that eventually, they became noisy: their bodies slammed together, their guttural cries of selfish lust carried through the walls. Saffie realised that they must be audible for some distance, but she did not care. They clung together, each ripping and clawing at the other's body as they fought for their orgasm. And when they came, it was loudly, with yelling and screaming.

Saffie was not surprised to become aware of someone outside the door as she came back to earth. She looked at Nikos, whose black curls hung low with perspiration over his somnolent eyes. His tanned body shone with sweat. She kissed his softened lips and then, with difficulty, rose from him. He stood and embraced her.

Constantine looked at them both in distaste. Feigned distaste, since they looked ravishing in their post-coital state, holding on to each other and regarding him levelly. His cock reared with the prospect of willing sex with them both.

'We need Saffie for a re-take,' he told them coolly.

Saffie grinned at the thought of sex with Yiannis now.

'We just need a shower,' Nikos said with assurance.

Saffie was intrigued as Nikos cast Constantine a look which could only be described as seductive as the older man ran his gaze from his eyes to his semi-flaccid prick, smeared with spunk and Saffie's sex-juices. It suddenly seemed to Saffie that the relationship between these two powerful men was more complex than she had realised. This thought was strengthened when Nikos put his arm round her as they went towards the shower: as they walked, he turned back to smirk at Constantine.

The filming for the 'Theseus and the Minotaur' episode went well. This would be continued on Naxos, mostly on Nikos' extensive property. Saffie was looking forward to seeing his house – or, rather – villa. Yiannis had told her that it was magnificent. On Naxos, Ariadne (Saffie) would be taken up by Dionysus, the god of ecstasy. And there would be initiated the rites of Dionysus, where people, liberated and maddened by wine, indulged in wild sexual orgies. When the Maenads, frenzied women, participated, the men were torn limb from limb in sexual rage. Saffie was interested in how Constantine would stage this.

Constantine planned for them to film a few more scenes whilst

170

on Crete. First, however, he thought that they should take a break. He deemed that it would be useful for them to see a Greek play. So they went to the theatre to see Aristophanes' 'Lysistrata'. This ancient comedy concerned Greek women holding a sex strike until their menfolk made peace. It contained plenty of bawdy jokes and sexual references. After this, they had dinner in an exclusive restaurant. Saffie sat with Rachel and Yiannis, which was nice, as she had a chance to catch up with her friend's reaction to events so far. Yiannis sat back and listened as the friends chatted away. Sometimes, glass of wine in hand, he gazed over the bay, glad of the refreshing breeze. Often, he glanced across the table at Nikos, who occasionally returned his look. It was good, to have this chance to adapt to their changed relationship. He wondered how Nikos felt. At present, he had resumed his unusual closeness to Eleni, and was sitting silently by her, whilst she chatted lightly to Mike and Jaspar. Saffie talked to Yiannis about the merits of the translation of the play they had seen, and Rachel said she'd rather have gone to the cinema.

'So . . .' said Saffie, watching Yiannis' reaction, 'Constantine plans to do "Hyacinthus" here, on Crete, before we leave to go to Naxos?'

She smiled as Yiannis coloured slightly – she liked such sensitivity in a man, and there was no doubt that Yiannis was a very sensitive man. Naturally, he looked across to Nikos and met his eye. It was almost, Saffie thought, as though Nikos was aware of their topic of conversation – or, at least, of Yiannis' private thoughts. Nikos turned away as Saffie smiled. She wondered whether Constantine had informed Nikos that tomorrow, he would be Apollo, and Yiannis, as Hyacinthus, a Spartan prince, would be his beloved. The first mortal man to be loved by a god. Soon, Nikos went off for a 'walk' with Eleni.

Saffie, confident partly on account of the wine she had drunk, and enlivened by the promiscuity of 'Lysistrata', invited Yiannis to 'sleep with' her and Rachel. Rachel looked at her incredulously, but nevertheless smiled and nodded in agreement as the polite Yiannis raised a questioning eyebrow to her. As they left, Saffie noticed that Constantine was engrossed in the decadent Georgiou.

★ ★ ★

In the deserted countryside of Crete, Nikos was adorned as Apollo, with his marvellous head-dress of laurel-leaves, intertwining with his black curls; and his short white tunic, and lyre. Yiannis was the beautiful youth, Hyacinthus. Apollo had to be shot over and over until Constantine was satisfied that he looked suitably enamoured of Hyacinthus. Whilst they fabricated (symbolically), the love of the wind for Hyacinthus, with Yiannis alone on film, Nikos sat and smoked desultorily.

When his beautiful youth went to him, between filming, Nikos was superior and untouchable. Yiannis thought of his pain and hostility during their private sessions, and thought, with trepidation, how Nikos would react under such pressure. Constantine came to them, smiling.

'You look very beautiful, Niko. Yes, I like the heightened colour, the air of tension: Apollo is wild with the jealous wind – an element over which the sun god has no control. A force as powerful as he.'

Nikos sneered, only a little taken with Eleni's helpful lascivious self-caressing behind Constantine.

'Now, Niko . . .' a note of warning crept into the man's cultured tone, 'I'm sure you don't want to shoot this scene more than once. And think of Marsyas, next.'

'So, I get to flay Yiannis alive?' Nikos' tone was alarmingly cruel.

'Niko . . .' said Constantine.

'I haven't found any myth which states that Apollo fucked Hyacinthus.'

'This is a sex film we're making, Niko . . . Anyway, I feel assured that Apollo did exactly as he wanted.'

'Unlike me, then,' responded Nikos cryptically, moving away from the man.

Riled, Constantine returned to the set.

'Hyacinthus – Yianni – you come back and look sultry and appealing. Lie down, that's right, and pull up your tunic – no, better, pull it up languidly, and then, too hot, take it off and lie under the loving beams of the blazing sun. He is your god. That's right, caress yourself . . . You know he loves you, as he looks down on you. Later, we will have you, whipped up to sexual frenzy by the amorous attentions of the wind. Negative ions, is it?'

Saffie was entranced as Yiannis lay, without shame or embarrassment, and caressed his golden body tenderly, leaning back his head and receiving the burning sun. He moved his head in its light, basking in its radiance. Saffie wondered whether he was imagining the glory of this most beautiful Olympian, dappling his naked body with a million tender kisses, sweeping his golden fingers over his face. Yiannis opened his mouth, as if to receive the god's heady, powerful kiss . . .

'Good, Yianni . . .' said Constantine, pleased with his performance, 'now extend your fingers and stretch them up, as if trying to capture the elusive golden light, watching the strands of gold go through your fingers. Try to open your eyes in his glory. He is licking and kissing you all over. Give him your body . . . Feel his invisible kisses. You are drunk on his love.'

Saffie watched at Yiannis complied, fingering the air in graceful movements, his expression one of bewilderment as he failed to grasp the light. His thrown-back head expressed ecstasy as he gloried in the warmth and strength of the burning sun.

'Touch yourself,' urged Constantine lasciviously. 'You are imagining your unearthly lover. He is watching you. He is in his golden chariot. He wants you. He will transform into a shape you love. You have to make him do this, Yianni . . . Make him come to you . . .'

Yiannis stroked his warm skin with sensual hands, caressing his body, going slowly towards his growing member. Saffie experienced stabs of unadulterated lust as she watched, enchanted by Yiannis' performance. He was a gifted actor.

'Now! Apollo . . .' ordered Constantine, 'stand before the sun. That's right, Niko – come out of the sun. Yianni, look at him – you are blinded by the light, you cannot see this magnificent, glorious deity.'

Nikos came slowly out of the sunlight, towards Yiannis. In his hand, he held his lyre. His expression was at once powerful and infinitely lascivious. Yiannis shielded his eyes with one hand, filled with awe at the presence of his god. With the other, he touched his erect penis, which sprung into yearning life at the sight of this glorious male. More than man. God. He trembled in anticipation, he even shrank away a little. Constantine urged and praised them. Apollo stood, dazzling, before Hyacinthus, surveying with wanton eyes this beautiful desirable human. He was possessed by his own glamour. He knelt beside the youth, placing his lyre by him. Evocative music would spring from it. Yiannis' body writhed in anticipation of Apollo's touch. He was beloved of the god.

Apollo turned his beautiful head to look at his captive. He lay beside him and kissed him. Yiannis fought hard to remain passive as instructed. Nikos was slow. Yiannis felt crazed. Nikos began to move his hands languidly over Yiannis, trailing his fingers tanta-lisingly around his straining cock. There was a glint of sadism in his dark eyes as he looked at Yiannis'.

'Fuck me, you bastard,' Yiannis hissed very quietly through clenched teeth.

For too long, Nikos remained looking at him, whilst through Yiannis' mind raced all the times his friend had driven him wild with withheld sex. Just when Yiannis had decided that he himself would screw Nikos, Nikos turned him over roughly, straddled him and forced his cock into Yiannis' hole. Nikos screwed Yiannis with truly god-like solipsism, doing exactly as he wished as he fucked wildly. Saffie saw Constantine smiling and nodding as everything was captured on film. Now Apollo had to take Hyacin-thus in his arms as the boy slept, satiated and happy. The sky would go dark, the west wind would whip up until it tore at them wildly, envious that the god had had Hyacinthus.

Then, lulled by stillness, Apollo would teach Hyacinthus the discus. He stood very close to the naked youth, his body against his, making him bend and stretch his arm, bend and stretch repeatedly, holding the disc. Their legs touched closely, Hyacin-thus' abdomen against Apollo's crotch. They repeated these graceful, practice movements, again and again, bending together, and stretching and leaning. Then, satisfied with the boy's progress, Apollo stepped away to watch. Hyacinthus released the disc. Here the jealous wind would take it and hurl it back at Hyacinthus, striking his head and mortally wounding him. This would be fabricated later on film.

Andy threw a rubber discus accurately towards Yiannis, whose head it hit. Yiannis fell. Carrie, who had been standing by, applied copious 'blood' to Hyacinthus' head. Apollo came to him in grief. They would later 'melt' his body, and fade it until nothing but the first purple hyacinth remained. So now Apollo stooped to caress

174

the hyacinth tenderly, to touch his mouth and transplant a kiss. Then, slowly, he retrieved his lyre, stood and walked gracefully away into the sun. Everyone clapped and cheered. Yiannis wiped the 'blood' from his head and smiled. Constantine went to Nikos.

'So you really did it,' he said, feeling his flaccid penis under his short tunic.

Nikos moved to strike him, his eyes blazing. Constantine prevented him.

'Do not try me, Niko. I am a very strong man.'

They remained locked for seconds, then Constantine added,

'There will be a real test for you later, hey?' He snarled in laughter.

Nikos walked off. Saffie watched him go, and then looked towards Yiannis who was happy and laughing.

Nikos was able to get rid of some of his rage when they shot the episode of Apollo and Marsyas. This showed the more sadistic side of the god of music. Yiannis as Marsyas challenged Apollo-Nikos to a musical contest. A suitable soundtrack, depicting Marsyas' skill on the flute and Apollo's on the lyre was to be added later. Apollo was envious of Marsyas' expertise and stripped him and tied him to a tree. Yiannis struggled but was weak against the strength of the god. He supplicated to Apollo, but the god was riled and immovable. Saffie wondered whether he imagined himself as Constantine, or at least derived his anger from him.

She saw that in reality, Yiannis yielded to Nikos' power. As soon as Nikos had begun to strip him, he had an erection. She saw Nikos glance at it in disdain. He began to whip Yiannis with such venom that Saffie feared that he really would flay him. Yiannis winced as Nikos lashed wildly at him. He saw the dark passion in his friend's eyes. He felt the pain as the whip ate into his tender flesh. Saffie looked in concern at Constantine, but the man's eyes were filled with sadistic pleasure. He would not stop Nikos.

'Cut,' said Mike, going to Nikos. 'Cool it man. You don't actually have to take his skin off . . . Temper it, concentrate on his prick, make him come – shouldn't be too difficult . . .' he winked at Yiannis. 'You don't actually have to act out the myths, Niko . . .'

Mike squeezed Nikos' shoulder. Obligingly, perhaps brought to a sense of reality, Nikos kept his strokes under control. It didn't take too long, now that Yiannis was assured Nikos didn't actually intend to kill him, for him to make Yiannis ejaculate dramatically. Saffie watched in pleasure as Yiannis' body contorted in ecstasy. Nikos dropped the whip and went off, avoiding Constantine.

Seven

Nikos' property on Naxos was based around an immense classical villa, built by his grandfather, Stavros Mandreas, some years ago. All ground floor rooms had access to the central courtyard which had a fountain and ornamental pool in the middle. There was a colonnaded walk surrounding the open space, so that the inner rooms were cool, with their marble floors and light furniture. Saffie was struck by Nikos' collections of paintings and antiques as she wandered around his house. She gasped silently as she entered the comprehensive library.

There was a huge mahogany desk in the centre. Drawn, Saffie traced her finger across its surface, imagining Nikos, lost to the world as he spun his fantasies. Nikos stood at his door, regarding her in silence. Slowly, she realised his presence, and turned to smile in appreciation. Nikos' answering smile was almost shy.

'I hope you don't mind, Niko?' she asked, 'It's such a wonderful room.'

Nikos activated his CD player, and Debussy's 'L'Après Midi d'un Faun' filled the air softly.

'I am very fond of it,' said Nikos sadly.

'Oh, Niko – you don't really believe that Constantine would show the pictures to your grandfather now?'

'I do not trust the man. I think that he may – in the future – even if I comply with all,' he scoffed, 'his increasing demands. Things have become more complex. He has even more to threaten me with now.'

'But, surely, he has promised? Did you not sign something? Yiannis mentioned . . .'

'You have seen what he is like. Even if this film is completed – and

177

a success – particularly if it *is* a success – he will soon have new ideas.'

'But, you will do all he requests?'

Niko looked uncomfortable, and shrugged with feigned carelessness.

'The "crunch" is near, hey? I think he has further designs than the film now, Saffie.'

Saffie had to agree, recalling Constantine's behaviour towards Nikos.

'So I have to be a high-class whore, Saffie, just to keep that which is already mine.'

He turned away. Saffie went to him and he turned into her embrace. His kiss was sweet and tender, seeming to derive from the integral Niko, here in his own home.

'I have written all my books here.'

'Even if your grandfather found out—'

'Make no mistake, Saffie, he would disinherit me.'

'Ttttt . . .'

Saffie hugged him.

'It's not so bad, Niko, making the film.'

'I hate him, Saffie . . .' Nikos said vehemently.

Saffie could feel animosity surge through his body. She pulled him closer, fired by his contained violent energy. She felt his erection pushing eagerly against her clitoris. She received his tongue hungrily into her hot mouth, sucking hard on it. She felt his hands rippling down her body and pressing on her buttocks. Her breasts were charged with feeling, needing his touch to appease. He obliged, getting his hand inside her dress and fondling her swelling breasts urgently. She wanted him, now. Her natural chemistry for him was increased by the ambience of his personal life.

Nikos released her, tried to release her, still kissing, taking her by the hand as he went to lock his door, draw down his blind. Debussy's seductive music played on. He drew her to his desk, cleared it with one fell swoop of his arm and lifted her on to it. He tore back her clothes, revealing her heaving bosom. For a moment, he stopped and held her eyes in dark intelligence. They smiled at each other slowly, in affection and overwhelming desire.

Then Nikos began a slow worship of her body, attending to her as though she was new, a tender virgin, and he an experienced lover. He made her wait, thus increasing her enjoyment. He encircled her aureolae with gentle fingers, kissing her neck and sucking at her ear-lobe, not allowing her eager fingers to touch him. Keeping her hands on the table. Saffie gave in, giving herself up to his generous pleasuring of her expectant body.

Nikos lapped at her breasts, seizing her nipples between his sharp teeth. He played on her flesh with tiny circles of rippling pleasure. He licked her, going down until he reached her clitoris, which he nibbled teasingly at. He placed his hand sideways between her thighs. Saffie could not help but writhe in pleasure as he awakened her deeply. She was aware of the hard leather of his desk under her. Here, where he spent his most enjoyable hours. Where he was most himself. Independent and strong. This knowledge added depth. She felt the hot flush of juices gather and flow. Nikos parted her legs and licked at the silvered liquid from the crimson depths.

He turned her over and parted her buttocks. He fingered at her sphincter. Very slowly, he inserted his index finger, making her strong muscle expand gradually.

Saffie pressed down on the hard surface with her sex and breasts. She raised her abdomen high and then slapped her fanny down. She knew that she could come like this if he allowed her. But he turned her over. She felt at his hard bulge, running her fingers along its shape under his jeans. Nikos smiled, and began to unbutton all the tiny silver buttons with difficulty. Then he pulled her along to the end of his desk, lifted her legs and enjoyed her look of rapture as he pulled out his prick. For a moment, he teased her, pulling strongly on himself, and then he penetrated her ready shaft.

He worked along her muscle, her vagina gripped him in reflex tightening as he pumped in and out. Saffie smiled gloriously at his expression of intense enjoyment, as Nikos threw back his dark head. His hands gripped her working buttocks with strength as he fucked her. He jerked her body powerfully, sending myriad spasms up through her vagina and womb, and thence to all of her body. She was bewitched by him as he strained to orgasm. When he came, pumping his seed forth, he cried out loudly in abandon, shuddering dramatically. Saffie experienced her own sweet orgasm as he finished. She felt its glow spread like golden heat through her body. Nikos released her and came and lifted her into his arms, kissing her and murmuring endearments. Now he was soft and pliable, warm and tender. She returned his kisses, filled with gratitude and tenderness, and a sense of glory that she had given him so much joy. They clung together, spent and satisfied.

'Let's go for a ride,' he said suddenly to her, dressing rapidly and urging her to do the same.

Saffie felt hysterical amusement as they stole out of the house before Constantine could accost them. They ran, laughing and liberated, across to the stables. Nikos showed her his horses with pride. He offered her his grey mare, Artemis, whilst he had the big black one, Astarte. With a sense of holiday, they galloped across his land.

Constantine had several ventures planned for Naxos. They would first complete the Theseus story, with Dionysus (Nikos) introducing Ariadne and the other women to his sacred, mainly sexual rites. He had also devised a scene with Saffie as the lesbian poet Sappho with her lovers and admirers. Nikos had to be Narcissus, and indulge in a frenzy of self-pleasuring.

After an evening of luxuriating in the relaxing surroundings of Nikos' lovely villa, and swimming in his pool, they got back to work on the film. Nikos had to be dragged from his library, where he had retreated to escape temporarily in his writing. Saffie saw that, albeit brief, this respite had given him strength. She herself understood this, though it was relatively simple for her, in comparison, to hide herself in sketches without appearing unsociable. Writing required complete withdrawal. People weren't even aware when she had gone from their attention when she began to draw.

Nikos' private land was extensive, as Saffie and Rachel had first discovered on an early-morning walk with Eleni, and Saffie, later, riding with Nikos. It contained all the landscape necessary for Constantine's filming. This included a large vineyard, adjacent to wilder, uncultivated land, suitable for the scenes with the god of the grape. Also close were low hills on which the Maenads could capture their male prey.

The following morning they all ate breakfast together in Nikos' dining-room, and Constantine gave them details on the day's filming before they went to dress and make up. The first scene – very simple for those involved – was Dionysus' (Nikos') seduction of the distraught Ariadne (Saffie), who had been abandoned by her lover, Theseus.

Constantine decided that Nikos, as the wine god Dionysus, would wear a leopard skin to denote his mythical connection with the beast. Theseus had gone. Ariadne/Saffie looked up from her prostrate weeping. Through her veil of tears came the shimmering inchoate image of a wondrous being. Around his sable curls, Nikos was wearing an intricate wreath of grapes and vine leaves. He walked stealthily towards her, clad in his leopard skin and with a short red chlamys hanging from his shoulder. In one hand he carried a jug of wine and in the other a bunch of grapes. At the sight of him, Ariadne/Saffie turned over from her grieving, recumbent position to an open one of welcome for this potent god. Instinctively, her legs opened invitingly, revealing, through her diaphanous robe, her naked sex. She massaged her thrusting breasts engagingly, and inserted a finger into her parted mouth. Her whole posture invited the wicked god in.

'He doesn't exactly have to seduce her,' laughed Mike.

'This is okay. Let their natural dynamics work,' Constantine replied, watching the lascivious Dionysus creep closer to Ariadne.

'What the hell? You can always re-take?' quipped Mike.

'Right,' agreed Constantine, knowing that Nikos, as Dionysus, was fully aroused by Saffie. The dynamism between these two was a bonus for his venture. He eyed Nikos' obvious erection as it lifted the soft skin.

Dionysus raised the jug drunkenly and poured the liquid lavishly into his mouth. It was delicious and potent, some of his best wine. He squashed some of the ripe grapes to his reddened mouth. He stood and looked down on Ariadne who lay, languid and unmoving, though he was aware of the yearning of her breasts and the thrust of her erect nipples beneath the transparent robe. He saw the sex in her green eyes. His seductive gaze travelled down to her crimson sex. He was fired by lust, dizzied with the need for her.

'Tear off her robe and pour the wine over her,' Mike called, realising that Nikos was just about to fuck her.

Nikos smiled and knelt beside Saffie. He cupped her elfin face tenderly and looked into her eyes. She smiled. Nikos/Dionysus then brought the grapes to her mouth and crushed them against her lips. The juice ran freely. It was delicious. Saffie opened her mouth to drink it in. She wanted Nikos to kiss her. So powerful was this silent command that Nikos complied, kissing the grapes and her mouth. She put her arms around his neck. Nikos moved away with difficulty. All he wanted was to make love to her.

He sat back on his heels, and drank more of his potent wine. Saffie was as intoxicating to him. He looked over her body, wondering at its tantalising light covering. Then, he placed his palm on her breast and ran it over her body. Ripples of acute desire followed in its wake. Saffie began to writhe gently under his soft touch. She basked in his sensuality as she watched his lovely face, made more romantic with its fantastical crown. Dionysus drank again, and then tore back the delicate robe to reveal her writhing body. His dark eyes dilated in pleasure. Ariadne-Saffie reached out to touch his erect phallus.

Dionysus rose and poured the remains of the wine all over her. Then he knelt and began to lick it off greedily, at the same time driving the lonely Ariadne crazy as she felt his tongue lap her roughly. Saffie delighted in his licking, especially as he reached her breasts and seized on them with his mouth, sucking strongly. Soon, he moved to her crotch, burying his dark head between her open legs, teasing at her inviting sex hungrily. Saffie bucked her body wildly.

Dionysus stood and took more wine, drinking and feeding it to Saffie. With passionate kisses, they exchanged the warmed wine in their mouths. Then Dionysus released his leopard-skin and revealed his standing phallus to the delighted Ariadne. He poured wine over his own body, challenging the woman as he lavished it on his prick. He emptied the flask over her sex and then lay upside down on her so that, whilst he began to mouth at her vulva, she was able to take his cock into her mouth.

The camera savoured this for a time as their bodies writhed together in mutual enjoyment. Saffie exulted as Nikos' tongue entered her hole, and his lips sought sweetness in her labia. She moved her mouth along his full prick, and fingered at his abdomen and balls. She delighted as he, in turn, felt at her breasts and bottom. They were lost to the camera, locked tightly in a private world.

'Fuck her, Dionysus!' Mike directed.

It took time for his words to penetrate Nikos' sensual haze. When they did, he rose obediently. Mike smiled at his drunken posture, while Constantine marvelled at his still glorious erection, now slaked with Saffie's saliva. His own prick reared greedily. Dionysus was more drunk on Saffie's sex-juice than on his vintage wine. Holding on to his crazy head-gear unnecessarily, Dionysus re-positioned himself to enter Ariadne's lifted vagina.

He thrust with gusto, pretending to be lost in inebriation. Saffie cried out in elation as he slid familiarly into her. Mike lit a cigarette and let the film roll, trained on them as they made love gloriously. He knew that Constantine was erect, as usual. He stole a look at his face, seeing that the man watched Nikos' pumping arse through narrowed eyes, his thinned mouth peevish. Ah, well, Mike thought, never a dull moment when working with this lot. He took a few drags and adjusted the lens. He looked forward to his own private filming soon.

They screwed for far longer than was necessary for the drunken god, relishing their practised ability to extend their enjoyment.

'Oh, come on, I'm going to run out of film!' shouted Mike in pretended exasperation, though really to hide his own arousal. 'Make it good.'

The lovers increased their pace frantically, becoming out of control in their need to peak. Constantine felt that his constrained prick would burst as he was riveted to them, kissing and fondling intimately, slamming harder and harder, emitting sexual noises as they neared their release. The god's rapidly penetrating prick seemed to be made of steel as he fucked her. Her body sparked with fire from it. Her burning clitoris welcomed his expert thrusts as he descended repeatedly on her. She felt her massive orgasm gathering, taking over her entire body. Nikos slid along her with ease, light and agile.

'Now!' Saffie whispered to him.

With a few more hard spasmodic jerks, Nikos emptied his sack. The madness of Dionysus was in her veins. Nikos was filled with euphoria as he ejaculated. Saffie let go. Her entire body was shaken with a thousand spasms as his glory filled her. Nikos smiled at her, and she kissed the mad god passionately.

'I think the one take will do,' said Mike complacently.

'Mmmm . . .' said Constantine sourly.

'See you back here after lunch.'

'Right. Thank you, Mike.'

Mike wrapped up his equipment and wondered how the randy director was going to slake his need before being exposed to more of his little Greek god. He put his thumb up to Nikos, who was dressing. At least he was being co-operative this time.

Yiannis and Rachel had prepared a magnificent picnic to which they now all adjourned. Georgiou and Eleni were making love not too discreetly in the woods close by. Constantine came to remind them of the scenes they were to film next, concerning their on-going 'actor' roles. Mike thought that Constantine was annoyed with Georgiou as he could have had him himself. He smiled as he saw Constantine visibly considering Yiannis or Rachel, but they were preoccupied with the food. He almost pitied the man as Nikos came to join them. He was flushed with the aftermath of sex.

'Jaspar is in the studio,' Mike told Constantine succinctly.

Constantine met his eyes briefly and gave a barely perceptible nod as he went towards the house.

Jaspar looked up as the door opened. He had been working on editing some previous takes. Constantine leant against the door. Jaspar quickly assessed the situation and named his price in drachma. Constantine nodded and took the notes from the leather wallet in his inside pocket. Jaspar pocketed them. Constantine locked the door, took a tube from his pocket and indicated that Jaspar should lean over the desk. Jaspar unfastened his trousers and complied. Constantine pulled them down and covered the youth's anus with KY. He then released his penis and creamed that also.

Then with selfish abandon, he buggered the young man, giving him no thought, but thinking only of Nikos. His anger caused him to smash Jaspar's prick repeatedly against the edge of the desk as he rammed forcefully into him. Jaspar held on to the edge of the table, gritted his teeth and controlled his own feelings as he consoled himself with the thought of the money he was earning.

Holding on to Jaspar only for support, Constantine sodomised him to the point of ejaculation, withdrew and left, quickly fastening his trousers. Jaspar remained, turned on and frustrated. On his return to the picnic, Constantine passed Eleni with Georgiou. He decided that he would have her or, better still, Saffie, next. He would have Nikos' little love! He decided then to change the order of filming and next do Saffie, as Sappho, indulging her female lovers.

Realising where Constantine had been, Georgiou and Eleni went up to the studio, concerned lest Constantine had hurt the young man in his rage. Jaspar was sitting, a little miserably, by the desk, not easily able to concentrate. He was attractive in a very English way, with his soft red-brown curls and grey eyes. He had a moustache and beard. His sexuality was as flexible as Georgiou's and they understood each other well. Now, Georgiou realised that, despite his acquiescence, Jaspar felt used. Eleni went and sat on his knee. He embraced her as she held and kissed him, feeling immediately at his hidden erection.

He rose in her hands, grateful for her care. Eleni sat astride his penis and undulated her vulva against him. He squeezed and kissed her breasts. Eleni rose and slipped off her pants. As she did so, Georgiou released Jaspar's penis and bent to kiss it. Eleni returned to ease it into her as she straddled him. Jaspar held onto her waist as she rose and fell on him, her tight vagina gripping his ready cock piquantly. Aroused by the selfish director, Jaspar soon reached his orgasm. He kissed Eleni gratefully as he felt her coming.

Saffie bathed in preparation for her role as the lesbian poet, Sappho. She had not expected to have to do this until the next day, but one never knew with Constantine. Carrie helped her to dress and make up, admiring her thick black hair and startling green eyes. Constantine hovered about, unusually interested in their preparations. Saffie had the distinct feeling that he intended to take a more active role than usual, and became a little uneasy.

This scene was to be filmed on the neo-classical terrace of Nikos' villa, with its marble table and scrolled benches, and its panoramic view. There was a grove of cypress trees to one side, and the walls of the terrace were covered with trailing plants.

Saffie was to sit, reading her poetry to a group of young girls – Eleni, Rachel and Lyndsay.

Whilst listening, the women were to touch each other's hair idly, looking shyly at this advocate of exclusive female love. When the time came for them to indulge, Constantine indeed took an inordinate interest in Saffie as she began to make love to Eleni. He kept stopping the filming and going over to her, telling her how to move, where to lie and what to do. Mike endured this patiently for a while, realising that Nikos was becoming angry with the older man handling Saffie so possessively.

'I really think she can make it, Constantine,' Mike told him in a strained voice.

Constantine shrugged. In fact, his constant handling and acute interest had turned Saffie on more and her scene of seduction of the supposedly innocent Eleni went very well. Since it was the libidinous Eleni herself who had introduced Saffie to the secrets of homosexual love, Saffie considered this scene to be highly ironic. Constantine watched in delight as the two highly sexed women rolled and writhed together on the stone terrace, naked under the relentless sun.

Their breasts thrust together, and their fannies kissed as they cleaved together in a deep lasting kiss. Mike had to instruct Eleni not to take the lead as she looked as though she was going to forget herself and, in her heightened need, go down on Saffie. At first, Nikos watched Constantine more than he watched the women's performance, but soon he was drawn absolutely towards Saffie and Eleni as their lithe bodies jerked rhythmically together. They were so engrossed in each other now that they seemed completely unaware of their appreciative male audience. Georgiou sat just off-film, drinking lager and shouting unnecessary advice and encouragement. Nikos leaned back and, narrowing his eyes, watched as Saffie's tight arse went up and down, her clitoris pressing against Eleni's. He knew each woman's body so intimately that he was able to imagine what each of them was feeling.

Saffie's body glowed gloriously in the hot sun as waves of electric joy passed between Eleni's sex and her own. Her thighs and groins received rapid buds of pleasure, which burst as she moved against Eleni, feeling her nipples against her own, and her soft lips as they kissed. They came gently, as directed, strangely, by Constantine. Saffie was sure that Eleni needed the comfort of a filled cock stuffed up her empty hole as much as she did. Eleni went to sit on Nikos' knee, as Saffie had to make love to Rachel now.

Nikos fingered Eleni's wet pussy as he watched the English girls making love. He knew that Eleni watched too, through lustful eyes. He felt at her breasts as Rachel and Saffie lapped at each other's quims, squirming in delight. He inserted his finger into Eleni's sopping hole as the women suckled at each other's breasts. His cock had been stiff for ages now, and it was easy to make love to Eleni. He bit urgently at her neck, rocking his prick against her thigh. Eleni smiled and nodded.

Constantine watched with a wry, self-satisfied smile as they went into the woods.

Saffie and Rachel reached their climax, and Saffie went off set with relief, looking round for Nikos, then realising that Eleni had got him first. She went to have a shower, leaving Rachel succouring to Georgiou. She was not sure where Yiannis was – perhaps he was with Nikos and Eleni? She sighed in exasperation. She badly needed a man. Still, she could save it for the impending scenes with Dionysus and utilise her energy for ripping up men – or at least pretending to.

She reached the shower and languished under it for some time, her body more needy when she stepped out.

'You were very good, Saffie . . .'

Saffie was surprised to see Constantine waiting for her. He advanced and she had to admit that her wayward body beat madly in response to this potent mysterious male. He reached out and squeezed her inviting nipple. Her vagina contracted immediately. Her blood quickened in her veins. She wanted him to kiss her, to demonstrate masculine dominance over her after forcing her to take this part with Eleni and Rachel. A flicker of a smile swept over his handsome features as he interpreted her stance.

He pushed her back on to the bed behind her and dragged the damp towel from her, though she clung to it. He pulled it out from under her buttocks across her soft, damp body. Her eyes held supplication, her feet were on the bed and she dropped her knees apart to reveal her wet, open sex to this dominant man. She just wanted a stiff prick inside her. She felt as though she had been teased to death by his control over her during the filming of the lesbian scene. Merely unzipping his flies, Constantine raised her legs, looked at her gaping hole and entered.

Nikos watched enraged as Constantine took Saffie. He ached to caress her yearning breasts, to kiss her parted mouth, to wipe away her frown of longing as Constantine merely gripped her bottom firmly and pumped into her. He did not touch nor kiss her. He grunted as he jerked into her, going deep but missing her longing clitoris in this position. He made her growl as he pressed her legs further back, and increased his rate of penetration.

Saffie felt some perverse enjoyment as his thick member slid up and down her vagina, fulfilling her need for a man. He began to press accurately and efficiently on her red bud until Saffie, who was already very ready, began to throb around him. Nikos realised that she was climaxing and made sure he could not be seen. However, as Constantine withdrew, his cock still erect and dripping, and looked round to see Nikos before putting it away, Nikos realised that the man felt he had gained some kind of triumph over him, making Saffie come without even bothering to himself.

Saffie saw Nikos' anger as he left. Constantine did not turn to look at her. Saffie sighed and went back into the shower, her vagina still throbbing from Constantine's ministrations.

To approximate the rites of Dionysus, there was to be some kind of fabricated ritual. The women – maenads – were to get intoxicated and liberated by the vine, and then run riot in the hills, capturing the men and doing as they wished. In antiquity, some thought that this involved destroying them. This fury was to be interpreted by wild, discordant music, and jagged images of what the actors actually did.

The women entered the vineyard in trepidation, looking for the wild god. Despite the cameramen, Saffie could imagine herself there, in ancient Greece, the land of culture, participating in this anarchic sacred ritual. Apollo and Dionysus – two sides of civilisation: control and chaos; culture and orgiastic indulgence. She caught sight of Nikos, again to be the god of ecstasy. His hair was wild, and ruffled, the vine-wreath tipsy on his head. He was naked except for the leopard skin, draped over his loins. His body was modelled by the shadows as he crept through the vines. Suddenly, he faced them in a clearing in front. They gasped to glimpse his gigantic phallus, poking through his skirt.

He held a wine-jar and goblet. The camera was trained on him as he poured and drank tipsily, red wine flowing from his mouth. His look at the robed women was leery and dominant. As he gestured them to him, Saffie looked at his false cock. All sensual nerves of her body soared in anticipation. For a fleeting moment, Nikos met her eyes. In this glance he seemed to be transmitting his rage at her and Constantine. Wild, unfamiliar music surrounded them. They went to him and lavishly, all the time spilling it, he drew wine into huge cups and thrust them at the women, urging them to drink. They were already drunk on his sensuality. The wine was potent and liberating, though Saffie thought that this was a medium through which to translate the dynamic effect of Nikos as the decadent god of ecstasy. Nikos played his part well. He looked wonderful, his jet curls dishevelled, his kohl-lined eyes lustful and intelligent, his demeanour suggesting intoxication, yet also expressing extreme eroticism.

He went to each woman, tilting her cup towards her, so that she imbibed more freely, tipping it down her pure white gown. At the same time, he touched each sexily, thrusting his hand masterfully between their thighs and parting their legs firmly. He thrust a finger into each willing sex, and nudged his huge phallus sharply against them. Saffie was certain from their noisy response that the other women were as aroused as she was. For her, as well as the natural fire of Nikos, there was the added piquancy of pretending that he was the wild and dangerous god who reduced all to their basic element.

Dionysus now tweaked at their breasts and began to tear their flimsy clothes from them, leering drunkenly into their faces, licking and kissing and inciting with his raw sexuality.

It was a good act. He seemed to Saffie to be more potent, possessing the sexuality his huge phallus promised. He was playing up his native lasciviousness, showing his intense sexuality. It was very exciting. His eyes were more alluring than she had ever seen them. She was very deeply thrilled: she was impatient for him. Longing, after Constantine's cursory possession. Though this had excited her, she wanted the more complete fulfilment of mutual love-making.

Dionysus stirred them to sexual frenzy, grasping and touching, supremely accurate at every spot. Eleni clung to him, her arms around his neck, her legs caressing his thighs enticingly. Saffie was moved by the reflex lust in his eyes as he seized Eleni. Her legs were up and around his waist. He supported her with his palms under her bottom as she moved on the stiff phallus. She leaned back, expressing delight and eagerness, her breasts exposed as the light garment tore fully away. Dionysus tongued her teats, lapped and sucked hungrily at her breasts as she began to slither along his huge dildo, crying out wildly as she did so. Her body tore through with savage delight.

Rachel moved ever closer to Saffie as they watched, transfixed, feeling the woman's joy, desiring it for themselves. They clung to each other, caressing and touching intimately in response to the naked expression of lust before them. Each thrilled as the other pressed on her sex and fondled her breast. Dionysus swung round and round with his willing conquest, then got her to the ground, pinned her down and continued his vicarious fucking. All the time, the camera panned around them eagerly, urging them to continue.

Saffie and Rachel watched, writhing together as the naked arse of Dionysus' pounded up and down, the animal skin trailing between his hot parting crack. Flashes of inflamed desire shot through Saffie's vagina as Eleni began to strain and grasp at her orgasm. Dionysus had her down by the arms as he supported himself to watch her. Eleni moaned and writhed, her face contorted in anguished pleasure as the spasms of burning joy exploded in the pit of her womb, causing her body to jerk spasmodically as she released it to course through her.

The 'inebriate' god released her peremptorily. He turned towards the other women. Saffie's body flashed through with electric fear at the wildness in his beautiful eyes. His entire body seemed to be raging with drunken, uncontrollable lust. His full lips were very red. He grabbed Rachel, who moaned with delight, and then squealed in alarm and trepidation. Dionysus quaffed his wine, and poured some into Rachel's eager mouth. He kissed her, whilst their mouths were filled with the delicious liquid and some, warmed by his mouth, went into hers. He raised the jug and poured the red liquid over her hair, then ripped her robe from her and doused her body. Rachel laughed in enjoyment, and the greedy god began to lick at her breasts and neck, nuzzling hungrily and biting.

He knelt to lap at her quim, drowning it with the hot alcohol from his eager mouth. He caressed her buttocks quickly, speedily bringing her to extreme arousal. She felt longingly at her own breasts, and hips, opening her legs for his eager fingers. Dionysus teased roughly at her labia, and then pushed his hand into her open sex. Then, with a sudden violent movement, he rose and rammed his huge artificial cock deeply into her. Rachel yelled out. Her cry of joy soared through Saffie, who stood watching in a state of vicarious pleasure and ardent longing.

Rachel felt the long pliable shaft penetrate skilfully as Dionysus supported her strongly. He rammed into her rapidly, putting exquisite pressure on her clitoris as he banged against her. Savage joy ripped through her. Her sexual arousal increased uncontrollably and she clung to Nikos as the waves of intense sensual pleasure coursed through her, shaking her body. She whimpered as she came, clinging to him, though the drunken god showed only passing tenderness before abandoning her.

He turned to Saffie, his black eyes burning. She backed away as required. She glanced shyly at her companions, quivering and clinging together in dazed shock and wonder. Saffie turned and fled through the vines, Mike followed her with the camera. The dark god stood for a moment, watching, and then took a lingering drink from his goblet as he surveyed her desperate-seeming flight. He sneered, then shook with drunken humour. As ordained, Saffie tripped and fell, breathing heavily in feigned fright. Then, sobbing, she struggled to her feet and continued on her stumbling way.

The fleet god followed, soon gaining on her as she pushed through the undergrowth. His feet pounded the dry earth. She tossed him a desperate glance, genuinely startled at the lasciviousness in his eyes. His desire seemed like wine. The more he had, the more he needed. He caught her, first by the arm, and then round the waist, and dragged her down, down with him to the hard ground. Saffie's friends followed in awe.

The wonderful, liberating god lifted her gown and went straight for her sex, parting her labia with eager fingers and inserting his wine-red tongue. Saffie yelped with pleasure as he tongued her, curling and hardening his tongue within her dripping muscle, drinking her sweet juices to mix with his red wine and further intoxicate him. He forced his finger into her anus and wriggled it, causing her to grunt gutturally and remember to struggle hard against his violation. Dionysus freed his prick, lifted her legs and rubbed her anus with its moist end. He forced the phallus into her gaping vagina and, looking her straight in the eyes, a secret smile on his red lips, he began to ravish her. Saffie knew that her eyes expressed her compliance, and her enjoyment of this game-playing. The false member was huge within her. She felt her face redden as it filled her. She was aware of Mike with the camera close. Dionysus raised himself to thrust his penis into her anus and Saffie smiled dirtily. Nikos now gave in to true sexual abandon, writhing and grinding in her. Saffie tore down his flesh with her nails, ripping at his back as he fucked her forcefully, ramming her back into the unyielding earth, squeezing painfully at her raised buttocks, and biting her breasts.

Saffie found that her pain and pleasure met on a plain where they existed alone, away from their audience. He took her high, giving her deep, dark joy. She scratched at his thighs and buttocks, yanked at his hair. She was aware that the pain she inflicted incited Nikos to more violent thrusting of both phallus and penis. He began to reach the tender neck of her womb with each thrust. He pushed his penis high inside her tighter passage, making her want to growl.

'Leave her wild, Niko . . .' Constantine cut in.

His words took a long time to reach Nikos. When they did, he withdrew suddenly, re-positioned his phallus and skin. Saffie roared at him, enraged. Constantine laughed, throwing back his head and she snarled at him.

'Good girl! Now, go on, chase the god, lose him and get your companions to join you in the hunt. This is too good to miss.'

Nikos paused to toss his head arrogantly at her, and then began to run, disappearing adroitly amongst the bushes. The camera followed as Saffie ran after him. She looked around, but he had already disappeared. Rachel and Eleni were behind her. Together, they raced up into the hills.

They were Maenads – wild women frenzied with sexual desire, eager to wreak vengeance on any male after having had their natural libido so enhanced by Nikos-Dionysus. The men ran before them, feigning fear, panting and hiding, though in reality fatally drawn to these wild women. They longed to be torn and clawed, groped and 'raped'.

Yiannis felt his heart thudding wildly in his breast. So taken up was his mental preparation – imagining himself to be an ancient Greek caught up in this primeval 'game' – that he felt the heady mix of lust and fear racing through his blood.

He wanted Rachel, the maenad intent on him, to catch him, but he knew that it made sense to try to escape her dangerous sexuality. She was close behind him, infinitely threatening: he had to imagine that she would rip him to pieces if she could, so savage was she, possessed by the liberating wine of the god. He clawed at the crumbling earth and roots as he felt his ankle grasped by Rachel. She dragged him down to her and began to tear off his clothes, ripping savagely at his flesh with her long nails.

Yiannis screamed in pretended terror, until her hungry, biting mouth clamped on his. Rachel clawed at him, ripping at his tender flesh in her urgent need. She was dominant, strengthened by the sacred wine. She pinned Yiannis down, yanked out his cock and shoved it into her. Yiannis could almost believe that she was possessed, so violent was she in her coupling. Also, her vagina seemed stronger and wetter than ever as she slid artfully along him. Yiannis held her waist and jerked her along his supremely excited member, feeling his cock thrill as she manipulated it expertly.

She made him come rapidly, squeezing him with her tensed muscles. As he ejaculated, yelling loudly as instructed, she got off him and, with the camera near, began to pretend to tear him savagely limb from limb. Yiannis screamed in horror. Nearby, the recently ravished Georgiou suffered a similar fate. The mad god watched from behind a huge tree, drinking his dangerous wine in enjoyment.

'It's a wrap,' said Mike. 'I really didn't think we'd make it in one take. It's been a long day.'

'We'll do "Narcissus" in the morning,' Constantine told him, 'and then,' he addressed the others also as they gathered wearily together in the clearing, 'we'll add in a few more of the "actors" scenes. We've come a long way. Congratulations, everyone.' His bright eye travelled over them, lingering affectionately on his star. 'You should get some rest tonight.'

193

The following morning, Nikos had to be Narcissus, the beautiful youth who rejected all suitors of both sexes, and eventually fell in love with his own reflection. Eleni was the nymph Echo, who pined away for love of him. Constantine had devised an artistic scenario, in which Narcissus, attired in a short tunic, which sometimes swung away as he walked revealing his naked penis, was to walk around the forest with his bow, hunting stags. He would constantly be waylaid by lascivious would-be lovers, who would grab him and molest him, swooning with lust, as he repelled them. The rest of the cast were to be these forlorn suitors.

Nikos waited moodily, smoking a cigarette and ignoring the preparations as Mike discussed technical details with Constantine. He had been ordered not even to get an erection, to show how disdainful he was of those enamoured of him. He must heartlessly reject his lovelorn wooers. He must demonstrate knowledge of his own beauty. Naturally, Constantine had interpreted all events sexually.

So the others enjoyed grasping at him, grabbing and kissing him, fondling his genitals, whilst he shoved them arrogantly away and went on glorying, as he walked, in his self-love. Nikos found it extremely difficult to control his reflex natural erection, brought on by touches from those whom he liked to make love to. He sought for things to concentrate on to prevent this. He hit upon his anger at the smirking Constantine, who sat with Mike and watched sedulously. Maddeningly, this rage aroused him perversely.

Constantine did enjoy watching the filming of these sexual and attractive young people. He took particular pleasure in seeing the difficult and untouchable Nikos discomfited. He was very sexy. Now, by the 'pool', and with the rejected Echo watching sadly, the handsome Greek youth lay down to drink from the untouched crystal water. As the ripples stilled he glimpsed his lovely face. Mike moved near to capture the image, and to train the camera on Nikos' face, as he portrayed his falling in love with that boy who looked adoringly back at him. The only person Narcissus had ever loved.

Narcissus slowly took off his clothes and began to caress himself, fingering his body fondly. He licked at his shoulders, ruffled his lovely black curls and ran his palms all over his bronzed body. Mike captured his controlled slow arousal as his full penis filled with joy of his self-pleasuring. Narcissus placed his hand between his legs and fondled his swelling balls. He stroked his muscular thighs, and then lay on his belly and thrust himself upon the earth so that Mike could linger on his jerking buttocks and his large testicles, as well as going close, with the camera's eyes, to his deep crack, and his red hole, which Nikos obligingly revealed as he pulled his buttocks apart.

As instructed, Nikos hung over the pool to eye himself reverently in the water. Andy filmed Eleni-Echo, caressing her own naked body in response to Nikos' self-pleasuring. Her dark hair was lovely around her perfect face as she felt at her small breasts and enlarged genitals. Nikos was very aware of her; the thought of her fired his playing, though he was not allowed to respond to her physically. He lingered over his masturbation, as commanded. With leisurely movements, he pulled his foreskin back to his root, repeatedly revealing the swollen head of his phallus.

He continued to caress himself as he would any woman, feeling his breasts and licking his warm shoulders. Constantine saw that his face was beautiful as he obliged them all. He was very good. They were all affected by this intensely personal display. Constantine had taken much pleasure in directing and filming these libidinous youngsters. It had given him a tremendous feeling of power to write the scenes, to arouse himself by imagining them. They were all highly-sexed. He was also pleased with the artistic content of the film. They had played their 'off-stage' parts well. Now the film was almost completed. He smiled wickedly at the thought of his final act.

Now, as he watched Nikos masturbate, his body thrilled poignantly. He had always loved sex – sex with anyone – but never had he desired anyone as much as he now desired Nikos. He wanted him. He must have him. He turned fretfully away, aware of his body's obvious arousal. He was becoming so lost in day-dreams of taking Nikos by force that he was in danger of his fantasies engulfing him and being unable to attend to technical points. It was fortunate that Mike was so astute. Nikos had closed his lovely eyes, so as to be completely engrossed in himself.

This slow masturbation, and his previous inability to respond to sexual advances were now driving him crazy. He had to prevent himself from ejaculating several times. When he came, the spunk had to hit the lens, and then he had to kill himself by plunging a dagger into his breast. His blood would soak into the earth and the white narcissus flower would spring up. Nikos controlled his breathing, and his pace as his hand gripped his burning penis.

He could not wait much longer, but he was required to come gracefully, not give in to the rapid panting and energised wanking he needed to relieve himself. The seminal fluid gathered in his balls. Nikos gripped his prick tightly. Mike moved closer. Nikos looked lovingly at the lens, making his face as lascivious as possible, dilating his eyes, pouting his lips. Then, with relief, he let the rushing seed spurt out at speed. His body jerked as it cascaded out. He hoped it hit the right spot. If it did not, they would have to fabricate something. He was damned if he was going through all that again.

He caressed his body, feigning an agony of frustration: as though he yearned for, and missed, actually being able to make love to his beloved self. Then, he reached for the dagger and, first trailing the sharp end down to his flaccid penis and fretting at its state, he plunged it into his breast. The generous blood-bag burst, drowning his chest, and ran down copiously to the ground. He lay still until Mike said:

'It's a wrap.'

Then he got up and grabbed the gown from Carolyn.

'I'm going for a shower,' he said irritably to Constantine, pushing the man away as he got too close.

He was angered by the lecherous look in Constantine's eyes, and his fawning posture as he cleaved his sweaty palms together. He longed to be alone, to be cleansed by running water, and he needed a drink. Constantine was possessed by sex, and at present not wise enough to leave the hot and sticky Nikos alone. He was motivated by his cock which reared at the proximity of the youth. He wanted to push him to the ground and force his buttocks apart, and drive home his greedy cock. He made the mistake of reaching out to touch Nikos. Nikos swirled and lashed out at him, punching him in the jaw. Taken by surprise, Constantine fell heavily to the ground, despite Yiannis' attempt to catch him. Nikos saw the dangerous fury in the older man's eyes. He said nothing, feeling that his own must be filled with equal fire, and continued on his way.

Eight

Mike had persuaded Yiannis and Eleni, Rachel and Georgiou to participate secretly in a sex-film. It was to be rough and basic, requiring no line-learning, relying on their basic talent, and perfect at first take. It was executed mainly at night, in Mike's suite. Their extra-official activities did not seem to curtail their libido whilst engaged in Constantine's project.

Mike invited the others to watch it when it was complete. The quality and general standard was nowhere as classy as Constantine's, but it was good fun, with plenty of raw sex. It had no pretensions to be an art film. Saffie cast surreptitious side-long glances at Nikos as they sat in the darkened room to watch the rushes. The scenario involved a couple who were involved in a complex sado-masochistic relationship. There was not a 'perversion' they did not explore, in their romps across Mike's screen. In between their savage sexual scenes, they carried on some kind of 'normal/ordinary' life – leaving for, or arriving from, the office, dressed smartly and complete with briefcases. Saffie saw that this was to counterbalance and enhance the decadence of the erotic scenes.

Some filming had taken place outside, as one or the other of them would sometimes await the other on his or her way home from the office, and waylay them, forcing them into some semi-public sex scene. The couple obviously could not keep their hands off each other, let alone their tongues, mouths, or genitals.

They now watched an extract in which Yiannis had 'forced' Eleni to strip off her scanty leather sex-gear and had tied her to a post especially for the purpose. She challenged him with wide kohl-darkened eyes as he began to whip her. She scarcely flinched as Yiannis rained down strokes on her writhing body. Saffie saw the wildness in his eyes as he wielded his weapon. He was tightly dressed in leathers. She saw his bulging crotch. It was refreshing to see him dressed in modern gear. His hair flew and he flung back the whip, and then brought it forcefully down across Eleni's pouting breasts. He lashed savagely at her nipples and pubis. He drew the fine leather through her labia and thrust at her clitoris.

The camera lingered on his swollen crotch. His expression demonstrated his lust as he beat Eleni. Still her dark eyes challenged him to continue as she writhed sexily. Saffie was turned on. She saw that Nikos' lascivious eyes were hooded as he watched his lover toss and strain against the pain. Yiannis cleverly encircled her breasts with the trailing thong, haughtiness in his enticing eyes. He prodded at her sex with the wooden end of the whip. Eleni's eyes narrowed. She spat at him.

Yiannis took off his black leather jacket and trousers. He wore a soft leather posing pouch. Its fine thong was hidden between the muscular hemispheres of his tight buttocks. His cock strained at its imprisonment. Eleni eyed it hungrily. Yiannis laughed and shook his head. He took up the familiar dildo and began to rub it over Eleni's clitoris and vulva. He pushed it into her dripping vagina, despite her shaking her head adamantly.

He released her and began to rub his clothed member against her reddened ridge. Eleni tried to tear the garment off him, to release his cock. She begged him to fuck her. Yiannis unfastened her, got her to the floor and, pinning her down by her arms, he began to move and press his hidden prick against her rising quim. He was between her widely-parted legs. He selfishly abandoned himself to rubbing his cock urgently against her pubis, appearing to enjoy himself hugely.

He retrieved the phallus from the floor. Eleni tossed her head in negation. Yiannis smiled wickedly and moved her so that he could get it between her buttocks. Eleni tossed and writhed, continuing to shake her head. He lit a cigarette and smoked in seeming pleasure as the desperate Eleni massaged her breasts and fanny, sticking her fingers inside herself, but indicating that this was not sufficient as she reached for his swollen penis. Every time she came near to touching it, Yiannis moved away. He laughed at her. He forced the dildo up and down her anus and prevented her from touching herself.

He took off his jock-strap and, with a wicked gleam in his eyes at his denial of what she so obviously needed, he began to wank rapidly. He uttered moans of enjoyment. He did not let her touch him. Eleni squeezed futilely at her breasts, needing his touch. She rubbed between her labia. The camera showed between her spreadeagled legs, her crimson, silver-trailed sex.

Yiannis masturbated until he came, and then he dressed and went from her. Eleni moaned and writhed, unable to bring herself to climax and getting angrier and angrier. She seemed to come to a decision and followed Yiannis.

In the next scene, Yiannis was tied to the bed. His cock stood up resplendently, though he could not stimulate it. His hands and legs were secured to the frame of the bed. He looked hot and uncomfortable. Eleni appeared before him with Rachel. She and Rachel stood within sight of Yiannis and began to undress each other, exchanging kisses and sexual touches they did so. This made Yiannis mad. He jerked himself wildly around on the bed, causing it to sway and creak with his passionate strength.

Eleni smirked at Yiannis as she played with Rachel's big breasts. All the time, she threw him seductive glances as she aroused the newcomer, fidgeting with her reddened nipples, and tweaking at the pink ridge poking through her pubic hair. Rachel uttered continual mews of sexual pleasure. Yiannis swore at Eleni, ordering her to release him, but she shook her dark hair adamantly. She was obviously relishing this reversal of power.

She pulled Rachel to her and concentrated on her, holding her bottom and forcing her sex against her own. The women appeared to forget the suffering Yiannis, whose angry cock raged to be handled. They lay down together on the couch so close to him. Eleni rode Rachel, manipulating the woman's eager sex with expert movements of her own as she lay between her legs.

They were lost in their consummate love-making, which Yiannis watched eagerly. Sometimes, the camera moved to his extended cock, sometimes it lingered on his face, capturing the naked longing. The women rocked wildly together in unison, their bodies as one as they mouthed and caressed and pressed. Eleni controlled her orgasm, saving sufficient to appease her wild lover. Rachel came noisily. Eleni got up, and leaving Rachel draped sexily over the leather chaise-longue, for the camera to caress, she stood and went to the bed.

She grasped her breasts and licked lasciviously at her lips. She reached out to Yiannis' cock, and he prayed that she would touch it, but she withdrew her hand. She made as if to suck him off with her puckered mouth and then rose, shaking her head and wagging her finger in denial. Yiannis moaned. Eleni left the room. The lens captured Yiannis' anguish as it swept slowly over his body, showing his fingers grasping at emptiness.

It portrayed the rage in his eyes as Eleni returned, leading the naked and rampant Georgiou by the hand. Georgiou smirked at Yiannis, his hand hovering over his friend's prick. Yiannis called out to him in supplication: he would have even him! Eleni positioned Georgiou in full sight of Yiannis and began to work on his penis, first jerking on it and then mouthing it, taking it deeply into her throat. She moved her agile mouth along it, at the same time fingering Georgiou's anus. Georgiou grasped her head and jerked his cock along her mouth and throat. He talked sexily, enjoying himself noisily.

He came with gusto, ejaculating forcefully into Eleni's mouth. Eleni swallowed his seed, rising and licking her lips deliciously at Yiannis. Georgiou stood behind Eleni, who smiled sweetly at Yiannis. Yiannis tossed and groaned as Georgiou fingered Eleni, pulling her against his hot cock as he massaged her swelling breasts, pummelling her swollen labia. Eleni rocked against him in sweet anticipation. Georgiou pushed his cock between her legs. Yiannis moaned to see its purple head between her lips. His own yearning cock longed to be there. Georgiou pushed his long prick into her.

Yiannis wracked his body wildly, in despair. The camera concentrated for seconds on his stiffened cock as fore-juices gathered, dripping from his glistening hole. Yiannis moved his head from side to side. Eleni held on to the bed as Georgiou pumped into her arse. He moved her breasts round and round and bit at her neck. Yiannis watched as Georgiou began to come slowly and noisily. They jerked against his bed, knocking it strongly against the wall. His own penis began to throb, ejecting semen. This too-weak emission made Yiannis wild.

He pleaded with the satiated, and awakening Rachel, who

nodded and began to untie him. Released, Yiannis struggled up, rubbed impatiently at his aching limbs and then seized Eleni, who screamed and pulled away. Georgiou embraced Rachel, who soon brought him back to life. They were further incited by the other couple, as Yiannis threw Eleni on to the bed and penetrated her, fucking her hard in punishment for her cruelty.

He slapped at her thighs and bottom, and breasts as he screwed her roughly. He raised her legs to his shoulders and rammed even deeper. Eleni growled and fought with him, but she also pulled him to her, seizing his buttocks and encouraging his rapid rate. Georgiou and Rachel had begun with more gentle intercourse, but they were soon affected by the other couple's wild passion and they too began to speed up.

Saffie glanced at Nikos. She wondered if he had realised that all of his friends had been involved in Mike's clandestine filming. He turned to her and shrugged. She was about to suggest that they leave: she was turned on by all this, when Mike expressed surprise at a tape he had just come across. He slotted it in. The small audience expressed approval as the opening shot was of Saffie lying back, holding on to the bed-head whilst the dark head of Nikos lapped at her spread labia.

Saffie saw that Nikos was enraged.

'When did Mike—?' she began.

'It wasn't Mike, was it?' he hissed impatiently, 'It was that bastard!'

'Constantine?' asked Saffie, bewildered.

'Obviously,' came the curt rejoinder. 'I expect he's filmed everything in my room.'

'Did you know?' asked Saffie stupidly.

'Of course I didn't know!' he said angrily. 'What do you take me for? The arrogance of the man!'

'Perhaps this negates the agreement you made?' suggested Saffie lamely, to placate him.

Nikos looked at her as if she was being very stupid and then stormed from the room. They looked at each other in bemusement. The rest of them insisted on watching the video, claiming that it was only fair, as Saffie had enjoyed theirs. Saffie had to admit that it was quite a turn on watching herself with Nikos and thinking how very good they were together. She wondered whether Constantine intended to market these, and whether he had copies, as Nikos was probably intending to destroy them. What was he saying to Constantine right now?

Constantine was only momentarily surprised as his hot-headed friend flung into his room. He himself had been enjoying a particularly arousing scene of Nikos masturbating, practising his ability to hold off orgasm and protract sexual pleasure. Nikos scarcely noticed as he began to rave at the older man. Constantine ignored him, allowing him to rage whilst he continued to watch the young man on screen in the freedom of his supposed private act.

'I'm glad you came, Nikos,' Constantine smiled at his double-entendre. He indicated the hand-written sheets beside him on his desk. 'I've written in some additional scenes for you to peruse. Take them.'

Nikos looked at him in astonishment, coming to a sense of himself and seeing his naked image masturbating on the television set. He watched himself as if in a dream.

' "Zeus",' explained Constantine pithily. 'He makes a visit to a mortal youth and, well, "seduces" him is perhaps too mild a word for the king of gods.'

Nikos felt his heart plummet. He did not need to be told who the mortal youth would be. And he had not specified in his ridiculous contract that he would not have sex with Constantine. What an idiot! He turned to go, not trusting himself not to kill the man on the spot. His beloved house was tainted with his presence. Would he *ever* be free of him?

'Oh, Ni-ko—' called Constantine.

Nikos froze, riled by his sing-song tone. He did not deign to turn round.

'No need to loiter at this point,' said Constantine. 'We will film tomorrow.' Then he added, as if reading Nikos' deepest thoughts: 'Your compliance won't be necessary.'

Nikos went to his study, his brain pounding in crimson flashes. His surroundings seemed unreal to him. It was as if he was in a trance. Perhaps, thought a tiny distant self, it's my blood pressure.

His wonderful room gave him no sanctuary. He wandered around, touching familiar objects, brushing his knuckles along the

202

spines of his treasured books. Then he went from this room and ran up to his bedroom, to check whether the video camera Constantine must have used for his private filming was still secreted there. Naturally, it was not. He had to restrain himself so as not to destroy things around him. The entire world seemed hostile and alien. He felt that he had been violated. The man owned him. He wanted to destroy him. Why? Nikos could not accept that all his vile acts came from desire.

He lay on his bed. The cigarette he lit tasted foul, rasping at his throat. He puffed perversely at it. The whole thing was ridiculous. He would tell his grandfather. His heart shrank. Not now. This was worse, far worse, than just the photos. In retrospect, it suddenly seemed an easy thing to prevent him from seeing the photographs. What a mess.

A sudden idea came vividly to him. He could burn down his house and kill Constantine. He knew that the man would torment him for ever.

'Niko?'

He realised that there had been knocking on his locked door for several moments.

'Go away, Saffie,' he said wearily.

'Let me talk to you for a minute, Niko.'

Nikos sighed and went to open the door to her. He lay back on the bed and continued to smoke desultorily. Saffie took a cigarette and sat by him.

'Mike told me about tomorrow. It's been planned for a while.'

'No surprise, really,' said Nikos dully.

He sounded very cold and distanced. Perhaps this was his method, of getting through, thought Saffie. It may be best to leave him, and he probably wanted that. However, he had never seemed so attractive to Saffie, his beautiful eyes smouldering; and his body suffuse with controlled violence. In any case, the days of the film were finite, and she may never see him again. She looked at his lovely mouth, now petulantly expressing his unhappiness.

'Let's go out, Niko,' she suggested brightly, rising, stubbing her cigarette, holding out her hand to him.

He looked at her in astonishment. Perhaps he felt like a prisoner in his own home.

'I'll just have a quick shower and get changed. You can take me somewhere good. I haven't seen much of the island.'

She left, not giving him the chance to reply. She raced up to her room, showered and put on her favourite dress. She was filled with trepidation, lest he should refuse. To her relief, he had also showered: his hair hung wetly over his brow in stray curls. He had on a white shirt and black trousers. He was very appealing. Saffie's heart turned.

'We'll go for a ride around the island,' he told her, taking her hand and leading her to the door.

He took her round the back of the house, not to the stables, but to the garages. Saffie felt his air of excitement, and wondered what he had in mind. He went to a smaller door, unlocked and opened it, then he took the black cover from a large object and stood back with an air of pride. Saffie smiled, going over to the gleaming black and silver motorbike.

She held onto him as he sped across the island. They ate caviare and drank champagne on the balcony of a restaurant with extensive sea views. The evening was balmy and gentle piano music played within. It was relaxing just to be with Nikos. He talked about his writing, and his family. When he talked of Anna, his eyes filled with affection. Saffie wondered what it would have been like, to be his twin, to have been part of his life, always.

Later, they went to a nightclub, where Saffie fulfilled her promise to dance for him. She loved to dance and her performance was enhanced by the appreciative attention Nikos gave her. When she had finished, everyone applauded and she bowed, laughing.

'That was lovely, Saffie . . .' Nikos told her, embracing her as she returned to him, and kissing her hair.

He continued to hold her as slow music began. They moved together across the room, close in each other's arms. This was a lovely, peaceful respite from Constantine's frenetic world.

'I'd love to meet your sister,' she said softly.

'I'm sure you will,' he promised.

Saffie hugged him close.

Nikos stayed separate from them as preparations were made for his scene with Constantine/Zeus. The god had not arrived yet. Despite her sympathy for Nikos, Saffie had to admit a certain excited sensual frisson at the prospect of the two powerful men, locked in a sexual power game. She thought of Nikos' love-making of the previous night. He was so definitively heterosexual that she believed that he did not enjoy sex with men. Unlike Yiannis, who obviously did, and Georgiou, who would have anyone and as often as possible.

Nikos was to be a youth who had been hunting stags, and become separated from his friends. He was lost in the forest, and a little anxious, as it was becoming dark and eerie. The forest appeared to come to life, filled with strange noises and sudden ghost-like traces of nymphs and dryads. Distant music – from Pan? – came through the trees. Nikos was appealing in his romantic-seeming confusion. For hours, he wandered through the woods, getting deeper and deeper away from the world.

Sometimes, in sheer exhaustion, he sat under a tree to sleep, but was assailed by frightening dreams, to be screened later, of animalistic orgies, of satyrs and nymphs. These were to be interpreted as the spirits of this wild place, and also as evocations of his deeper fantasies.

These dreams aroused him, and he attempted to appease his need by self-stimulation, but only succeeded in turning himself on further. He was becoming sexually hungry and hot. He needed a mate. He slaked his desperate thirst in a river, and then tore off his clothes to bathe. Constantine had been trailing him for some time, watching in relish his anguished frustration. Nikos saw naked water-nymphs and appealed to them, imploring them to take pity on his famished state. But they scorned him, and laughed merci-lessly, demonstrating their preference of engaging in sex with their own kind. However first Saffie, Rachel and Eleni came to him and tantalised him by caressing and masturbating him, then they abandoned him.

Nikos watched hopelessly as they writhed together libidi-nously. He was excruciatingly aroused by their sport as they touched each other, ignoring him. The camera trained on Nikos' painfully erect penis. He jerked on it, hanging on to a tree and panting, but he could not come. He saw Yiannis and Georgiou, who gave him to realise that the only sex here available was with one's own kind. Nikos shook his head. He could not help but watch them jealously as Yiannis fucked Georgiou. He would far prefer that to what was in store for him.

Then the all-powerful Zeus arrived, accompanied by wild and furious music. His demeanour was foreboding. Nikos backed away. Zeus uncovered his gigantic member, throwing back his head and laughing at the terrified Nikos.

Nikos tried to run away, but the god ran strongly and was very close behind him as the youth crashed through the undergrowth, grasping desperately at branches. The others followed. Zeus grasped Nikos and flung him to the ground. He held him down on his belly. Here, Nikos' struggles had the aura of authenticity. He hated Constantine and he made up his mind to destroy his film.

Constantine parted Nikos' legs and without preamble forced his throbbing prick into him. Constantine was filled with enormous pleasure as he held this beautiful man completely in his power. He intended to savour every long second of his illicit intercourse, and he was going to make it last. Selfishly, he moved to benefit from ultimate dominion. He wriggled around, gasping with controlled pleasure.

Nikos was flooded with pure hatred. He felt the man's unwelcome intrusion, his firm hot prick filled his raw hole, sending spasms of pain through him. The others encircled them in a maddened dance of sexual frenzy. They chanted and encouraged with lewd calls. They tore at each other's flesh, and groped and squeezed lasciviously. They paused for sexual bouts. But all the time, they draw near to watch and incite to further lust, the god having his way with the unwilling sexual being.

Constantine urged his massive cock up and down Nikos' tight, muscular passage, aware only of his own heady pleasure. Spasms of delight shot through his nerves. He had the scent of the man in his nostrils, mixed with the aroma of the damp forest.

He was only too aware of Nikos' extreme reluctance as he lay rigid on the firm ground, his cock pressed hard against the soil. Time after time he thrust his penis deeply into the man, and then teased himself by withdrawing almost to his tip. He knew that he could come, much too soon. He had been practising for this, withholding his orgasm, increasing his capacity. Whilst realising this would be his one and only time, he was already wickedly devising future opportunities for having him. He must!

Nikos was annoyed that this ordeal was already going on for

much longer than the damned film required. He knew that Constantine was delaying, slowing and sometimes even pausing so that he could humiliate him for longer.

He tried hard to retain his detachment, but he felt his prick begin to pulse as he came. Constantine was delighted at this. Nikos' spontaneous ejaculation made him fuck wilder, no longer able to contain himself. The watchers increased their rude chanting, clapping and jeering. Constantine felt his nerves fill with anticipation and extreme awareness of his genitals as all of his life seemed to gather and shoot rapidly from his tightened testicles and at speed along his throbbing penis. He held Nikos tightly as he shuddered and strained and came with loud bellowing cries and jagged thrusts of his powerful abdomen. He rolled off Nikos, who groped to his feet, fell into the bushes and vomited. Constantine laughed uproariously as he put on his robe, deliciously satisfied. Nikos felt his sickness rise and rise. He was angry as he wanted to punch the man. At last, he rose, shook off Saffie, who had come to him in concern, and walked off with dignity. Eleni draped him with a towel, and kissed his head tenderly.

'What are you making, Georgiou?' Saffie asked, drawn to the kitchen by the delicious aroma emitting from it.

Georgiou smiled.

'A special concoction ordered by Constantine, supposed to be what the ancients used as an aphrodisiac. Part of a special feast to liven you all up,' he jested. 'Grapes, olives, goat's cheese, shellfish, artichokes . . . honey – the ambrosia of the gods.'

'Can I have a taste?'

'Ffssfff . . . I don't know, Saffie. We can't have you too lively, can we?'

Saffie punched him playfully.

'Cheek!'

The aromatic sauce tasted delicious, its potency developing as it slid deliciously down her throat.

'Good idea, to see if it works,' said Georgiou. 'Yes, I suppose we should test it. What do you think, Saffie?' he asked, coming close to her and whispering huskily in her ear.

He eyed her breasts, loose and provocative under her thin dress. He pushed her against the edge of the table and lifted her dress to touch her. A deep thrill rushed through Saffie as his hand lingered so teasingly close to her quim, without touching. Georgiou kissed her, at the same time, he released his prick and pushed it between her welcoming thighs. Saffie gripped him tightly, beginning to move along him as he kissed her more deeply, his tongue exploring her mouth. She thought of him, with Rachel, with Georgiou, as the Minotaur, in Mike's film.

He massaged her thrusting breasts, warm and inviting in the soft material of her dress. Saffie urgently wanted him to feel their nakedness and became impatient at his teasing. She parted her legs and reached down to shove his hard cock into her gaping hole. Georgiou prevented her with his hand, removed his mouth, still slowly tantalising, and explained:

'I don't think we should, Saffie . . .' But still he pleasured himself, sliding his throbbing cock between her thighs.

Saffie pushed him forcefully back against the wall. Unprepared, and preoccupied with his self-stimulation, Georgiou was taken aback and easily pinned to the wall by his arms. He smiled sleazily: this was sweet and unusual. He pretended to struggle, shaking his head from side to side and moaning in refusal. Nevertheless, he groaned in pleasure as he felt his yearning cock grasped. He closed his eyes and followed with his mind the movements of Saffie's fingers as she squeezed him. Then she released him. Georgiou smiled and returned to the table.

'Anyway . . .' said Saffie, nibbling at his culinary delights, 'I thought we'd more or less finished.'

'Mmm . . . I expect Constantine has one or two scenes in mind – including some kind of endurance test. Who can satisfy the most number of partners, that kind of thing, you know . . .'

'Sounds more Roman decadence than Greek classical to me . . . but it would probably suit him – or you . . . Is it your own idea, Georgiou?'

'Cheers.'

'Seriously, though. I reckon that Constantine would really be pushing his luck if he asked Nikos to do anything else. Actually, I think I'll have a word with him.'

'Do you think that's wise?' asked Yiannis, coming in to help Georgiou.

'I doubt it can do any harm. Where is Nikos?'

'In his study, of course, writing. Eleni is in there too, studying. Really. She is doing a PhD – in Decadent Art, would you believe?'

'Mmm . . .'

Before she began to hesitate, Saffie went, with determination, up to Constantine's room. Her mind went back to the two men in the kitchen; she wondered whether Georgiou would encourage Yiannis to finish him off. She was not surprised to find Constantine cloistered with Mike, watching the various bits of film, and putting them together. Deciding no doubt, thought Saffie, what else he could fit in!

'I need to have a private word with you, Constantine,' she said icily.

Mike looked up, smiled at her and left, taking the reels and projector with him. He probably thought that Constantine would be occupied for some time. Saffie went to the window and looked out into the garden for a moment, then she turned to confront Constantine, who was leaning back in his chair behind the desk and regarding her with interest.

'You are pleased with your film?' she challenged.

Constantine merely inclined his head.

'Yes . . .' Saffie mused, 'I do think it's good. Interesting. I expect, when Mike and his team have added all the effects, it will be – very artistic.'

Constantine could not help but smile.

'Much of its appeal is due to Nikos. You can't deny that?'

'There's no reason why I should deny that,' Constantine agreed. 'I've made no secret of the fact that he is primarily why I made the film.'

'Personally, I think that he's more than fulfilled his side of the deal with you,' she told him.

'Do you, Saffie?'

'Yes, I do. You can't really want to destroy a young man's life – the son of your dead friend – by retaining this hold over him.'

Saffie was riled to see the amusement in his eyes at her audacity. He came to join her at the window. She did not like his proximity.

'I don't want sex to be involved here, Constantine,' she warned him, realising that he would think that she was offering herself in exchange for Nikos' liberation.

She wondered if she would agree, and if, then, he would really hand over the photographs. She knew that if this happened, Nikos would feel that it was dishonourable, and would not want to achieve his release in such a way. Saffie wanted to retain his friendship. This could not be so if she had sex with Constantine in return for the photographs.

'I've come to warn you that Nikos really has had enough.'

She saw his eyes darken at her continued serious tone. He turned away from her, fighting down his anger at her interfering impudence. He lit a cigarette. Saffie noticed that his hand shook slightly with suppressed annoyance.

'You come to my room at twelve, and I will give you the photographs.'

'Constantine. You're not listening. This isn't about sex.'

'Ha!' he laughed, his deep, rich voice conveying much, and thrilling Saffie. She was annoyed at her body's natural response to him. Still, despite everything, the man retained his innate charm.

'It's very much about sex, Saffron. This has all been to do with sex, right from your initial attraction to Nikos – which, after all, is why you are here, isn't it?'

'Yes . . .' she murmured. 'Look, Constantine. You know that this has not been easy for him.'

Whilst she really hoped for some kind of sympathy or compassion from the older man, all she saw in his eyes was a flash of triumph, or cruel amusement.

'I think that he has fulfilled his role with dignity,' she added.

'Oh, that's what you call it, do you, when your cunt thrills to see his arse?'

Saffie did not move away in time to escape his deft caress of her crotch. Her body did indeed thrill, lightning-like flashes spreading up her. She turned away, seeking to hide her vulnerability. She had been crazy to think she could come here and speak to this man without sex coming into it. Despite his seeming cultural aspect, there was nothing he had done which did not relate directly to this subject. If he was not so rich and handsome, with such a respectable position, he would just be a dirty old man. But it was impossible to interpret him as such, for he possessed these qualities in abundance. Saffie threw her thunderbolt.

'Nikos intends to destroy your film.'

For a moment she enjoyed his look of bewildered astonishment, followed by apprehension, before he managed to resume his mask of control.

'He can't do that—'

'And the copies,' she looked at him slyly, 'if you have any.'

'But—'

'I've told you. You have pushed him too far. I reckon that he will go away, begin a new life. Even if his grandfather disinherits him, he will still look after the rest of his family – his twin sister, and mother and younger brother and sister. Stavros will leave his estate to his daughter. Nikos' cousins will care for the family, just as Nikos was to. He loses his personal wealth, and his position of respect. But perhaps, Constantine, he feels he is losing more than that now. You belong to the same society. You must understand better than I. I myself think this would be very sad. He takes his responsibilities very seriously – which is, after all, how you got him in the first place. But he can write. He has that. He has already had success.'

'You care deeply for him,' Constantine sounded resigned.

'It's unjust, Constantine and, actually, I think it would be a pity if you lost your film. But Nikos really intends to destroy it.'

'How?'

'He'd find a way. Perhaps he'd burn the house down?'

'He'd destroy his villa?'

'His?'

'Where is he now?' asked Constantine, narrowing his eyes at her suspiciously.

Saffie realised that he thought that she had been sent to occupy Constantine whilst Nikos sabotaged the films. She felt a pang of pity for him. It would indeed be a good time to destroy them as there were as yet no more copies. She thought that it had been a little lacking in foresight for Constantine not to imagine that Nikos would, in a sudden fit of temper, decide to do such a thing. He could, if he tried, get round one of the crew to help him. Jaspar, for instance, could perhaps be induced for money. He felt bitter towards Constantine. Perhaps Constantine imagined that Nikos was seducing Mike, who was often critical of him anyway.

Could Constantine really believe that Mike would help in the obliteration of his own work? Did he think that he too could be bought?

'He's in his study. Writing. I just came to advise you – of his plans.'

'Right.'

Constantine stood smoking and looking over the garden. Saffie felt that he was weighing up the situation. The film was complete. It was possible, even now, that Nikos could fulfil his threat – the others would probably help him. After all, they had only participated for Nikos' sake: to free him from Constantine's threats. If Nikos felt that would not be honoured, then, naturally they could be induced to destroy the film. Even if Constantine protected the film at this stage, he could not feel safe. For, if Nikos thought that he would be revealed anyway, he had little more to lose by attempting to stop its release later. He also had friends and influence in the film world. As did Yiannis, who was a successful part-time actor in commercial films. Constantine could not afford to risk sabotage of his precious film.

'So—' he turned back to Saffie, 'you want me to hand over the photographs to you?'

'No,' she replied, 'I think you should give them to Nikos, with an absolute assurance of there being no copies and, if any should come to light, that you will not show them to Stavros Mandreas.'

Constantine sighed and nodded. He stubbed out his cigarette and went to the drinks cabinet to pour himself a brandy. He offered Saffie one silently. She shook her head.

'I would enjoy making another film with Nikos – with all of you. I will not easily find another group of such suitable people.'

'There's no reason why you shouldn't make another film with Nikos. Perhaps from one of his books. There's sure to be some sex somewhere. And his friends are always available to him.'

He lifted his head and smiled at her.

'That may be an idea, Saffron. Now, please go and tell Nikos that I will speak to him.'

'Alright.' She smiled and went to the door, relieved.

'And, Saffie—'

She turned back at his softer tone.

'Yes?'

'Will you come to me tonight?'

'Not in return for the photographs?'

'No. That is done. Merely to say goodbye.'

'And, you will think of me, also?'

'I promise.'

'Alright.'

Saffie was interested in discovering a little more of this other, kinder side of Constantine. She ran down to Nikos' study. He scarcely looked up from his computer.

'Constantine wants to speak with you.'

A dark shadow crossed Nikos' clear features as he met her eyes. He rose to go. As he passed her, she caught him and kissed him.

Constantine was smoking a fine cigar and drinking brandy. He poured one for Nikos and held up his in 'salut'. Nikos drank his down, not knowing what the man wanted and eager to get back to his book, where half his mind was, anyway. He was keen to regain the lost weeks and would be glad when they all went and left him alone. Constantine watched him thoughtfully for a moment, and then opened the drawer where he had just placed the precious envelope and handed it to Nikos. Nikos coloured and looked at him through hooded eyes. Constantine smiled at the expressiveness of his full lips. He should have made Saffie bring Nikos along tonight. He cursed himself.

Nikos opened the envelope and took out the high-quality black and white studio photographs. He looked through them quickly; they all appeared to be here. He looked questioningly up at Constantine, who shook his head slowly.

'I haven't even kept one, though I'd like to, and I haven't had any copies made. You know that Damianos had the negatives. Perhaps they have been published in magazines you don't even know about.' Constantine smiled. 'So, now you are free, Niko.'

He drew the pad towards him, wrote a few lines and signed them. He slid this across to Nikos. The elaborately hand-written phrases assured Nikos Mandreas of his integrity, and that he would not approach Stavros, or any other member of his family, or anyone who knew him, or could do him harm, on the subject of the photographs, and he would not mention the film to any of them.

'You need not worry, Niko. The gifted young actor in the film

213

could easily be any other beautiful Greek youth.'

Nikos met his eyes for a moment and then rose.

'So you will not find it necessary now to destroy my wonderful film? Now – or later?'

Nikos frowned and shook his head.

'Why should I have done that? You would still have had the photographs and would, in anger, have taken them straight to Stavros.'

'But you have your writing?'

'Yes – I could survive. But I could have before the filming. Why would I go through all that and still risk you revealing me to my family?' Nikos seemed genuinely puzzled.

'In anger?'

'You do make me very angry, Constantine,' Nikos admitted. 'But I have my father's honour to consider, even if my own is tainted now.'

He recalled, when he was angry, telling Saffie that he felt like destroying everything. He smiled. Constantine made the same realisation.

'She is very clever . . .'

'Would you have withheld the photographs?'

Constantine shrugged.

'She made me see clearly. Let us shake hands, Niko, and be on our former, more seemingly friendly footing. I have no hold over you now. Though you continue yours, over me . . . it only gave me some advantage, for a small time.'

Nikos met his gaze in understanding, then he held out his hand and the men shook hands firmly.

'Your honour is intact, Niko,' Constantine sought to assure him.

Saffie had waited in Nikos' study. She curled up on the window-seat and looked out into the courtyard, listening to the splashing of the fountain. It was very quiet, the others had gone for a walk, or were resting in their rooms. Eleni was asleep over her books. She looked to the door as Nikos came in. He tossed the large brown envelope across to Saffie.

'Yours, I believe?'

Saffie held the package to her in relief. She watched Nikos as he poured a drink, lit a cigarette and sat in his desk-chair, leaning back as he felt the strain of weeks dissolving. Saffie took out the photographs and looked through them. The photographer had begun with two very attractive men, but he had made them look absolutely wonderful. The pictures ranked with any beautiful painting she had even seen. Whatever Nikos said, he could not have fabricated his response to and relationship with Yiannis in these lovely, beautifully erotic pictures. The photographer had merely brought out what was there.

Saffie felt that she was in the presence of an extremely intimate revelation. She fully understood Nikos' apprehension. Stavros Mandreas was a highly intelligent, and sensitive man. He had made his success partly on his ability to read people. In looking at these revealing photographs, he would believe that his beloved grandson was in love with this young man, whom he had welcomed as a friend, and he would fear for the future of his 'empire'. Old-fashioned, misguided in his expectations, but no-one could blame him.

Nikos watched her. She was aware of his heightened colour, his liquid eyes. Was he recalling that day, so long ago, when he had innocently posed with Yiannis? Why had he done it? He didn't look drunk, or appear to have been coerced, but then, as she had seen, he was a consummate actor.

'You should give these to Yiannis,' Saffie told him, recalling Yiannis' admission, in Delphi, of his love for his friend.

'Yiannis has me,' Nikos said quietly. 'One day I will marry his little sister. Maybe he will marry mine . . . He doesn't need photographs. Anyway, they are safer with you, Saffie. Yiannis had them before, remember?'

Nikos narrowed his eyes at her as he saw the expression in her face. He nodded.

'Okay, Saffie – let me guess, what do you want? You are as spiteful as Constantine.'

'It is not to impel . . . It is only for my own pleasure. And you and Yiannis began it, on the boat to Crete.'

'Okay – if Yiannis agrees, we will see you tonight.'

'You think Yiannis will not agree?' asked Saffie.

Nikos smiled ruefully.

'I'll see you later. I'll leave you to your writing. I have an appointment to cancel.'

'With Constantine?' Nikos asked, his eyes narrowing.

Saffie smiled.

'Keep the photographs safe, Saffie . . .'

'Of course I will, Niko,' she touched the envelope to her lips as she left the room. 'And – thank you.'

'Thank you, Saffie.' Nikos smiled enchantingly.

Tomorrow, they were all leaving – except Nikos. Saffie was going to join her parents in Florence, where she planned to do some sketches in the Uffizi. In a few days, she would meet Rachel in London, where she was returning directly. Eleni and Georgiou were going back to university – Eleni to Athens, and Georgiou to Thessaloniki. Yiannis was also returning to Athens, to his post as lecturer in Literature at the University. Constantine and Mike and co. were going to Paris to make preparations to release the film, as well as to work on the last details, such as the music and special effects. They were all supposed to meet in Paris, in autumn, to see it.

They drank champagne, and ate smoked salmon, and Georgiou's 'ancient' concoction in the shade of the cypress trees in Nikos' garden. They exchanged addresses, and were sure that they would all meet again. Saffie felt a little of the artist's sadness at passing time as she looked around at them all and wondered whether they would. She caught Rachel's eyes and smiled. This had been a very special Grecian holiday. Which had taken them through time as well as space. She attempted to dispel her poignant mood by thinking positively about Florence. She decided that she would sketch Michelangelo's 'Bacchus' in the Bargello. She smiled as she thought about Nikos as Bacchus (or Dionysus). It would be most interesting to see the film, she decided.

She looked across the garden to Nikos. He had been watching her; trying to fathom her expression under her wide-brimmed hat. He smiled and gestured her over, to his more secluded spot. Yiannis and Eleni handed round caviare and asparagus tips. Georgiou poured more champagne, sloshing it around. Saffie met Nikos' eyes once more and they laughed. She went to sit beside him. She was aware that Constantine watched them from his chair at the edge of the group.

'I have decided to come to London in the autumn.'

Saffie, looking down at the glass in her hands, smiled.

'After the film is released?' she asked.

Nikos shrugged, his eyes sliding away for a moment.

'So, you can put me up, yes?'

Saffie laughed to think of this rich and luxuriant Greek man in her flat in Richmond. She shrugged, still smiling.

'And perhaps – Yiannis will come too, hey?' he suggested.

Saffie glanced at the laughing Yiannis and smiled at him.

'I hope so,' she said to Nikos.

Nikos raised his glass of champagne to her and she lifted hers to touch it as their eyes met once more.

Adult Fiction for Lovers from Headline LIAISON

SLEEPLESS NIGHTS	Tom Crewe & Amber Wells	£4.99
THE JOURNAL	James Allen	£4.99
THE PARADISE GARDEN	Aurelia Clifford	£4.99
APHRODISIA	Rebecca Ambrose	£4.99
DANGEROUS DESIRES	J. J. Duke	£4.99
PRIVATE LESSONS	Cheryl Mildenhall	£4.99
LOVE LETTERS	James Allen	£4.99

All Headline Liaison books are available at your local bookshop or newsagent, or can be ordered direct from the publisher. Just tick the titles you want and fill in the form below. Prices and availability subject to change without notice.

Headline Book Publishing, Cash Sales Department, Bookpoint, 39 Milton Park, Abingdon, OXON, OX14 4TD, UK. If you have a credit card you may order by telephone – 01235 400400.

Please enclose a cheque or postal order made payable to Bookpoint Ltd to the value of the cover price and allow the following for postage and packing: UK & BFPO: £1.00 for the first book, 50p for the second book and 30p for each additional book ordered up to a maximum charge of £3.00.
OVERSEAS & EIRE: £2.00 for the first book, £1.00 for the second book and 50p for each additional book.

Name ....

Address ....

....

....

If you would prefer to pay by credit card, please complete:
Please debit my Visa/Access/Diner's Card/American Express (Delete as applicable) card no: